"It must be terrible," Cass said.

"What's that?" Bolan asked her, taken by surprise.

"To live this way. To trust no one."

Once again the Executioner felt the prickly sensation of awareness that somehow she'd picked up at least his general train of thought.

"I make exceptions."

They reached the shop and separated. As Bolan put the car into motion, he was troubled. He could lay no claim to psychic powers, but experience had taught him to rely on his instincts. They were talking to him now, in whispers, but he read the message loud and clear.

The too-familiar voice was telling him that there was danger on the streets, and in the very air he breathed. A lurking menace waiting to explode in the warrior's face, devour everything he touched.

So be it.

MACK BOLAN®

The Executioner

DON PENDLETON's EXECUTIONER

MACK BOLAN.

Night Kill

A GOLD EAGLE BOOK FROM

WORLDWIDE.

TORONTO • NEW YORK • LONDON • PARIS
AMSTERDAM • STOCKHOLM • HAMBURG
ATHENS • MILAN • TOKYO • SYDNEY

First edition April 1989

ISBN 0-373-61124-2

Special thanks and acknowledgment to
Mike Newton for his contribution to this work.

There is compelling evidence of the existence of a nationwide network of satanic cults, some aligned more closely than others. Some are purveying narcotics; others have branched into child pornography and violent sadomasochistic crime, including murder. I am concerned that the toll of innocent victims will steadily mount unless law enforcement officials recognize the threat and face it.

—Maury Terry
The Ultimate Evil

I'm ready to confront the threat, if no one else will. Let the cultists come . . . and find out what hellfire is really all about.

—Mack Bolan

To the members of Believe the Children,
and the American Cult Awareness Network.
God keep.

PROLOGUE

The warehouse stood on Chicago's South Side, in a run-down neighborhood dominated by light industry and condemned tenement housing. Sixty years before, during Prohibition, it had been a staging center for the Spike O'Donnell bootleg gang, persistent rivals of Capone, and it had seen its share of liquor come and go. In modern times it served a different clientele, but many of its shipments still departed in the middle of the night.

For the past three days Mack Bolan had been tracing shipments to and from the South Side warehouse, verifying his impressions of the owners, lining up his strike. By now all doubt had been eradicated from the soldier's mind.

The warehouse was a Noraid drop for arms and ammunition traveling to Northern Ireland, where the IRA would use them in its endless war against the British. Various donations made to "Irish charity" had purchased M-16s, Uzis, shotguns, automatic pistols and a crate of frag grenades originally stolen from a military post in West Virginia. Delivery could be a problem, but the Provos had become proficient at evading the security patrols.

Bolan's task was to stop the shipment here, before it could proceed.

He knew the warehouse inside out; its floor plan had been permanently branded in his memory. A squat two-story structure, with the second level served by elevators large enough to hoist a flatbed truck, it featured loading bays in back, a normal entrance for the business offices in front. Employees used a side door on the east, but Bolan planned to circumvent the various alarms and move directly to the second floor, effecting entry there.

The fire escape had been maintained in fair condition, everything considered, but it qualified as a legitimate antique. The Executioner scaled the flimsy metal staircase, pausing every time the steps let out a groan and shifted underneath his weight. If there were sentries on the job, they had a decent chance of tracking his approach.

The second-story windows had been painted over years before, but it had been a sloppy patchwork job, and Bolan managed to secure a glimpse of the interior. A single row of bulbs provided dim illumination, and he saw the cargo waiting for him, crates marked Farm Equipment stacked in pyramids in the center of the floor.

A stiletto blade released the latch on Bolan's second try. He slipped inside and left the window open as a possible escape route if the soft probe went sour. Easing off the safety on his Ingram stuttergun, he crossed the stretch of open concrete floor to crouch beside the crated weapons.

The IRA had been engaged in war with Britain since the early days of 1916, and there seemed to be no end in sight. The Executioner didn't have any answers to the problem, but he knew the Provos had been getting arms from Libya, the Soviet Union, Iran and other sources hostile to the interests of America. In Bolan's view the Noraid shipment had traveled far enough.

He set the charges quickly, wedging C-4 between the larger crates and seating detonators, synchronizing timers. Doomsday would arrive in seven minutes, giving Bolan time to execute a smooth withdrawal. He should be at least a block away before the fireworks started.

One final charge and he was rising from his crouch, prepared to exit, when the cargo elevator grumbled into life, ascending from the lower floor. Despite its age the rig was fast enough to catch him short of safety, totally exposed between the crates and open window. Bolan cursed and huddled back against the pyramid, mere inches from the nearest plastic charge.

The new arrivals numbered at least three. Their exit from the elevator placed them thirty feet in front of Bolan, slightly to his left and closing fast.

The Executioner had no more time to waste.

If they were armed, he'd be forced to deal with them as best he could. If not, a warning burst should send them scattering for cover while he made his getaway.

Emerging from the shadow of the crates, he darted for the open window, conscious of the sudden lag in conversation at his back.

"Hey, you! Hold on there!"

Bolan swiveled, bringing up the Ingram in time to see a muzzle-flash. The bullet whistled past his ear as Bolan let the little subgun rip, rock-steady at a range of something under fifty feet.

The shooter took three rounds and staggered, going down before his comrades had a chance to reach their concealed weapons. Bolan counted four men as he emptied out the magazine, reloading on the run.

Someone had begun to shout, and heels pounded on the concrete floor. Another pistol shot went wild, the slug releasing drifts of plaster from the ceiling. He was in the window now, the rusty landing underfoot.

Below him, lounging against a year-old Cadillac, three hardmen craned their faces toward the sound of gunfire. They were digging underneath their jackets, hauling hardware into view before they saw their target, one of them gesticulating at the sight of an intruder on the fire escape.

They opened fire together, wild rounds peppering the wall and coming closer as the shooters concentrated on their aim. Pinned down between the window and the alley, Bolan felt a stab of sympathy for every housefly that had ever been discovered on a windowpane.

A bullet grazed the rail beside him, peppered him with rust and metal shavings. Blindly, reaching through the grillwork, Bolan answered with a burst that scattered his assailants, sending them to ground.

A smoky flash shattered every window on the second floor. The warehouse rocked on its foundation, dust and plaster raining down inside as fissures opened in the second floor. The fire escape was jolted loose and swung through space, a rusty pendulum, as several of its anchor bolts ripped free of ancient mortar.

Bolan caught himself and clutched the handrail, dangling twenty feet above the ground. The Ingram swung from its shoulder strap, but Bolan had the weapon well in hand before his adversaries on the ground began to cautiously emerge from cover.

One of them was smiling as he raised his pistol, sighting on the human fly. Bolan wiped the smile off with a stream of 9 mm parabellums, tracking on to tag the other guns as they recoiled from the reality of sudden death. The Ingram emptied out a second time, but there was nothing he could do about reloading at the moment.

At the moment there would be no need.

He scrambled halfway down the fire escape, let go and cleared the last ten feet in free-fall, dodging clear as something groaned and snapped above him. Folding in upon itself, the staircase buried his assailants, setting up a makeshift monument to mark their passing.

Bolan's car was parked two blocks away. He slid behind the wheel as sirens started keening in the distance, drawing closer. He was on the move before revolving colored lights flashed past him, first police and then a fire truck closing in on the disaster scene.

Tonight, he thought, disaster might have been averted . . . or at least postponed. The war in Northern Ireland would continue, but the next man killed wouldn't be slain with *those* guns, blown to shreds with *those* grenades.

It was a fair night's work and he was almost done.

Almost.

There was the matter of a phone call to be made, a brief report to put the bureaucratic mind at ease. He drove for half an hour, found a pay phone in suburban Brookfield, had the all-night operator patch him through.

"Hello?" The gruff, familiar voice had been called from somewhere on the verge of sleep.

"It's done."

"No problems?"

"Nothing major. Go back to sleep. I'm standing down."

"Oh, Striker?" Bolan scarcely recognized the tone of hesitance. "Before you disengage, there's one other thing. . . ."

1

The drugs were kicking in, and Susan settled back against the back seat of the van, eyes fading in and out of focus on the colored lights that flickered past outside. She felt detached and distant from the street scene, traffic crawling, people jostling along the sidewalk in defiance of the hour. Some of them might be her friends. They might appreciate an invitation to the party, but she couldn't pick them out, and Susan thought her new acquaintances wouldn't have stopped the van in any case.

A sudden stab of paranoia lanced the swirling mist inside her skull. Where were they taking her? Would she be home before her parents missed her in the morning?

The girl giggled, apprehension pushed aside, forgotten. She'd stumbled onto a golden opportunity, and if her parents learned that she'd crept away from home in bald defiance of their orders, if they grounded her forever, it would still be worth the hassle. She'd seen the concert of a lifetime.

Better, she was off to meet the band.

At first she'd been wary of the tall man who approached her in the milling crowd, inquiring whether she would like to meet "the boys" and share a little celebration afterward. It seemed peculiar, when she thought about it, that the meeting hadn't taken place backstage. But then again, she knew the members of the band would want to split as soon as possible, head back to their hotel and party down while roadies handled all the dirty jobs, like breaking down the set and packing up the instruments. You couldn't honestly expect the stars to hang around and waste their time like everybody else.

And she would see them soon. *They* would see *her*.

She noticed fewer lights outside and dimly realized that they were almost out of town. She didn't recognize the neighborhood and couldn't read the street signs as they ran together in a dancing blur of green and white.

The darkness wasn't friendly anymore.

For just an instant Susan thought of screaming, lunging for the door, but they were doing sixty-five or better, and anyway, there was a guy—the tallest of the three—prepared to cut her off if she attempted to escape. He didn't *look* prepared, but there was something in the way he sat, hands folded in his lap, that made her think of that old television show she sometimes watched on Sunday reruns.

Fading now. What was the name?

Kung-Fu. Of course.

She almost giggled, despite her fear. The tall guy didn't look Chinese. In fact he wouldn't be half bad if he could shake the air of latent menace that surrounded him.

Another rush washed in from nowhere, unexpected, lulling Susan's fears. Whatever else these men might be, they scored some bitchin' party favors. Susan realized she was getting paranoid, surrendering to her imagination and allowing fantasy to run away with her. Her new friends didn't want to hurt her. They were taking her to meet the band.

But where?

She understood that superstars might have to find themselves a hideaway where they were safe from groupies, hustlers and wackos like the dude who shot John Lennon when Susan was a child, in elementary school. The really great groups attracted freaks the way a magnet draws iron filings. You could never be too careful in this world.

So why the hell was she sitting in a van with three guys she'd only met that evening, cruising through the dark to who knows where?

To meet the band.

Despite her relatively tender years, she understood that superstardom was a cosmic gift bestowed upon the chosen few. It struck like lightning, picking out this one or that one, and the generated heat was such that most of the elect burned out within a year or two. Some died or lost their minds; most merely faded out of sight, reminding Susan of those mornings when you caught the sun and moon together in the sky and you could barely see the moon at all.

Most people only dreamed of greatness, never coming close. Aware that she didn't possess the seeds of anything remarkable within herself, she would be satisfied to bask in the reflected glow of fame and fortune for an hour or two. Perhaps, with any luck, a little of the magic might rub off.

The van was slowing, turning off the highway. Susan had a fuzzy glimpse of wrought-iron gates with ornate figures—were they angels?—on an arch above the drive. There was a short guy dressed in leather waiting at the gate to let them in.

"Where are we?" Susan asked of no one in particular.

"You'll see," the driver replied.

They drove on through and Susan saw the short guy hustling to close the gates behind them. Dark trees loomed on either side, their branches tangled in a canopy above the curving drive. They seemed to wind forever through the darkness, driving aimlessly, but Susan realized she couldn't trust her sense of time and distance. She was thrashed and there were no two ways about it.

When they finally stopped she craned her neck to scope in on the party house, but there was no sign of any buildings. Wait. There was a little structure that resembled a blockhouse, barely visible from where she sat, with faint light emanating from inside. She felt another stab of apprehension, but the drugs were good and strong. They did their job.

She wobbled on her feet as she got out of the van, and they were there to help her, strong hands taking Susan's arms and keeping her from falling. She felt the grass beneath her feet and tried to focus on the stones that thrust up from the earth on every side. The stones inscribed with names and dates she couldn't read.

"What is this place?"

"Relax. It's party time."

The small building loomed before them, and she watched the door swing open, trailing chains along the ground with rasping sounds that set her teeth on edge. Inside, a warm, seductive light was flickering and casting shadows on the walls.

Four men were waiting for them in the bunker, wearing robes of midnight black that hung below their knees. Torches had been mounted on the walls around the claustrophobic chamber, and there were candles—fat and black—arranged before her in a circle on the floor. She saw that something resembling a giant star was painted on the wall directly opposite the door, except the star appeared to have a face. In the center of the candle ring, an elevated slab of marble stood approximately level with her waist.

"So where's the band?" she asked, a small worm of anxiety uncoiling in her bowels.

"They'll be along."

The words were spoken by the tallest of the four robed strangers. He had tawny hair that fell about his shoulders, and a Fu Manchu mustache that framed his thin, unsmiling lips. His eyes reflected torchlight like an animal's, and Susan was reminded of the way her dogs looked when a flashlight was turned on them in the dark.

Susan was distracted by the sounds of rustling cloth behind her, and she turned to find her three new friends all slipping into black robes of their own. The driver caught her watching him and smiled.

"Where's everybody else?"

"You must prepare yourself," the tall guy with the funky eyes informed her, circling around the altar stone until he stood before her. Susan's face was level with his chest.

"Where's everybody else?" she persisted.

"You have been chosen."

Susan didn't like the sound of that. She loved a party, but she didn't want to *be* the party. Not with seven guys, at least. The way she felt just then, she might have taken on the band, but these were strangers, with the emphasis on *strange*, and Susan wished with all her heart that she was safe at home.

Pale hands came up before her face and passed a vial of something sweet beneath her nose. She didn't even have to snort it this time. Suddenly the room began to spin, and she would've fallen if the helping hands had not reached out, permitting her to keep her balance as her clothing fell away. Her bra went last, and Susan felt her nipples harden from the sudden chill.

She offered no resistance as they lifted her and placed her on the altar stone, slick marble cool against her naked skin. She didn't know what kind of shit the man had given her just then, but she would have to ask before they took her home. Her body was on fire, and Susan felt a pleasurable tingling in her loins. The drug was dynamite.

Seven faces ringed the altar stone, eyes studying her body. Susan didn't mind. The way she felt just now, it wouldn't be so bad to share the wealth with newfound friends. That way she would be ready when the members of the band arrived.

The tall man with the funky eyes was saying something that she couldn't understand. At first she thought the drugs had scrambled her reception, but she finally realized that he was speaking in a foreign language. He would pause from time to time, and his companions would repeat whatever he had said, their voices echoing in mournful chorus.

It was trippy lying there with seven guys around her, the center of attention in her birthday suit. Seven guys with one thing on their minds, she thought, and giggled. It was kind of flattering, all things considered, that they wanted her this much.

She thought of giving them a little show to get things started, and the notion was so radical that she had to laugh out loud. Both hands were sliding down across her hips and homing on the target zone, when someone grabbed her wrists on either side. Her arms were pinned against the altar stone, and when she tried to rise, another pair of hands secured her shoulders. Susan tried to kick but someone had her by the ankles, levering her legs apart.

The knife came out of nowhere, hovering before her eyes, the blade reflecting torchlight. Everyone was chanting in unison now, and Susan was reminded of a scene from some forgotten horror film, the kind her dorky younger brother watched on weekends when their parents weren't around. She tried to struggle but found the chemicals had robbed her of her strength.

A sudden ringing silence descended on the scene, and the tall man with the knife was bending down to whisper in her ear. "You have been chosen, child. Rejoice."

And then he straightened, the knife poised overhead in both his hands. The fog had lifted and her eyes were crystal clear. She saw death coming and there wasn't even time to scream.

2

The motel sat on Highway 40 near the South Platte River, west of downtown Denver. Mack Bolan recognized the place as one of several thousand look-alikes that marked the map from coast to coast. For twenty dollars, give or take, you would be guaranteed a room that looked the same in Terre Haute or Tuscaloosa. Everything would be identical across the board, from tacky bedspreads and the mass-production "artwork" on the walls to strips of paper promising the toilet had been Sanitized for Your Protection. Menus in a thousand different coffee shops would be identical, and everything you ate would taste the same.

The place wouldn't have been his choice, but Bolan wasn't choosing this time. The meeting place had been selected for him. He'd promised. He was here. Case closed.

The urgency in Hal Brognola's voice came back to Bolan, nearly audible despite the intervening hours and miles. "I've got this guy you oughta talk to," the big Fed had said.

"So, what's the deal?"

Brognola hesitated. "I don't know if you'd believe me. I don't know if *I* believe it all. Go see the guy, okay? Just hear him out and make your mind up for yourself. Whatever you decide."

"That's pretty vague."

"Just humor me, all right?"

"I'll need a name, some background on the guy."

"He's Amos Carr—that's *Dr.* Carr, the Ph.D. variety. His doctorate's in sociology, with emphasis on mind control and behavior modification. Brainwashing, dig it? He's also been a cop for close to twenty years. Retired three years ago, as chief of some department up in Minnesota. Since he packed it in he works full-time as a consultant to the boys in blue.''

''And what do they consult him for, exactly?''

''That's the part you'll have to scope out for yourself. Okay? You'll go?''

''I'll go.''

And here he was. The room he sought was ground floor, rear. Its single window would provide a narrow river view, if anyone should care to open up the curtains. A cardboard sign suspended from the doorknob indicated that the tenant didn't wish to be disturbed.

Too bad.

The soldier slipped a hand inside his jacket, felt the reassuring weight of the Beretta in its armpit sling. He thought the other hardware would be safe where he'd left it, in the trunk. Before he locked the driver's door, he set the tamperproof alarm and promptly put it out of mind. If anybody tried to monkey with the car, it would produce a shrilling loud enough to wake the dead.

He listened briefly at the door, made out the manic patter of a television game show, knocked. The TV died before Vanna had a chance to turn her letters, and he caught the sound of footsteps cautiously approaching. Bolan took a backward step and slid the zipper on his jacket down, providing better access to the piece beneath his arm.

The door inched open and a face appeared. Its owner was a stocky man of middle age, perhaps five-nine, with wavy hair that had begun to thin and lose its midnight sheen to creeping gray. He wore a dress shirt, chinos . . . and he kept his left hand out of sight behind the door.

''What is it?''

''Dr. Carr?''

''You're Blanski?''

''In the flesh.''

''Small world.''

''And getting smaller all the time.''

The password had been Carr's idea, relayed by Brognola. The Executioner was used to cryptic meetings, but his present contact seemed a tad uncomfortable in the role of secret agent.

"Welcome to my home away from home."

It was the room he had expected. Carbon copy. Spic-and-span. At Carr's direction Bolan closed the door, made sure that it was locked. His face was deadpan as the older man replaced his Smith & Wesson Magnum on the nightstand.

"Hunting grizzlies?"

"Maybe. Maybe worse."

"Look, Dr.—"

"Make it Amos, will you? Keeps me humble."

"Fine. I think you ought to know—"

"You're here at Hal's request, and you're a busy man. Brognola ran it down for me already. I appreciate your coming here to see me, and I'll try to make it worth your time."

"Okay." He found a chair across from Carr and settled into it.

"How much did Hal explain?"

"I got your name, a twenty-second bio. Nothing more."

"Okay, I'll start at the beginning. Did he tell you that I used to be a cop?"

"He mentioned it."

"For damn near twenty years. I came up through the ranks, from beat patrol to captain, finally chief. Along the way I figured it was time to get my ass in gear and try a few new tricks. I started going back to school at night, and pretty soon I couldn't get enough. It seemed like everything I learned could be applied, somehow, to law enforcement."

Bolan nodded, waiting for the punch line.

"Anyway, I mention that to let you know I'm not some fuzzy-headed academic out to revolutionize the system. I believe in punishment to fit the crime, but first you have to catch the bastards. Education helps."

"I understand."

"I guess Hal told you my department wasn't very large. Big fish, small pond, okay? The point is that I got to know my neighbors, on and off the force. Good people for the most part. Seven years ago we had a suicide. A teenage boy. Seems like I'd known his parents half my life. They found him in a cemetery five miles out of town. He opened up a grave and cracked the coffin, crawled inside with what was left and slit his wrists. The note he left said, 'Father Satan, I am coming home.' ''

"It happens."

"Not in small-town Minnesota. Not to friends of mine, for Christ's sake. I was stunned. The whole damned town was stunned. The undertaker found tattoos—Satanic symbols, runes—and self-inflicted scars that might have been as much as two years old. This kid spent two years dying, don't you see? And no one even noticed."

"Like I said, it happens."

"Right. I read the papers, too, but I decided that it couldn't hurt to run a background check and find out how he plugged into the devil-worship scene. I went in looking for the motive to a teenage suicide, and what I found was seven other kids who knew he planned to kill himself. He told them all about it at a meeting in the woods. They sat around a bonfire, smoking grass and casting spells. One night he up and told them he was going home to Satan. Everybody thought it was a great idea."

Carr fetched two cans of beer from a cooler on the dresser, offered one to Bolan, cracked the other for himself.

"The more I dug, the worse it got. These kids had organized a coven—that's a witch's circle—and they were experimenting on their own with Satanism, voodoo, anything that had to do with sex, drugs and power. They were robbing graves and vandalizing churches, selling pills around the elementary schools and mutilating pets. Before we wrapped it up I had a dozen kids hauled into juvey court on thirty, forty different charges."

"But you cracked it."

"Wrong. I stumbled on the tip of one ungodly iceberg. Like a flash, before the newsprint dried, I'm getting calls from all around the country, other cops with suicides and homicides and every other crazy thing. I started finding out the trouble wasn't only in my own backyard. It's everywhere."

"I've heard about these so-called covens," Bolan said. "From what I understand, they're mostly kids plugged into dope and heavy-metal rock, rebelling any way they can against their families, their schools, 'the system.' The majority don't know a demon from a dump truck.''

Carr was nodding. "Right. You've put your finger on the problem. Every time the subject's raised we see another headline: Juveniles Arrested, No Substantial Evidence of Cult Involvement Found in Local Crimes. Because the kids are amateurs. The kids get caught. How many adults have you seen sent up for cult-related crime?''

Bolan couldn't think of one. He said so.

"Right again. In fact there've been a few, but every time the bastards come to court, some prosecutor says the crimes were drug-related, sex-related, pick your poison. What D.A. would stake his reputation on a charge of human sacrifice? You might as well ask jurors to believe your perpetrator flies around in UFOs. It's too bizarre to be believed, and that's the secret in a nutshell.''

Bolan frowned. "From what I've heard, there doesn't seem to be much evidence. Some child-molesting cases, bargained down or dropped when stories didn't gibe. Those digs a few years back when everybody was expecting bodies and they came up empty.''

"I was there," Carr said. "Toledo, back in '85. You're right about the bodies. Zip. We *did* find daggers, fetishes, inverted crosses, children's clothing. Sixty-three right shoes. No lefts, you follow? And a few miles down the road, in Marysville, they had 260 animals found sacrificed and mutilated over eighteen months. No bodies, though. You've got me there.'' Carr smiled. "I got a call around the time the stories broke and everybody started laughing at the sheriff there. Guy wouldn't give his name. He said, 'You had us worried. You were getting close.' ''

"It could have been a crank," the Executioner suggested.

"Sure. I thought so, too, at first. But then I started picking up the rumbles out of California, New York City, *North Dakota*, if you can believe it. Something heavy going down among the covens. Wackos closing ranks, I guess you'd say. The same names started turning up at crimes scenes all across the country. Everywhere I looked, the story was the same.''

"What names?"

"Are you familiar with the Chingon cult? The Black Cross? Children of the Flame?"

"Can't say it rings a bell."

"I'm not surprised. There aren't a hundred cops in the United States who care enough to learn the inside story." Carr was on his feet and bustling around the room, removing pictures from the wall directly opposite the bed, returning to produce a slide projector from his luggage. Setting up a tray of slides, he crawled on hands and knees to reach an outlet tucked away beneath the nightstand. "Will you catch the lights?"

A wedge-shaped photograph was thrown up on the wall, its surface mottled by the pattern of the stucco "screen." For all of that, the warrior had no trouble recognizing beachfront, with a pair of naked, headless bodies lying in the foreground.

"California, 1968," Carr told him. "It's the first time anybody caught a whisper of the Chingon cult. They also called themselves the Four Pi Movement. God knows why. These kids were camping when their luck ran out. Investigation turned up mention of a devil cult that dealt in drinking blood and eating human hearts. No names, you understand. That all came later."

Bolan recognized the grinning features that replaced the beach scene. Wild eyes flashing through a veil of tangled hair. A swastika carved deep into the crinkled forehead.

"Charlie Manson. Now, I *know* you've heard the 'Helter Skelter' rap, and he believed it to a point. But we've got information now that indicates the Tate thing was a contract, probably retaliation for a drug burn. Manson was connected with the Four Pi Movement and a couple other fringe groups well before the murders. More important, the surviving members if his 'family' are still in touch with various Satanic covens in the Chingon network."

A mug shot, next.

"Meet Stanley Bowers. He was picked up on a moving violation by the CHP in 1970. Before the officer could finish writing out his ticket, Bowers said, 'I have a problem. I'm a cannibal.' He meant it, too. They found a set of human knuckle bones inside a pouch he carried on his belt. He led them to the rest, near Yellowstone. A ranger. Mutilated and dismembered. Bowers ate his heart and bragged about it.

"For a while, they couldn't shut the bastard up. He talked about the Chingons, Charlie Manson, biker gangs, you name it. He confessed to murdering an artist up in San Francisco right around the time the Manson trial was under way. He says the Chingons wanted to distract police and make them think the killers from Los Angeles had headed north. It didn't work."

"And Bowers?"

"Oh, Montana gave him life. They had a bit of trouble with him in the joint. It seems he kept on trying to recruit his fellow inmates for a cove he was organizing. Anyway, they don't have problems with him now. He's been released. Address unknown."

The next face was familiar.

"David Berkowitz. The Son of Sam. No possible connection, right? You've got eight years and better than 2,000 miles between the crimes. Except we know from Berkowitz himself that he was tied in with a devil cult in Yonkers, called the Children of the Flame. Investigation indicates the Children are connected with the Chingon network, hand in glove."

"You're getting this from Berkowitz? As I recall, the guy was diagnosed a schizophrenic."

"Granted. He was also found to be completely competent for trial. The fact is we have eyeball witnesses from the vicinity of every shooting done by Son of Sam. I figure Berkowitz is good for two or three of them at best. The others, he would have to lose a hundred pounds and sit for plastic surgery to measure up."

"You've had enough experience to know eyewitnesses are mostly unreliable."

"I'm way ahead of you." Another slide came up, a chart of sorts: dates and names arranged in columns on the left; more dates, with cryptic names of holidays, presented on the right.

"The bastards struck eight times," Carr said, "and every homicide fell kissing-close to a Satanic holiday. Myself, I'm no believer in coincidence."

"That doesn't link the Sam and Manson cases," Bolan said uneasily.

"You're right. This does."

The next slide was a photographic reproduction of a book, held open so that two opposing pages were displayed. The running head told Bolan that the book concerned itself with Satanism. Passages that mentioned Manson and the so-called Chingon cult were underlined in red, but Bolan's eyes were drawn to comments written in the margins of the left-hand page. Above the running head, someone had written "Stanford U." Along the outer margin had been written "Arliss Perry, hunted, stalked and slain."

"The notes were made by Berkowitz," Carr said, before he had a chance to ask. "The book was smuggled out of prison to a newsman in New York. Analysis confirms the penmanship, in case you're wondering."

He had been, but Bolan kept it to himself. Instead he asked, "Who's Arliss Perry?"

On command a lovely smiling face was cast onto the wall. The hair was blond, eyes bright. It was a face to cherish, and to die for. In the next shot he could scarcely recognize the face. Instead he forced himself to concentrate on the mutilated body, steeled himself to wonder if the wounds had any ritual significance.

"Before and after," Carr pronounced. "She left her dorm at Stanford on October 12, 1974, and never made it back. They found her in the chapel, as you see her here. An ice pick killed her, single blow behind the ear. The other wounds were all inflicted prior to death. And those are altar candles, by the way, between her breasts . . . and down below."

"Is there a possibility that Berkowitz picked up the name from someone doing time in New York State?"

"It's all been double-checked. He has no friends inside—at least no friends with any California time behind them. Anyway, there's more."

A car crash, next. The vehicle had slammed into a bridge abutment. Blood was painted on the inside of the windshield, where the driver's skull had made explosive impact.

"Tommy Pearson, named by Berkowitz—along with brother Joseph—as a member of the Yonkers cult. According to our boy, while he was talking, Pearson was the trigger on a couple of the shootings laid to Son of Sam. We'll never know. He bit the big one in October 1980. No vehicular malfunction the mechanics could discover."

Another change of scene, and Bolan saw a faceless body stretched out on a carpet that had once been green. The spreading pool of blood had changed all that. A shotgun lay beside the corpse.

"Joe Pearson," Carr informed him, "one month after brother Tommy took his dive. Apparent suicide in Fargo, North Dakota. Did I mention Arliss Perry came from North Dakota? Anyway, the theory is that Joey was distraught about his brother's death and he decided to check out. He put the muzzle of that shotgun in his mouth, and whammo! Problem is, he couldn't reach the trigger with the muzzle in his mouth. Impossible. The sheriff's men have checked it out. He also had his shoes on when he died, in case you were about to mention toes. The Black Cross hit them both."

"Which is?"

"They're designated hitters for the Chingon network. Got a problem in the coven? Drop a dime, it's taken care of. Just like magic."

"Let's assume there is a cult. They're killing one another off. Why interfere?"

"Because they're only killing off the members that we know about, and they're enlisting new replacements every day." A stately, academic structure was projected on the stucco. Bolan vaguely recognized the name.

"This private college in Los Angeles is funded by the Chingons," Carr informed him. "We have documented evidence of covens active on the campus."

"So go in and pull their damned credentials. Put them out of business."

"Guess again. The First Amendment guarantees them freedom of religion. Even devil-worshipers have rights."

The next five shots were mutilated bodies, young and female. There was something similar about each scene, aside from wounds, and Bolan finally caught it. All the corpses had been photographed in cemeteries.

"Something new," Carr told him, leaving up the final shot of what appeared to be a mausoleum's interior. "Six months, five bodies. Teenage girls, their blood drained, hearts removed. The killer gets around. So far they've seen his work in Dallas, San Francisco, Memphis, Birmingham and Cleveland."

"All identical?"

"The slice and dice is carbon copy. Also, we find this at every scene."

The next slide showed a wooden plank that had been decorated with inverted crosses and a pentagram. A message had been added, painted on with something that resembled blood.

Woe to you, O earth and sea,
For the Devil sends the Beast with wrath.
Let him who has understanding
Reckon the number of the Beast, for it is
A human number.
Its number is six hundred and sixty-six.

"That's lifted from the Book of Revelations, more or less intact," Carr said. "Our killers read the Bible, it would seem."

"You make that plural. Is there evidence of group involvement?"

"Semen and saliva tests make different blood types for the perpetrators. We've got casts of footprints, tire tracks. Everything we need, in fact, except a bunch of suspects sitting in the tank."

"It sounds like one for VICAP. They're equipped to handle serial investigations."

"They're equipped, and understaffed. Last time I checked they had eight men assigned to cover the United States. That's eight against an estimated forty random killers presently at large. The forty that we know about. On top of that, the FBI isn't convinced it should be hunting witches. Anyway, not *this* kind."

"Well..."

"I ought to mention one more link between the recent killings. Each and every one took place immediately after an appearance by Apocalypse."

"The heavy-metal band?"

"*Black* metal. There's a difference. Groupies call it death metal or thrash metal." Carr made a sour face. "Your basic heavy-metal bands are party animals. You check their lyrics out, and get an overdose of sex and drugs and rock 'n' roll. Black metal is a different rap entirely. The message is occult, death oriented, rape and mutilation, sex at gunpoint—all the finer things in life."

"And you believe the band is killing girls?"

"I wish it was that simple. Frankly I'm not sure exactly what to think, but there's a tie-in. I can feel it in my gut. The past few months, each time those bozos play a gig a young girl winds up dead and mutilated."

"Only in the past few months?" He frowned. "This band has been around for what, two years?"

"It's more like three, and sure, I understand your question. Back in January they acquired a brand-new 'spiritual adviser,' one Lucian Slate. Informants on the fringes of the devil-worship scene had made him as a member of the Chingon-Four Pi network."

Bolan focused on the face that filled the opposite wall. A brooding countenance, all lines and creases, shaggy brows that met above a Roman nose, dark eyes set deep in pools of shadow.

"Cheerful, isn't he? You're looking at the brains behind the new Apocalypse. Unless I miss my guess he's got a handle on five homicides. I'd say the odds are good that he could crack the Chingon net wide open, given proper motivation."

"Where do I come in?"

"Hal tells me you're a motivator."

"What's your angle?"

Carr turned off the slide projector, turning on a lamp beside the bed. "So far the murders coincide with concerts by

Apocalypse. By sheer coincidence, they're playing gigs at Mile High Stadium the next three nights.

"Coincidence?"

"So sue me. Are you game?"

He thought about it, nodded. "We'll need tickets."

"Done. I had to pay a scalper, but they're in the bag."

"When do we leave?"

"Right now. It's pushing show time."

3

It was an easy quarter mile from Amos Carr's motel to Mile High Stadium, but crawling traffic slowed them down. Carr used the time to brief him on the band that called itself Apocalypse.

"Light reading," Carr advised him, dropping half a dozen magazines in Bolan's lap before he put the car in motion. From the titles and the photos on their covers, Bolan gathered they were all directed toward a teenage audience, with emphasis on heavy-metal rock and roll. The articles about Apocalypse had been secured with paper clips, and Bolan checked them out while Carr kept up a running monologue.

"This gig is part of what they call the Slaughter Tour, okay? Road tours are basically designed to pump an artist's latest album, whipping up big bucks at record stores. In this case *Souls for Slaughter* is the album, and the title gives a pretty fair synopsis of the message."

Bolan's eyes were on a two-page color spread in *Metal Madness*. It depicted five young men in studs and leather, naked arms defaced by serpentine tattoos. Their faces had been blanched by makeup that reminded Bolan of mortician's paint; their hair—four dark, one blond—was past the shoulders, spiked on top, with an electric frizz. Each held his left hand in a common gesture, with the thumb and middle fingers folded, index finger and pinky raised.

Carr caught his interest in the fold out. "To your basic metal groupies, that's the 'power sign,'" he said. "In fact it comes direct from Satanism, as a recognition symbol passed between members of a coven. Cultists call it the horned hand, symbolizing Lucifer." Carr grinned. "It also frightens the bejesus out of Hare Krishnas at the airport. You should try it.''

Bolan laid the magazine aside and riffled through another. Action snapshot of Apocalypse in concert. Singing. Sweating. Stretching out their tattooed arms to young girls pressing close around the stage.

"The blonde's Clay Deatheridge," Carr said. "But you can call him Death. They all use 'heavy' stage names for the benefit of prepubescent Walter Mittys in the audience. Clay sings the leads and holds the band together when their spiritual adviser's not around to pull the strings.

"John Beamish is the drummer, a.k.a. Mephisto. Long on rhythm, short on brains, from what I hear. He couldn't punctuate a sentence if his life depended on it, but he gives the band that special beat you can't forget—or so they claim.

"The lead guitarist is a self-styled ladies' man named Mike O'Neal. He goes by Skull onstage. Six months ago he ran a stop sign in Topanga Canyon, flying high on booze and what-the-hell. He hit another car head-on and killed the driver. She was all of seventeen. His record company picked up the funeral tab and put another hundred K on top for icing. Skull got off with ten days in the lockup, and they let him serve the time on week*days*, in between his gigs.''

"A prince."

"You're mispronouncing 'prick,' my friend. That's Freddy Sykes on bass guitar. His stage name's Ripper. Back before he got religion Freddy had a thing for teenage girls. Still does, for all I know. He served eleven months with L.A. County on a charge of statutory rape, with half a dozen priors for contributing, indecency, you name it. PR has it that he's changed his spots. You buy that, I've got a lakefront property in Arizona you can have real cheap.''

Carr made a risky lane change, edging toward the curb and falling in behind a line of cars directed toward the parking lot of Mile High Stadium, still about twenty minutes away.

"The skinny guy on keyboards," Carr continued, "is a cokehead by the name of Tommy Piersall, known as Ax to his adoring fans. No record as an adult, but he spent a lot

of time with CYA—that's California Youth Authority—
before he started making music. You could park a semi-
trailer in his sinuses and Tommy wouldn't know the difference.''

Bolan thought it sounded like the profile on a hundred
other bands. Much of the modern rock-and-roll business
lived on drugs, rebellion and the theory that there was no
such thing as bad publicity. He had to know what made
these rockers different.

"What's the bottom line on this Satanic rap?" he asked.

"A valid question. One way or another, damn near every
metal band employs demonic trappings. Most of them are
money-hungry poseurs. They run around with pentagrams
and scribble 666 across their foreheads with a magic marker,
but it doesn't stand for shit. A few bands, like Apocalypse
and Venom, make no secret of the fact they dabble in the
arts. Word has it Deatheridge installed a ritual chamber in
his house at Malibu. Check out the lyrics on their albums
and I think you'll find it pretty heavy going. Then there's
always backward masking.''

"Come again?"

"You know, the messages you only hear when someone
spins the record backward. *Souls for Slaughter* has a dozen
different inserts, give or take. All kinds of shit like 'Satan is
my savior,' 'Lucifer is love' and whatnot. They've got one
track—I think it's 'Blood for Beelzebub'—that's more coherent backward than it is in normal time.''

"But isn't that a gimmick, really? Spinning all those records backward wears them out, I understand, and then the
suckers have to buy a whole new batch.''

"That's part of it, I guess. The PR men from Acid records—that's the label handling Apocalypse—might tell you
it's the only motive, but I'm not so sure. Remember all that
hoopla in the early sixties dealing with subliminal advertising in movies?''

"The popcorn flashed on-screen?"

"You've got it. One or two frames, carefully inserted in
a motion picture running two, three hours, and it still made
people hungry. Five, ten minutes after those two frames ran
by, too fast for anybody's conscious mind to register, the

snack bar was a mob scene. The technique was outlawed, incidentally. You still can't use subliminals in movies or on television. Records, on the other hand, are virgin territory.''

"What's the difference?''

"Loopholes in the law, for openers. Besides, the band will tell you they're not selling anything. It's not commercial. No one hears an album and runs out to buy a quart of Lucifer. It's silly, right? Unless you've got some disillusioned, coked-out youngster running through the same damn song a hundred times a day.''

They crept into the lot and spent another fifteen minutes searching out an empty parking space. The stadium appeared no closer, and from where he stood, the warrior thought it might have saved them time to walk from Carr's motel.

"Your ticket," Amos told him, handing off a strip of purple cardboard. "If we happen to get separated, meet me back here afterward.''

Inside, the stadium was playing host to orchestrated chaos. Bolan didn't even try to estimate the numbers, sticking close to Carr and feeling years out of touch as youngsters ranging from their early teens to college age surrounded them on every side. He felt conspicuous, but nothing seemed to phase the audience, as everyone sought places closer to the stage. Police were very much in evidence, indifferent eyes disguised by mirror shades, and Bolan noticed that they traveled everywhere in twos or threes.

The faithful were a human rainbow representing every race and ethnic background, unified by shaggy, unkempt hair and style of dress. The favored uniform was leather, with the kind of chrome and stainless steel accessories once found exclusively in biker bars or taverns where assorted masochistic gays went shopping for rough trade. If all the chains and studs and cartridge belts and handcuffs had been melted down, there might have been enough steel in the audience to build a fleet of limousines.

The faces were vacant for the most part, slack-jawed, demonstrating animation only when a squeal of feedback echoed from the speakers placed strategically around the stadium. At each eruption of electric sound the crowd responded in unison with a shout, and several thousand hands were raised together, brandishing the power sign.

Carr nudged him in the ribs and drew him toward the stairs that sloped away, in the direction of the stage. "Let's boogie. Don't be bashful now. It's party time."

HER PARENTS WOULD BE FURIOUS if they could see her, but the prospect didn't trouble Amy Hatcher at the moment. She was in her element, surrounded by her old and future friends; the band was warming up backstage, and she was high enough that retribution from her family still seemed years away.

In her own defense, she hadn't lied. Not really. She'd told her parents that she planned to spend the night with Jill, her closest friend, and that was true. Last time she noticed, Jill had been around somewhere, talking to a great-looking guy.

And Amy hadn't lied.

She never said they meant to spend the night *alone*.

It should have been ridiculously easy, picking up a guy with so much beef to choose from. Jill had managed well enough, it seemed, but she had always been the more outgoing one, less bashful once she fixed her sights upon a designated target. Not that Amy was a shrinking violet by any means. She simply didn't have the talent for seduction that her oldest, dearest friend possessed. And if the truth were told, she didn't have Jill's body, either.

Amy sometimes hated Jill, but only for a moment at a time. It wasn't Jill's fault that Amy had a boyish figure and her braces wouldn't be removed until next spring. You had to put the blame where it belonged: on Mother Nature and the old familial gene pool. Amy's mom was pretty and petite, but she'd never pass for Dolly Parton, either. On her father's side, the lanky frame and crooked smile had been transmitted nicely, thank you very much. Her parents told her she would be a knockout "some day," but she needed some attention *now*.

The crowd was warming up in preparation for the openers. A band called Spasm would be opening the concert, but Amy wasn't thinking of the music now. Her eyes were on the faces and the bodies that surrounded her, observing, taking mental notes for future reference.

She decided she was dressed all wrong, for starters. Jeans were passable, but she felt almost dowdy in her blouse and denim jacket. All around her girls were sporting leather, fishnet and a scattering of outfits that resembled lingerie. Unwritten guidelines called for maximum display of merchandise, but Amy didn't have that much to show, and guys were clearly going where the action was.

At least she had the music, and the ludes that Jill had lifted from her mother's stockpile. Amy wasn't into major drugs, but she enjoyed a party, and from time to time the chemicals forestalled depression when she thought about her love life.

No, correction: *lack* of love life.

Going on sixteen and she was still a virgin. There were others in her school, of course, but they were dogs, geeks and bitches. Amy didn't fit in any of the outcast categories. She had dated sparingly, could party hearty with the best of her contemporaries, but the guys still went for Jill, or any one of fifty others she could name. It was humiliating, when she thought about it. And, of late, she thought about it plenty.

This would have to be the night. She had decided. There might never be another concert quite so radical, a crowd so large and free of inhibitions. She might wither up and die before next week was out, but Amy was determined that she wouldn't take her cherry with her.

She was going all the way. Tonight.

No sign of Jill. They had arranged a rendezvous for later, granting each other some privacy if they got lucky. Amy didn't miss Jill at the moment. She would only be an obstacle, distracting guys who might be interested in Amy. Granted, those were few and far between, but in a crowd this size there *had* to be at least one boy who didn't find her totally repulsive.

Amy wasn't desperate enough to settle for a sleazoid. There were always geeks around, although you wouldn't find too many of them turning out to hear Apocalypse. In this crowd she worried more about the heavy stoners, guys who didn't know what they were doing half the time, who liked it rough when they were wasted. They were dangerous, and while she felt a tiny shiver of excitement at the prospect, Amy knew that she was absolutely dead if she went home with bruises she couldn't explain.

So she was looking for a *decent* guy, no monkey on his back, no obvious diseases, who would take the time to turn her life around. She wasn't shopping for a serious relationship; a quicky might be adequate, if it was handled with a sense of style.

She worked her way in the direction of the stage, deliberately brushing up against a hunk or two and getting no response. In the confusion, if they noticed her at all, they probably mistook her for an awkward little girl. A new approach was indicated, but she wasn't really sure—

The hand on her shoulder startled Amy, made her jump. She turned to find a tall, sharp-looking guy regarding her with something like amusement.

"Did I scare you?"

"No. Not really."

Amy tried to peg his age and quickly gave it up, deciding that he might have been eighteen or twenty-five. You couldn't always tell with guys, but he was gorgeous, no two ways about it, with his long blond hair and steel-blue eyes.

"You here alone?"

She shook her head. "With friends." She made it plural on an impulse, feeling vulnerable as he looked her over, blue eyes taking time to check her out.

"Where are they?"

Amy shrugged. Her smile was hesitant. "I'm s'possed to meet them later."

"So you're on your own right now?"

She took a chance. He seemed so nice. "I guess."

"I'll bet you'd like to meet the band."

It took her by surprise. "What band?"

"*What* band? Get real. Apocalypse."

"Oh, sure."

"I'm serious." He did a magic trick and held up two backstage passes before her startled eyes. "You game?"

"Oh, wow!"

"I'll take that as a yes," he said. And smiled.

"So, where the hell is Lucian?"

Clay shrugged off the question. "Stuck in traffic. I don't know. He'll be here."

"Yeah, I hope so."

"Never fear." He turned to face the others, smiling. "Has he ever let us down?"

"Not yet," the drummer offered, putting final touches on his makeup.

"Hey, first time for everything," said Freddy Sykes. He looked a little green around the gills. Not Ready Fred at all.

"He's coming. Keep your shirt on."

Deatheridge was feeling edgy, too, but he would never let the others see it. He was still the leader, and a leader couldn't let it all hang out each time he suffered an attack of nerves. There were examples to be set, an image to maintain. He had to be a rock or everything could fall apart before you had a chance to scratch your ass and holler "Mayday!"

Lucian was late, so what? Outside the stadium the traffic must be backed up for a mile or more. There had been pressing business, consultations with another acolyte, and Lucian was called away. It wasn't like they owned the guy or anything. Some days Clay thought it might have been the other way around.

Out front he heard the heavy-metal strains of Spasm cutting loose. The crowd responded with a single voice, a fair reception, but it wouldn't count for shit when the Apocalypse brigade came out onstage. There would be celebration then, and no mistake. The Master would be pleased.

Success had been a long time coming, from the days when Clay was still in high school, practicing with friends in a garage, through dead-end gigs he'd played for chump change, working overtime to build a reputation for himself. There were so many metal bands around, you couldn't tell the heavies from the poseurs any more, unless you had a built-in crap detector. Breaking in was basically impossible without a gimmick or a helping hand.

He thanked the Master for providing both. At first he wasn't sure they had a chance. So many bands were pseudo-Satanists these days, with their tattoos and bullshit videos of Dracula and all that crap, that when the real thing came along, most fans could hardly tell the difference. Education was required, along with reams of "bad" publicity, to drive the message home. It helped when homicide detectives in New York declared their latest subway slasher was "addicted" to the music of Apocalypse. It didn't hurt when teenage fan clubs—known as covens—started sacrificing pets and vandalizing cemeteries. They were rolling by the time hundreds, thousands, started answering the "alter calls" that climaxed each performance.

And they had reached the pinnacle when Lucian Slate had walked into their lives.

Clay hadn't gone out looking for him. It had been the other way around, from all appearances, though Lucian would never spell it out. He liked to say their steps were guided by the Master, steered by Fate, and that was fine with Clay. As long as Lucian got results.

So far so good. Slate's presence in the entourage had been a major draw in terms of new publicity. The Parent's Music Resource Center had been screaming bloody murder, calling for congressional investigations of the "heavy metal plague," and every time they hit the airwaves, Clay could count on better album sales next week. The past few months they had been dominating magazines like *Cream* and *Metal Madness*; there was even talk about an interview with *Rolling Stone*, provided Lucian would hang around to speak his piece.

Whoever said that it was lonely at the top was full of shit. Clay had his friends around him, all the woman he could handle plus a few besides, and he had Lucian to keep him on the straight and narrow if he ever lost his way.

Above all else, he had the Master in his heart.

The contract, in comparison, was trivial. It had been Lucian's sole condition on accepting a position with the band. He had been adamant, and in return he had been happy to accept a salary that barely put a dent in petty cash. Not that he *needed* money, after all. With patrons all around the country—hell, around the *world*—he never had a cash-flow problem. Living with the band, he had no overhead to speak of, and if Lucian had any private vices, Clay had been unable to discover them.

It had been eerie, writing out his name in blood, but still, a guy got what he paid for. Fucking ay.

He turned on impulse, facing toward the door as Lucian entered, smiling. Instantly Clay felt as if a monumental weight had just been lifted off his shoulders. He hung back and let the others crowd around, some of them reaching out to touch the man they held responsible for their success.

The dark man smiled at each of them in turn, then raised his eyes to meet Clay's gaze. Clay couldn't help but smile.

"My children." Slate stretched out his hand. Clay took it, linking up with Tommy on his left, and so on, right around the circle. "Let us pray."

He closed his eyes and felt the power humming through his soul. *"In domine Dei nostri Satanas Luciferi excelsi . . ."*

4

The Reverend Mr. Jordan Braithwaite listened to the fading strains of "Onward Christian Soldiers," smiling to himself as he surveyed the sea of faces spread before him. Eager faces. Hungry for the Word. They trusted him to meet their needs, conduct them on a tour of hell and bring them back again, unscathed. He knew the vast majority wouldn't be disappointed.

Brother Trent had launched into the prayer that always paved the way for Braithwaite's sermon. Soothing words at first, all glory and forgiveness, building to a climax that would call upon the godly to prepare themselves, gird up their loins for war against the Prince of Darkness. It would set the perfect tone for Braithwaite's message. He could *feel* the hush, a living, breathing thing, as he approached the podium in Denver's Municipal Auditorium. A heartbeat later and the lights were in his eyes. He might as well have been alone, rehearsing for his mirror, but he knew the crowds were out there, and the knowing was enough.

"Good evening, children," he began. "Of course, I call you children here tonight because we all are children of the living God who sired creation. If you live to be a hundred, you are still a child of God. You can reject your father, but our Father who created the heavens and the earth will not reject *you*. Can you say 'Amen'?"

It came back to him, weak and indecisive, from the first few dozen rows.

"I asked you, can you say 'Amen'?" he bellowed, and they got the message this time, answering with gusto. In the cheap seats, someone even started to applaud.

"That's better," Braithwaite told his people, visibly relaxing. "If the man or woman sitting in the seat next door can't hear you witnessing, the Lord might have a little problem with reception when you need him. Can you say 'Amen'?"

"Amen!" This time they got it right.

"Before we really start I want to thank each one of you for coming out tonight. I know that most of you have other things to do. I won't say *better* things, oh no. There's nothing better on this earth than an injection of the Holy Spirit. Let me tell you, it can keep you going when the times get lean."

"Amen."

"But some of you, I know, have *other* things to do." He dragged the "other" out until it sounded like a groan of pain. "Some of you here tonight have let the world sneak in and take the place of Jesus in your hearts. Admit it! You've allowed the world of men and things to occupy your time and occupy your mind so fully that you have no time for God. I'm here to tell you, there must be a change in those priorities and those behavior patterns *now*, or some of you are going to be mighty disappointed when the Judgment arrives!"

"Amen! Amen!"

He had them now, and he was rolling.

"Some of you have *better* thing to do than talk with Jesus. Some of you have got careers that need attention, country clubs and sports and countless other things that take your time away from God. You may be so caught up in the pursuit of money and possessions that you're gambling with your immortal soul and you don't even know it yet. I'm here to tell you that your Savior knows it, and the Devil knows it, too.

"You all remember Satan? I believe he might have slipped your minds. That doesn't mean he's gone away, of course. The Devil loves to be forgotten and ignored. Like any thief, he does his best work in the darkness, when his victims are asleep and he can take whatever suits him with a minimum of opposition. When the Devil slips your mind and you forget about the holy laws of God, you might as well put out a welcome sign, because I guarantee you Satan's going to be there!''

Braithwaite paused to let them soak that in, allowing scattered thoughts to form and coalesce. He seldom outlined sermons these days, and he never wrote them out. It simply wasn't necessary, when you knew the words by heart.

''Now some of you may be aware—you all *should* be, but this is where distractions get you down—that Satan and his imps from hell are putting on a show tonight, right here in Denver. Not two miles from here, while you sit back in comfort and delude yourself that everything's just fine as frog's hair in your own backyard. How many of you know exactly and for certain where your children are tonight?''

A whisper in the audience, responding to his question, escalating to a rumble.

''As I thought! Of course, you *hope* your sons and daughters are at home, tucked up in bed or finishing their homework, but I want to tell you there's an estimated sixteen *thousand* souls in need of Jesus packing Mile High Stadium right now, this minute, waiting for the hosts of hell to prance onstage. And while they wait they're smoking dope. They're taking pills. They're drinking alcohol. They're sneaking off behind the grandstands, in the washrooms, anyplace at all, to rut and fornicate like animals. I pray to Christ *your* children aren't among them, but you don't get sixteen thousand souls from nowhere. There are sixteen thousand families in danger of a grievous loss tonight, because they've tried to be so liberal and understanding that their children have no solid Christian values to fall back on in a time of trial.''

''Amen.''

''You *say* 'Amen,' '' he challenged them, ''but do you *mean* it, people? Do you mean 'So be it,' or are you content with 'Let it be'? The choice is yours. Your children look to you for an example in this world, and they can spot a hypocrite a mile away, I'm here to tell you. Some of you believe your children are so ignorant and blind that they won't recognize your little sins, but I've got news for you tonight. Your children recognize it, and your Savior recognizes it. Amen!''

"Amen! Amen!"

"All right, then, let's get down to basics. I don't gamble, but if I was forced to make a wager, I would bet that there are some among you who allow your sons and daughters to pursue a life of sin. You heard me! *Sin!* I didn't stutter! I'll lay odds that some of you have turned away while children trusted in your care tuned in the television set to MTV and let those godless, sinful images roll through their eyes and ears, straight down into their tender souls. I'll wager there are those among you who allow the filth of so-called heavy-metal music in your homes on tapes and record albums. I believe I'm safe in saying there are some among you who are absolutely unaware of *what* your children listen to when they turn on the radio or record player."

Guilty silence.

"Am I right?"

"Amen."

"I knew it! Well, I'm here to tell you there's a band made up of Satanists right here in Denver, playing at the Mile High Stadium tonight, tomorrow and the next night. They call themselves Apocalypse. It might as well be Anti-Christ because their message is demonic and licentious. They make no attempt to hide the fact they worship Satan, Prince of Darkness, Father of the Lie. Their music reeks of decadence, corruption and depravity.

"But I can tell you one thing, people, and I'll tell it to you straight. The members of this so-called band may be in league with Satan, but at least they're straight about it. They make no attempt to hide their light beneath a bushel. Have you seen their latest album? No? It's titled *Souls for Slaughter*, and they got that right the first time. Sixteen *thousand* souls in Denver, and that doesn't count the next two shows.

"No, this may come as a surprise, but music isn't simply music anymore. It's politics and it's religion all wrapped up together. This may shock you in your blissful ignorance—I hope it does—but when Apocalypse and several of your other so-called heavy-metal bands are finished pouring out their filth through song, they have an altar call. For Satan! Yes, you heard me! Even as you sit here in your comfortable chairs tonight, a crowd of sixteen thousand boys and girls are pledging their immortal souls to Satan. Not two miles away!''

The audience was silent now, and Braithwaite thought he heard the sound of someone weeping.

"Each and every one of us has a responsibility tonight. We owe a debt to Jesus for His intervention in a cause already lost, His sacrifice to make us whole and pure in His Father's sight. There might not be a thing that you and I can do to keep the filth of so-called artists like Apocalypse from poisoning the air waves, but there *is* a remedy. You can assist this ministry in counteracting the infernal damage done each day, each night, by Satan and his minions. When the ushers come around and pass those buckets, you can reach down *deep*—

DEATH PROWLED THE STAGE with microphone in hand, absorbing frantic energy that radiated from his shrieking, chanting audience. He played no instrument, so his hands were unencumbered as he raised one fist to flash the two-pronged sign of greeting to the faithful. Thousands gleefully responded, stamping on the bleachers with their combat boots and crowing to the heavens.

Death enjoyed an audience. It turned him on like nothing else.

Ax was warming up the keyboards, running through hellacious riffs and deafening the kids who jammed in close, against the stage. You might have thought that there would be a ceiling to the volume, an inherent limit to the sheer ear-splitting fury, but Skull and Ripper cracked the barrier when they unlimbered their guitars. Raw, squealing sounds of power burned inside Death's brain and set his soul on fire. And it was crazy; through it all, he didn't have a bit of trouble picking up Mephisto on the drums.

They opened every show with "Blood for Beelzebub," and Death could hear the Master's children echoing the words before he started singing. It was comforting to know they were ready, waiting, totally receptive as he joined in the cacophony and sang.

"Listen up now, Master's calling.
Shades of brutal night are falling.
Flames behind us, flames before,
Master's craving more of what he needs.
It's time to feed him now.
I'm bringing blood for Be-el-ze-bub,
A little taste of human kindness,
So much waste and so much blindness now."

The screaming faithful ate it up, and Death moved closer to the footlights, teasing them, permitting them the fantasy that they could just reach out and touch him any time they pleased. A couple of them tried it, and were violently repulsed by outlaw bikers hired to work security down front. Screw Altamont. If people got their heads cracked or their throats slit, it would guarantee a sellout in the next town down the line.

Each time he sang Death felt the spirit moving in him, gaining strength. When he was out onstage, committed to a song, he didn't think about the party that was bound to follow, or the girls who would be hanging out backstage and praying for an opportunity to be humiliated, used by anyone connected with the band. The sex, drugs and liquor didn't matter when he sang.

The lights and smoke that were a trademark of Apocalypse transformed the stage into a burning hellscape. Death moved through the writhing, twisting vapor like a wraith, accepting the ovation of his faithful, serving as a temporary stand-in for the Master. If they only realized...

He ran the chorus down again and faded back as Skull kicked off his solo, torturing the strings of his guitar until they took on almost human tones and cried for mercy. Standing close, with batteries of giant speakers banked on either side, the sound was nearly lost, but Death could feel the sweet vibration in his bones. He let the moment run and knew precisely when his cue was coming, magnetism from the masses drawing him toward center stage.

The audience was going wild, and Death slid back to let the instrumentals end it, winding up and up until he thought the heavy-metal shriek would separate his skull from its connection to his spine. Eyes tightly closed, he rode the crest of sound, and when the music broke with an explosive crash, he felt the pull of gravity exerting its control, reclaiming him and binding him to Mother Earth.

Behind him Skull and Ripper had the next song rolling well before the echoes of the first had died away. He recognized the strains of "Abaddon," the first of the infernal names, and gave it everything he had.

THE TWELFTH OR THIRTEENTH SONG was winding down. He couldn't be precise about the number; some of them had run together in the early part of the performance, and to Bolan's ringing ears they sounded much the same. He could remember bits and snatches of a few—"Love Weapon," "Lucifer Excelsis," "Bed of Pain"—and by the time they finished "Chainsaw," he would gratefully have traded his position, near the stage, for a secluded mountain cave.

"They're getting ready for the altar call," Carr told him, leaning close and shouting to be heard.

"What?"

"Hang on. You'll see."

The music faded, Gothic organ strains replacing frantic rhythms, and a hush descended on the crowd. Apparently the kids knew what was coming, and they seemed prepared to play their role dutifully.

Clay Deatheridge was pacing onstage like a big cat in a cage. The frontline troops, a greasy pack of bikers wearing leather, studs and sleeveless denim jackets, eyed the audience with dark suspicion, fingering the sawed-off pool cues they wore tucked through their belts. A few of them seemed disappointed by the fact that there had been no opportunity for cracking heads.

"We're almost finished now," Death announced, and there was instant opposition from the crowd. A moan that came from everywhere and nowhere, rippling around the stadium.

"We're almost finished now," he said again. "Almost. Not quite. There might be one thing left."

"All right!" A skinny kid near Bolan started jittering and rubbing grimy hands together. All around him others shifted in their seats or shuffled on their feet in time with music no one else could hear.

"His royal, exalted highness, Lucifer, requests the pleasure of your company," Death continued. "He offers you a chance to make your dreams come true. Tonight. Right now. No guilt, no inhibitions. Freedom, children. Can you dig it?"

From the rising sound of voices, Bolan gathered that they could.

"The time is now. No time for hesitation. He who hesitates is lost. The world is waiting, children, but you have to take it for yourselves."

A restless shifting in the audience as hundreds rose from bleacher seats and crowded toward the aisles.

"He's waiting, children. Can you feel Him? *Come on down!*"

They came, a human tide that clogged the aisles and jammed the stairwells, emptying the cheap seats. Carr and Bolan wedged themselves against a pillar, islands in the human stream, as Death turned back to face the band and flash a hungry smile. Without another word Apocalypse kicked into "Souls for Slaughter."

"Priceless diamonds on the line tonight,
A soul that shines so pure, so clean, so bright,
A living sacrifice the Master can't refuse,
We're bringing souls for slaughter. Spread the news."

Down front, the bikers didn't have a prayer of holding back the masses that surrounded them. If anyone had tried to reach the stage, they could have overwhelmed the scruffy guards with ease. But no one tried. In contrast to the mood that had prevailed throughout the concert, boys and girls pressed close together, solemn, nearly silent, answering the altar call.

"Can you believe it?" Carr was scowling at the spectacle, a small vein pulsing in his temple. "Jesus, what a scam."

When Bolan craned his neck to scan the stadium, he saw that roughly half the audience was crowding forward. Most of them could never hope to reach the stage, but they were answering the call as best they could. Of those who stayed behind, a few looked vaguely troubled; most were simply stoned.

As Bolan watched, Death raced across the stage, his microphone forgotten, scooping up a bucket from its place behind a bank of amplifiers. Grinning like a madman, he ran back in the direction of the footlights, winding up before he let the contents of the bucket fly. A crimson shower caught the lights in living Technicolor. Ruby droplets spattered upturned faces, streaking hair and decorating uniforms adopted by the faithful.

Blood.

He wondered what the band had used to thin it and prevent its clotting while the show was underway.

"I baptize one and all of you in Satan's name!" the singer bellowed.

Near the stage, the faithful had begun to slam-dance, butting heads and punching one another, smiling all the while. Fresh blood was added to the offering. A girl ripped off her top, displaying blood-streaked breasts, and eager hands began to paw her, smearing it around her torso. On the fringes of the crowd, police made no attempt to intervene.

"You seen enough?" Carr asked.

"And then some."

"Right. Let's see if we can make our way upstream."

5

The blond guy wasn't eighteen, nor was he twenty-five. He had in fact turned thirty-one the previous Thursday, but it didn't show. He still got carded sometimes when he went to bars, and while it was a nuisance dragging out the old ID, there was a fair amount of flattery involved, as well.

Clean living, something in his brain suggested, and he nearly laughed out loud.

He felt the girl beside him, giving off her vibes. She was a decent specimen—no prize, perhaps, but not half-bad, considering it was his second time at bat. And you could hardly count the one in Cleveland, she had been so wasted when he found her. Easy pickings, but in spite of everything, she sobered near the end. They *always* sobered at the end, and he supposed the latest catch would be no different.

This one wasn't in the bag exactly, but he had her on the line, and he was certain he could reel her in. York would appreciate another plump young lamb. He hated working with the older specimens, when there was so much youth available, just waiting to be tapped. When York was happy, everyone was happy. When he wasn't . . .

Michael Shirky didn't want to think about the grim alternatives. His job involved procuring the meat; no one had asked him for opinions or analyses. In truth he wasn't qualified to judge their leader, any more than he was qualified to take orders directly from the Master.

Shirky glanced around him, lit a joint and offered it to Amy What's-her-name. She hesitated, finally took it, tried a little puff without inhaling properly. He showed her how, and after three or four deep drags she started to relax. He thought the pills could wait a while.

The drugs were tricky, just as York had told him. Sometimes when you chose a mark she was already so far gone you had to hit her with the hard stuff right up front, or lose her when her mind began to wander. Other times—like now, he thought—you ran into a little girl who got her kicks by playing grown-up. Chances were, this one had done a little wine or beer, but Shirky would have bet his life that she had never smoked a joint before, and he suspected her experience with pills was limited to aspirin and Flintstones vitamins.

No problem. Physical corruption of the innocent was half the battle. Half the fun. He might score extra points with York for picking off a cherub. Hell, if she turned out to be a virgin—

Shirky smiled and shook his head. Now *that* would be a miracle. He pegged her age at sixteen, give or take; her looks were average-plus, with possibilities. He didn't know if there were any virgins still at large, outside of preschool, but he hadn't met one lately.

They were waiting near the stage, not actually in the wings, but close enough that she could get her hopes up. Shirky didn't want to lose her in the backwash from the altar call, and he could feel her watching the display of raw emotion—make that raw *devotion*—with the slightest trace of queasiness. He offered her the joint again. She thought about refusing, finally took it, and she got it right this time without a lot of coaching.

Better.

It was time to work the magic, just as York had taught him.

"I'll be back in just a second, okay?"

A ripple of anxiety played over features that were definitely average-plus. "Where are you going?"

"Just backstage," he told her, nodding in the general direction of the wings. "I want to guarantee there isn't any problem for the party after."

"I'll come with you."

"Sorry, no can do." He pointed to the stage, where Death was standing, trancelike, with a bloody bucket in his hand. The other members of the band were getting down and dirty with the background music for the altar call. "They don't let anybody back there while the show's in progress."

"How will *you* get in?"

The little bitch was clever. Shirky smiled. "I work here, babe. Remember?"

"Oh . . . that's right."

Another problem taken care of through the powers of persuasion and the modern miracle of marijuana. Shirky wondered if he ought to kiss her, settled for a quick caress along her jaw. She smiled, and even with the braces he was forced to give the chick an upgrade. Average-plus was shifted, in his mind, to pretty-minus.

"Stay right here?"

"Okay."

"I wouldn't want to lose you."

Drifting toward the wings, he waited for the crowd to close behind him, cutting off her view, before he changed direction, homing on the men's room. He wouldn't attempt to go backstage. The bikers didn't know him—no one with the show would recognize his face, his mission—and the passes he'd shown to Amy were as bogus as the day was long.

Inside the crapper he was more or less alone. Some dipshit was puking up his guts behind closed doors, the last stall down, but wimps and stoners didn't count. He stood before the urinal and let his bladder empty, concentrating on the pattern of the tile before him, hoping that his pigeon would agree to the suggestion he already had in mind.

Just one more "Yes," and she was his. To keep.

There was a certain kick he got from trolling on his own. In Cleveland there had been a chaperon assigned to make damn sure he didn't fuck things up. It didn't hurt to miss a pickup. Guys were running down their bullshit make-out lines at every concert in the country, and a chick would have to have some heavy-duty ESP to pick his brain from any of the standard openers. The danger lay in fumbling the later moves, when drugs were offered, propositions made. A mark who might suspect too much was dangerous; allowed to slip away, she might seek help from friends, or even the police.

And legal heat was something Shirky definitely didn't need.

He made his way back through the milling crowd and found his pigeon where he left her. Some guy with acne in the third degree was trying hard to beat his time, his flaming face pressed close to Amy's, thick lips grinning like a circus clown.

"Fuck off."

"Who says so?" Pizza Face was talking brave until he turned around and got a glimpse of Shirky in the flesh. "Hey, man, is there some problem?"

"You're the problem. I don't like you bothering my woman."

"Right. I didn't know, you know? I mean, you weren't around."

"I'm back."

"Uh, yeah, I know."

"So blow."

He almost caught her smiling, but she hid it with a practiced ease that females must acquire around the age of two. His own smile, when he offered it, was rueful, every bit as practiced as her own.

"I'm sorry, babe," he said. "We've got a problem."

"What's the matter?"

"Change of plans. The guys are splitting any minute, and they won't have time to party here—"

"Oh *no*!"

"—so they've invited us to join them for a little something private, back at Ripper's place."

Her eyes went wide. "He has a place in Denver?"

Shirky realized that he was skating on thin ice. "Well, sort of. It's a rented place, you know? They send a guy around before each tour and pick out crash pads they can use, to get away from all the rat race back at their hotel."

"Hey, that's a great idea."

"I thought so." Shirky felt his confidence returning. "Will you come?"

A ghost of hesitation appeared in her eyes. "I ought to find my friend."

He noticed she had dropped the plural. Getting better all the time.

"Where is he?"

"*She*. I haven't seen her for a while. If I know Jill she's found some guy, and—"

"There you are, then. Everybody's happy. You can call her from the party, put her mind at ease, and I'll provide the transportation when you have to split."

"Well—"

"Hey, if you'd rather not—"

"Oh, what the hell. Let's go."

"SO, WHAT'S THE VERDICT?" Amos asked Bolan when he had the car in motion. "Still think good ol' rock and roll will never die?"

The soldier shook his head. "I've never been a fan of censorship."

"Hell no. Don't get me wrong," Carr said. "I don't care what they sing about. These guys have got the right to be repulsive assholes, just like everybody else. It's not about the *music*. It's about the *murders*. If I'm right—and I believe I am—there'll be another sacrifice within a ten-mile radius of Denver while the band's in town."

"And if you're wrong?"

"I'm tickled pink. It means some little girl goes home alive."

"You think the victims are selected from the audience?"

"I'm betting on it. Hell, the joint's a supermarket, wall-to-wall with lean, choice cuts. For someone who can strike a pose and talk that trash, it's easier than picking out which socks to wear tomorrow."

"And the motive?"

"We've been over that. The Chingon cults are hard-core Satanists. They live for evil just the way your basic Christians are supposed to live for good. The sacrificial ritual has several purposes. Release of psychic energy at death. An offering of blood to Lucifer. Sadistic pleasure, coupled with the opportunity to break a young girl's faith and steal her soul. On top of that, they need party favors.''

"Party favors?"

"Remember Stanley Bowers? Well, he wasn't just some wacko chowing down on hearts because he got a sudden hankering for protein. Blood and flesh are prime components of the Chingon ritual. That's *human* blood and flesh."

"You think the members of the band are cannibals?"

"I wouldn't rule it out, but at the moment I'm inclined to think of them as bait. They draw a crowd, go through the motions, and the hunters have their pick from six, eight thousand girls. If half the crowd gets psyched on Satan while they're choosing . . . well, that's gravy. Something extra for the cause."

The Executioner was frowning. "I'm waiting for the theme song from *The Twilight Zone*."

"I know the feeling, guy. It's weird, and I'm the first one to admit it. That's their strength. It's *too* weird. Who can possibly believe in devil-worshipers and cannibals today? Well, I can. And I'm concerned about a string of brutal homicides that show no signs of letting up. I want these bastards off the street forever."

Bolan wondered how much Brognola had actually shared with Amos Carr. As they pulled up outside the ex-detective's room, he asked.

"We kept it basic," Carr replied. "I realize a lot of what you do is need-to-know, and I don't qualify. No problem. Hal says you can do a job. I've got a job needs doing."

"I don't make arrests."

Carr chewed on that one for a moment. "No," he said at last. "I didn't think so."

"Anything we do together would be strictly unofficial. I can't offer you protection if it all goes sour."

"No sweat. I've got my eyes wide open."

"You might not like what you see."

"I've seen the worst already. Anything from here on in has got to be a definite improvement."

"Well, you're the expert, Amos. Tell me how you start a witch hunt."

"I prefer to think of it as exorcism," Carr responded.
"And we start off bright and early. Make it seven, in the
coffee shop?"

"I'll see you there."

"Hey, listen . . . I appreciate this, really."

"Save it," Bolan said. "We aren't home yet."

AMY HATCHER DIDN'T recognize the highway landmarks,
but she knew they were headed out of town—to Lake-
wood, possibly, or Wheat Ridge. She was blurry from the
grass, both visually and mentally. It frightened her a little,
but she also felt extremely free, released from inhibitions,
and on balance she was satisfied.

The blonde was driving. She had mustered up the nerve
to ask his name—Mike Something; he had mumbled the last
name and she didn't feel like having him repeat it—and his
age. She didn't know if he was really twenty-two—some
guys were prone to lie about their age and make themselves
seem older, more experienced—but at the moment Amy
didn't care. He was a hunk, she had him to herself and they
were headed for the greatest party of her life.

It was incredible, the way she'd stumbled into it. A chance
to meet the band, of all things, when a few short hours earlier she hadn't been entirely certain she would make the
show. It only went to prove that lying served a purpose in
the family unit. If her mom and dad could see her now . . .

She put the grisly image out of her mind, afraid to think
of their reaction. Neither of them was a hitter, anyway, but
she would certainly be in for major grounding, possibly until she reached the legal voting age. She couldn't blame
them, really—looking out for children and attempting to
control them was a parent's job—but kids had certain duties, too. Like testing limits, flying in the face of tired con-
ventions, getting down and going for the gusto.

Amy glanced at Mike, relieved to find that he was coming back in focus. So far he'd been a perfect gentleman, but
she suspected that would change when everyone began to
party hearty. Amy *hoped* that it would change. The prospect frightened her a little, but she had her mind made up.
With any luck at all tonight would be the night.

A little warning voice began to whisper from the back of Amy's mind. Disturbing words like "pregnancy" and "AIDS" kept cropping up, and she did her best to turn the volume down. You had to figure that on any given day a couple million people in the state got laid, and the majority would walk away from it with nothing but a smile and pleasant memories. With odds like that, she thought it might be worth the risk.

Assuming that they ever reached their destination. They had been on the road for something like a quarter hour. Jill would be concerned, but she was smart enough to figure Amy might have headed for the car. She would go back and check it out before she started making calls.

And she would find the note.

Mike had considered it a waste of time, but Amy had insisted. Even with the marijuana kicking in, she still knew right from wrong, and it was cruel to leave a good friend hanging, wondering if Amy had been kidnapped by a motorcycle gang or something. Worse, if Jill got scared she might try calling Amy's home, and then the possibility of punishment would be a certainty.

No thank you.

Mike had gone along when Amy showed him she was adamant. He made a little joke about it, smiling, and she knew that everything would be all right. It would be *perfect*.

Still, they had been driving quite a while. It seemed unusual that members of the band would book a room so far from downtown, where the action was. It made a certain kind of sense, if they were after privacy, and yet—

"Where are we going, Mike?"

"We're there."

The pillars looked familiar. There was sculpted writing overhead, above the open gate, but Amy didn't have a chance to focus on it as he took the Firebird through and left the entryway behind them. In the distance Amy saw a long, low building ringed with lights outside. It seemed familiar, vaguely reminiscent of a shopping center after everyone goes home, but Mike was taking them along a different track, away from the light, toward the darkness. Amy felt a prick of apprehension, instantly supplanted by excitement.

"Will they be here yet?"

"Don't know. They might have had a problem getting out, with all the people."

"Yeah, I guess so."

He was slowing, coasting to a stop beneath some trees. On Amy's left a rolling lawn rose gently to a crest some thirty feet above the drive. Atop the knoll, she was surprised to see a gleam of what she took for firelight. Human silhouettes moved back and forth before the flames.

"Somebody's here," she said.

"Let's check it out."

"Is this supposed to be a barbecue, or what?"

"You never know with these guys. Could be they're cooking up a little something special for the party."

Amy took his hand and let him lead her up the slope. He seemed to know his way, and it was good to follow him. To touch him.

Closing on the fire, she realized there were several persons—six or seven, anyway—already waiting by the fire. It took a moment for her mind to register that all of them were wearing hooded robes, and all the robes were midnight black.

"You didn't tell me were going to a costume party."

"Never mind. You're perfect as you are."

She swallowed hard, around the lump his words had planted in her throat. "Okay."

The fire had been constructed on a slab of rock—or was it marble?—planted in the grass. Black candles ringed the fire, and one robed figure stood inside the circle while the others formed a broken ring outside.

Everyone was watching Amy as she followed Mike across the grass, revealed to them by firelight. She didn't like their eyes.

"I don't see anybody from the band," she whispered, desperate not to blow it, frightened she would hurt his feelings. Simply *frightened*.

"Fact is, babe, they won't be coming."

"What?"

"They never make these gigs. I think they're just a wee bit squeamish, if you want to know the truth."

Her thoughts had outrun comprehension, and she didn't grasp the import of his words.

"So where's the party?"

"I thought you understood," he told her, casually releasing her hand and clamping his own around her wrist like a vise. "You *are* the party, babe."

LUCIAN SLATE GOT NERVOUS any time he had to wait for York. The man was trouble, plain and simple. There were no two ways about it. Granted, he performed a necessary function—one that Slate wouldn't have taken on himself at any price—but York enjoyed it. That was fine in theory. Servants of the Master were supposed to love their work, exalt themselves by honoring His name, but York was something else entirely.

Slate lit a cigarette and checked his watch again. Five minutes. York was never early. He was never late. He came on time, precisely, and he did his job without a lot of excess small talk. York was a professional, and yet...

Professionals were theoretically objective, dammit. They weren't supposed to *love* it.

Slate supposed that York had simply been around too long and seen too much, absorbed too many chemicals and shocks along the way. The bastard had been at it for over twenty years, and that was well beyond the estimated life span of an active hunter. Most burned out or fried their brains with drugs around the time they hit their stride. It was a waste of personnel, but in a war you had to count on casualties from time to time.

Slate could have been a hunter—there had been some opportunities along the way—but he had recognized a fundamental weakness in himself and channeled his creative energies toward other avenues. He had, of course, participated in the ritual initiations, and in later ceremonies as an interested observer, but the new crusade lay well beyond his private capabilities.

No matter. There was room enough for everyone, in different roles. Without Slate's leadership and guidance, York and others like him—*were* there others like him?—would be wasting precious time and blood to no avail. Together they comprised a living whole, and they would triumph in the end. Along the way, with careful handling, a few of them might make a profit in the bargain. Lucian Slate believed the Master would approve.

He jumped as York appeared beside the driver's door. The bastard hadn't made a sound, approaching like a wraith and popping up that way because he knew damn well it set Slate's teeth on edge. A sudden flush of anger warmed his cheeks, but Slate resisted the temptation to express his feelings verbally. You never knew how York might take a word of criticism. He would probably just smile and walk away, but on the other hand...

Slate rolled the window down. "You have it?"

York was smiling. "Of course."

He held the paper bag in one hand, fingers curled around the jar concealed inside. Slate didn't have to see the contents; he could hear them sloshing gently as he took the offering and placed it on the seat beside him.

"Any problems?"

"No."

"Tomorrow, then?"

"As usual."

Slate nodded, had the window halfway up when York reached out and rapped his knuckles on the glass. Slate cranked it down again, suppressing his exasperation.

"What?"

"Drive carefully," York chided him. The man was grinning like a shark. "Don't spill."

Slate put the car in motion, had to catch the jar as it began to wobble on the seat. He wanted out of there, and fast. There was no time to roll the window up, and he could hear York's mocking laughter as he floored the pedal, looking for the nearest exit from the parking lot.

6

Jinx Haversham had earned his name the hard way. Not his given name—the hated Eustace—but the nickname he had carried like a badge of shame for close to forty years. He *was* a jinx, and Haversham had learned to live with that.

When he was called to serve his country in Korea, he'd been the first man wounded in his company. It was a minor wound, devoid of glory, self-inflicted when his M-1 rifle jammed and he'd tried to clear the chamber with the muzzle pointed downward, toward his feet. A little toe was nothing, really, in the scheme of things, and they had shipped him back as soon as he could walk without a hobble. One month later he'd been the only man *not* wounded when a screaming yellow tide broke over his detachment on Hill 415. And it was worse the second time, to walk among the dead and maimed, to feel their eyes accusing you for being whole. No one had called him on it then, but he'd been Jinx Haversham from that day on.

The name had followed him into civilian life, a shadow he could never lose, though he *could* lose jobs—eleven in the next three years. And while he told himself that he was being silly, that all those accidents could happen anywhere, to anyone, Jinx had begun to wonder. Breaking dishes he was hired to wash had been a relatively minor problem, but the job on Ford's assembly line had been disastrous. In the end the union hadn't even tried to save him from the ax, and Jinx was sure the local rep had let his private feelings interfere with the decision not to fight dismissal. Hell, why shouldn't he? It had been *his* ass that was nailed—quite literally—after Jinx experienced his difficulties with the rivet gun.

The obvious solution had been flight. Escape. It might have been the coward's answer, but that didn't make it wrong. In distance there was hope, and he had run as far as Denver, working little jobs along the way and bungling the vast majority, before he saw an advertisement seeking men to "handle things" around Mount Olivet.

A cemetery might not be the most exciting place to work, but it had compensations. Like the fact your clients wouldn't raise a stink and get you fired because you accidentally jostled them—or even dropped them on their heads, as Jinx had done on only two occasions in his twenty-seven years of "handling things." Most often what he handled was a shovel or a rake. They didn't dig the graves by hand these days, but there was always gardening and maintenance. It kept him busy forty-nine weeks out of every year; the other three he spent at home, absorbing daytime television shows and trying not to break things.

Most of all Jinx enjoyed the silence of his work. Mount Olivet was large enough that he could almost always find a corner to himself and work without the others hanging over him. He wasn't antisocial in the normal sense, but Haversham had learned the hard way that his problems, for the most part, came from interaction with his fellow man. Alone, he rarely stumbled, and he *never* had those major Jesus-how-did-I-get-into-this accidents that plagued him when he had an audience. Sometimes, alone, Jinx Haversham felt positively graceful.

Saturday wasn't his normal shift, but they were putting on a "special" service, and they had asked him nicely. It wasn't as though he had a lot of vital chores to do at home. The cats could spare him for a while, and it was double time for weekends, which was better yet.

They wanted everything just perfect for the special ceremony. Not that Jinx regarded one deceased as any better than the rest. If anything disposed of differences, he thought it must be death, but this one's family had the kind of money that you might try taking with you when you went. They had a special plot, removed by several hundred yards from the intrusion of the freeway overshadowing the cemetery's southern quarter. Mr. Moneybags was going out in style.

Jinx had his rake, broom, trowel and assorted other tools that he might need as he approached the family plot. A little wrought-iron fence had been erected to surround the headstones and the family monument—a burly angel, praying on one knee—as if the spirits of the dead could be penned up or held at bay by ornamental spears. The waist-high fence would scarcely slow a vandal down, but that had never been a problem in the years Jinx had worked around Mount Olivet. He smiled and wondered if he might have finally brought someone—even dead folks—decent luck.

His luck ran out upon arrival. Jinx had stacked his tools and was about to use his passkey on the lock securing the ornamental gate, when he was startled by the sight of feet protruding from the shadow of a headstone. Naked feet, and legs. No shoes, no stockings.

It's a joke, he told himself, already disbelieving. Got to be a stupid joke.

Inside the fence he circled warily, eyes squinted, following the feet and calves to dimpled knees, trim thighs, a bit of pubic fluff and—

Jim recoiled, his breakfast coming back on him, and there was nothing he could do to keep it down. A second spasm rocked him, and a third, before he found the strength to put his feet in motion, gaining distance, fighting for control.

He hadn't seen that kind of damage to another human being since Korea. Getting popped with rivets in the ass was nothing next to what the child had suffered.

He wore a little walkie-talkie on his belt, to keep himself available. Most days it simply dragged his pants down on that side, but now he was immensely grateful for the link to other living humans.

"Cotter? This is Haversham. You hear me?"

"Yeah, I got you, Jinx. What's up?"

"You'd better meet me at the Tomlin plot, and call the cops before you come."

"The cops? Don't tell me we've got vandalism, Jinx."

"No vandalism, Herb." He felt his stomach rolling, closed his eyes against the images of death. "I'd say we've got ourselves a murder."

IT WASN'T THAT UNUSUAL to find a stiff dumped in a cemetery. Every week, across the country, suicides and murder victims were discovered in or near major urban boneyards. Killers sought the places out, it seemed, as if, too late, they tried to strike a bargain, cling to the proprieties. Besides, the other tenants wouldn't mind.

Norm Grant suspected he'd seen it all, with twenty years behind a badge, thirteen of those in homicide. At least he *thought* that he'd seen it all. Before today.

Except for visits to the morgue, Detective Norman Grant had never seen a body opened up that way outside a morgue, and at the morgue they didn't play sadistic games like Hide the Heart. Forensics found the organ missing when they gathered up assorted scattered bits and made their inventory. Everything had been accounted for except the heart and all that missing blood.

The way this kid was mutilated, waders should have been the order of the day, but they were high and dry. There were residuals, of course, but no more than you might expect when you brought home a juicy rump roast from the supermarket. That told Grant the girl hadn't been murdered where they found her, and it made his job that much more difficult. If not impossible.

Statistically the odds were three to one she'd been butchered by a friend or relative. Grant knew that he would have to go through all the motions, but his gut was telling him they had a psycho on their hands. Dissection in a cemetery wasn't on the list of top ten crimes of passion. Someone— maybe several someones—had invested time and twisted thought in the production of his latest nightmare.

His partner, Miller, had a few more questions for the medical examiner before they started grilling members of the staff. Grant left him to it, studying the body from a distance, wondering precisely what a kid that age could do to make somebody so damned angry.

Suddenly Grant wished he had a sheet to throw across the body. Sheets were for the movies, rarely used at real-life murder scenes unless the stiff had been discarded in a public place, and even then it would be left uncovered while the people from forensics did their work with cameras, yardsticks, calipers and tweezers. Ambulance attendants mainly used the rubber body bags these days. The bloody sheet of yesteryear was now passé.

And Grant still wished he had one. More than ever.

Swiveling around, he lit a cigarette, hands cupped against the breeze. He wasn't getting squeamish. He could never last in homicide without a stomach made of stainless steel, but there were times—like now—when the accumulated blood and bestiality crept up and took you by surprise. You never really understood your fellow "human beings." They could still amaze and terrify.

He heard his partner coming, turned to face him, deadpan. "Well?"

"No heart," Bruce Miller told him, shrugging. "I'll get uniforms to run a sweep, but I don't think we'll find it here."

"Goddammit."

"Right."

"I guess you know we've got a fucking head case on our hands."

"Just what we need."

"Like I need clap."

"I know where you can get some, cheap."

"Terrific. Did the M.E. let you have an estimated time of death?"

"He figures six or seven hours prior to the discovery. Whoever did the chop job didn't kill her here."

"I figured. What about the blood?"

"Drained off before they dumped her from the looks of things."

"Drained *how*?"

"Can't say until they do the full postmortem."

"Looks like someone beat them to it."

Grant was wishing that the ambulance would get there and remove the pitiful remains. Instead, a dark sedan pulled up and two men came across the close-cropped grass to meet him. One of them was short and stocky; his companion stood a full head taller, broad across the chest and shoulders, with an athlete's grace.

"Detective Grant?" the short guy asked them both at once.

"I'm Grant. And you are...?"

"Amos Carr." He pumped Carr's hand perfunctorily. The name had a familiar ring. "And this is Michael Blanski, FBI."

Grant flicked his cigarette away and studied Blanski's face. "What brings the Bureau out so early in the morning?"

Blanski's smile was tinged with ice. "I work with VI-CAP," he replied. "That's the violent criminal apprehension—"

"I know what it stands for. What's your interest here?"

"A string of homicides, with similarities, across four states. We're looking into possible connections, and it sounded like your victim might fit in."

"You people monitor our calls?" If Grant was actually surprised, he hid it well.

"Let's just say bad news travels fast."

"Okay, let's say that." The detective turned his gaze on Amos Carr. "You with the Bureau, too? Your name's familiar, but—"

"That's *60 Minutes* for you," Carr responded. "Catch a little air time and the whole world knows your name. They just can't place it when they meet you in the flesh."

"You're on TV?"

"Occasionally. Make that rarely. When the networks have a question in my field of expertise, they sometimes drop a dime."

"What *is* your field of expertise exactly?"

"Hey, I've got it!" From the sidelines Grant's companion shouldered forward, frowning as he aimed an index finger at Carr's face. "The witchcraft guy."

"You're warm," Carr told him. "Cults in general actually. At the moment I'm involved with Satanism."

Grant glared his partner into silence. "So, you're working with the Bureau now?"

"It's strictly temporary. We have certain common interests."

"And you think our stiff was . . . what? A human sacrifice?"

"I wouldn't rule it out."

"You missed the boat on this one, pal. We monitor our crazies here in Denver. We've had violent crime related to the cults before, be we're on top of it. It's mostly kids these days. They do a little drugs—okay, let's cut the crap, they do a *lot* of drugs—they listen to some heavy metal, sometimes kill for Halloween. We haven't had a homicide related to the cults in seven years."

"You're overdue."

"You say."

"All right. Convince me there's no evidence of ritual involved in what you've got here, and we're on our way."

"It's not my job to go around convincing stray civilians, *Mr.* Carr. The last I heard, you weren't a working lawman any more."

"I'm working, Grant. I simply haven't drawn a city paycheck lately."

"What's your angle, then?" the partner asked. "A book? Another TV spot?"

"Try half a dozen teenage girls ripped open. Gang raped, gutted like the trout you had for supper."

"Yours were gutted?" There was something in Grant's eyes that told Carr he had touched a nerve.

"Extensive mutilation, with exsanguination."

"Say again?" The partner look confused.

"Their blood was drained," Grant answered for him.

"Right," Carr snapped. "In every case the heart was gone. Three times the killer walked away with reproductive organs."

"Jesus, Norm—"

"Shut up!" Grant's sudden animation drove his partner back a space. "What ties this in with cults, in your opinion? I mean, who's to say we haven't got another Jack the Ripper on our hands?"

"The lab says we've got multiple assailants, based on blood types from saliva samples, sperm, what-have-you.

Granted, numbers get a little hazy after the third or fourth rape, but we're talking at least four assailants. In Cleveland they're sitting on casts made from tire tracks—two vehicles. Birmingham picked up some footprints—three sizes.''

"Okay, so your wacko's a whole *gang* of wackos. It happens. Those guys in Los Angeles five, six years back. They were roaming the freeways and knocking off kids like for the hell of it.''

"Sorry, no go. We've got ritual artifacts found at the crime scenes.''

"Say what?''

"Cult graffiti. Wax residue—always black candles, you follow? A ritual circle in Birmingham. Hell, the selection of murder sites spells it all out. Every victim so far has been killed in a graveyard, at night.''

Grant was shifting his feet, glancing nervously back toward the place where forensics technicians were doing their postmortem thing. He looked edgy. Carr thought it might go either way.

"We've got none of that here. No damned candles, no pentagrams, nothing.''

"She die where you found her?''

A soul-searching look between partners, and Grant shook his head. "We're not sure where she died.''

"Find the killzone," Carr told him. "You'll have all the proof you need.''

Behind them, somewhere, static emanated from a walkie-talkie, voices crackling and fading in and out. Carr didn't try to catch the message. He was busy watching Grant, attempting to anticipate the gruff detective's choice. A uniform approached and muttered something in Grant's ear. He waited for the blue suit to retreat before he spoke.

"I think we've got our kill site.''

"And?''

"They haven't done a thorough sweep, but they've got bloodstains, evidence that someone lit a fire, some kind of vandalism to a couple of the tombstones. They've got wax. Black wax.''

"We'll need to check the site ourselves," Bolan said, asserting spurious authority.

"But first," Carr told his captive audience, "I need to see the girl."

THE EXECUTIONER HAD SEEN his share of death, dismemberment and sundry other mutilations. In the steaming hell of Vietnam, remains had often been reduced to such a state that positive ID was strictly hit-or-miss, and who would ever know the difference, anyway? He'd borne witness to atrocities on both sides of the DMZ, and the inauguration of his private war against the savages had added new refinements in the realms of pain and suffering. Before his stateside war was three months old, he had been introduced to "turkeys," the pathetic relics of sophisticated, utterly sadistic "questioning" by mafiosi and the med-school ghouls they kept on staff for such contingencies.

The girl was different.

She wasn't a turkey. Death, from all appearances, was relatively swift, if not precisely painless. The evisceration had come later, when her killers finished up their chores.

He didn't bother checking out the details of the mutilation. Bolan saw enough from where he stood beside Detective Grant, but Amos Carr was on his knees beside the body in an instant, peering closely at the wounds, the organs that had been removed and scattered in a seemingly distracted, aimless manner.

"Have you found the heart?"

"Not yet," Grant said.

"You won't. Unless I miss my guess, you've got some other pieces missing in the pelvic region. It's a little hard to tell."

"I guess. What makes you think the heart won't show?"

Carr grimaced. "Never mind. You wouldn't buy it, anyway. Let's check that murder scene, okay?"

The grassy knoll, by daylight, offered a commanding view of Mount Olivet. In darkness, Bolan thought, it would seem isolated, terrifying to a young girl in the company of strangers.

Carr was everywhere at once, a human bloodhound, poking at the ashes of the fire, examining the headstones that had been defaced with pentagrams and phrases lifted from the Book of Revelations. Where the girl had died, atop a grave, the grass was stained a rusty brown. He spotted residue of candle wax at ten or twelve strategic points around the makeshift altar, etching out a circle, which last night had penned the victim and her killers.

"It matches," Carr informed the locals. "There are minor variations, mostly predetermined by terrain—they couldn't find a mausoleum the way they did in Cleveland—but the kill is carbon copy."

"So?"

"So you've got trouble."

"Jeez, no kidding? That's the big announcement? Can you help us out or what?"

"I don't have names or faces. I can tell you it would be a good idea to watch your local cemeteries for the next few days, including this one. These sick bastards appreciate the setting, follow? Every kill so far has been inside, or just adjacent to, a cemetery."

"That's not much to go on."

"No."

"Your other kills . . . were they repeaters?"

"No," Carr said again.

"What makes you think these shits will hit again in Denver?"

"Just a hunch."

"I don't believe in hunches."

"You should try them sometime."

"Maybe." Grant was eyeing each of them in turn. "I'll tell you something straight. I think you guys are holding out on me, and I don't like it. If you're sitting on a piece of information, or anything at all, I want it. Now."

"You know as much as we do, Grant. We're all just groping in the dark on this. I don't know who we're looking for exactly, and I don't much give a rat's ass who gets credit for the collar. If your bluecoats bag this scum, it's all the same to me."

Grant stared at Bolan. "What about the Bureau? You've been known to go for ink at the expense of interagency cooperation."

Bolan spread his hands. "Right now I'm tracking. Nothing more. If you know VICAP, then you know we're spread too thin to dominate a case like this. I'll want to interview your prisoners on interlocking cases, if and when arrests are made."

"You'll get your interviews," Grant said, "if any of the bastards are in any shape to talk."

"I'll go for a solution either way."

"We understand each other?"

"I read you loud and clear."

"All right, then. If you pick up anything—"

"You'll be the first to know," he lied.

They walked back to the car in silence. Bolan kept his question to himself until Carr slid behind the wheel.

"Were any of the other victims moved from where they died?"

Carr shook his head. A scowl was carving furrows in his face.

"So, what's your read?"

"I figure it's a stall," Carr told him. "Someone's buying time."

"For what?"

"I hate to think. Let's just say Denver is the first place that Apocalypse has played three nights in a row."

Bolan didn't have to ask the ex-policeman what he meant by that. His meaning was as clear as crystal, bright as fresh-drawn blood.

7

The duplex in Aurora, on the Denver outskirts, would have passed for normal at a glance. In fact it had been purchased with normality in mind, to throw off any chance suspicion of what might be happening inside, behind drawn blinds.

If anything the draperies would have to be the giveaway. It seemed unnatural, the neighbors would agree in retrospect, for anyone—especially a nice young couple like the Abernathys—to live that way, without admitting so much as a ray of sunshine to their dwelling place.

It seemed unnatural . . . and yet, for eighteen months not one neighbor had remarked upon the oddity or sought an explanation from the tenants. Neighbors in Aurora simply weren't the nosy type. They liked to live and let live, which meant leaving well enough alone.

The neighbors didn't know that Tom and Mary Abernathy were in fact not married. Neither were they Abernathys. Other names had been recorded at the time of their arrest—in Massachusetts and Connecticut, respectively—and they had served their time for forgery, solicitation, drug offenses, long before they met.

The address was a tip from Amos Carr, obtained through channels he hadn't explained, passed on to Bolan as a favor. The warrior had no interest in the source, as long as he or she was accurate, and Carr was vehement on that score. He'd offered Bolan samples of the merchandise prepared behind those blinds, but Bolan had declined.

The duplex was a cut-rate motion picture studio, producing kiddie porn for customers who liked their action unencumbered by the frills of plot and dialogue. Among those clients, Carr informed him, was a group of Satanists in San

Francisco, others in Los Angeles, New York, Miami. Some of them allegedly repaid the favor by supplying "actors" for the raunchy dramas filmed within. If Amos was correct in his surmise, a number of the "stars" were featured in the Have You See Me? advertisements dotting billboards and dairy cartons from coast to coast.

It was enough to rate a closer look, and in the spirit of the operation Bolan had rehearsed his role en route. He wore a flashy suit and mirrored shades, the sleek Beretta snug beneath his arm. The wad of bills he carried in his pocket could have choked a hippopotamus; the slim incendiary sticks were every bit as hot, but less obtrusive.

Bolan parked his rental in the driveway, shunning stealth. He slipped the button on his jacket, granting instant access to the pistol, as he mounted concrete steps and jabbed a finger at the doorbell.

Several moments passed before a sallow creature in a leather jacket answered.

"Yeah?"

"I'm here to take a delivery."

"Huh?"

"Come on already. Read my lips. I'm here to get the reels."

"What reels? Who are you, man?"

"For Christ's sake, are you serious? The movies."

Anger flared behind the rodent eyes, but Bolan had the guy off balance, groping for an explanation.

"I don't know, you'd better talk to Tom."

"I guess I'd better."

Bolan moved before the doorman had an opportunity to close the door. He shouldered past and found himself inside a narrow foyer, facing a corridor, with dingy rooms on either side. The lights were on, but it didn't seem to help.

"Hey, man, you can't just walk in here an—"

Bolan fed the talking rat a bullet, eased his scrawny carcass to the floor and went in search of bigger prey. The well between two sections of the duplex had been punctuated with connecting doors, permitting access back and forth from either side. He tried each door in turn, found several locked before one opened onto a set where lights and cam-

eras were recording some preliminary action on a wa-
terbed.

He took the girl for ten years old—eleven, tops. She wore
a flimsy baby-doll, and heavy makeup couldn't hide the
terrified expression on her face. It scarcely mattered in the
long run; Tom and Mary weren't concerned with method
acting, just as long as profits kept rolling in.

The girl was flanked by two men wearing party masks and
nothing else. Besides the "stars," he made a cameraman and
a director—Tom. No sign of Mary, but he let it go and settled for what he could.

The scene was frozen as he entered, ten eyes riveted on
Bolan and the pistol in his hand. He shot the actors first,
without a second thought, the silencer reducing muzzle blast
to something on the order of a muffled sneeze.

The cameraman retreated, bolting for another door behind him, exiting stage left. A parabellum round between
the shoulders helped him get there, flattening his face
against the doorjamb.

Tom found the strength to rise, but it appeared to wear
him out. The bastard wasn't going anywhere.

"Police are on the way," the Executioner advised him.

Tom couldn't think of anything to say, although his lips
were working, silently.

"It's up to you, the way they find you," Bolan said. "As
you can see, I'm not particular."

"Okay." The voice was somewhere on the faint side of a
whisper. "Right, I'm listening."

The guy had raised his hands in a pathetic gesture of surrender, and Bolan saw the pentagram that had been tattooed on his inner wrist.

"You push your garbage to the Chingons, am I right?"

"Say what?"

"Wrong answer."

Bolan had the pistol out at full arm's length before Tom
broke.

"No, wait! Don't do it!"

"Give me one good reason."

"Chingons, man. You want 'em? I've got contacts."

"I'm still listening."

The movie mogul gave him names, a San Francisco number.

"I want something local," Bolan told him.

"Local?" The confusion in his captive's eyes struck Bolan as sincere. "They don't have any local coven, man. That's straight."

"You're telling me they never come to watch you work?"

"Well...sure, sometimes. But none of those guys are from here. They like the big town, dig it?"

"Yeah. I've got a message for them. Think you've got the brains to pass it on?"

"Just try me."

"From today, this moment on, the free ride's over. Someone knows, and someone's taking action."

"Okay. I've got it."

"Not just yet."

The shot drilled his kneecap and dragged a scream up from the cellar of his soul. Bolan crouched beside him. "You're out of business, guy, and I mean permanently. I'll be checking back from time to time, assuming that you make parole with all your priors, and the first time I suspect you're dealing chicken, I'll come back and *really* hurt you. Am I getting through?"

"Uh-huh."

He rose and turned to face the girl, a travesty of youth. She had retreated to a neutral corner, crouching there and covering herself, knees drawn up against her chest. Her eyes seemed flat and dead, without a flicker of emotion in their depths.

Too late, perhaps, but he would leave it to the juvey officers and staff psychologists. With any luck they might break through.

He caught the sound of distant sirens, drawing closer as he put the house of death behind him. Given time he would have liked to trash the neighborhood and wake some people up, but time was one thing Bolan didn't have. There was another stop to make, and precious little breathing room to spare before he had to rendezvous again with Amos Carr.

DEALING DREAMS MADE Mickey Treacher's day. It put good money in his pocket, kept him dressed in flashy threads and boosted his charisma with the fairer sex. As long as Mickey had connections, he suspected he would never want for anything.

Connections, on the other hand, could be a problem.

Lately Mickey had been forced to deal with bikers for his stock of methamphetamines, and while the Harley crowd indulged in showers with a greater regularity these days, they couldn't shake the smell of violent death. It made him nervous, haggling with men who killed for sport and business interchangeably, but when your product was illegal, there were certain limitations on your right to pick and choose.

At least with syndicate suppliers there was something in the way of courtesy, decorum. Mickey knew that his Italian contacts were as lethal as the bikers—never mind the grim Colombians who had monopolized the coke trade recently—but they had style, a certain flare. Before they blew your brains out they would kiss you on the cheek.

A touch of class.

It was a mark of Treacher's business that his buyers sometimes sparked the same uneasy feeling as his sources of supply. His favorites were upscale businessmen and yuppies, snorting on the weekends, partying with friends or chasing Wall Street migraines with a potion that their local drugstore didn't carry. College kids were fine, but Mickey sometimes used a cutout in his dealings with the younger crowd, ensuring that the tales they carried out of school wouldn't rebound to his misfortune.

On the other hand you had the stone-cold junkies, hanging on from one fix to the next and stealing anything their scrawny arms could carry in a desperate bid to make their daily quota. Treacher viewed them with distaste, avoided touching them at any cost, but he would bag up their money and bank it with the rest. While junkies were around, he knew that there would always be a market for his services.

Among his several types of customers, it was the witchy crowd that made him nervous. He could understand the party side of drugs, and he'd seen the rigors of addiction firsthand, but the "religious" side was something else entirely. Treacher sometimes wondered what the goofy bastards saw when they were wolfing down his special numbers, baying at the moon and killing chickens.

Wrong.

It wasn't chicken blood that made him nervous. And he wouldn't think of asking what his witchy buyers saw around their bonfires, any more than he would voluntarily attempt to kiss a buzz saw.

He'd seen their eyes, burned out and dead, like bullet holes in soulless faces. And the eyes had been enough.

He would have dumped the witchy trade entirely, passed them on to any one of several cronies in the business, but they paid top dollar for their shit, and it was income, after all. In seven years of trading with the cults, no one had ever tried to make him sign the dotted line in blood. They paid in cash, showed up on time and brought no heat.

What more could any self-respecting dealer ask?

The witchy crowd was on his mind this morning, since a cryptic phone call had awakened him at half past one. The voice had been familiar, and he hadn't asked for names. A buyer was in town, the caller had told him, and a special shipment was desired. Could Mickey handle the arrangements, or would he refer them to another party for the deal?

Incensed that anyone would question his connections, Mickey told the caller it wouldn't be a problem. He would have to wake some people up, but they were getting paid, so what the hell? Of course, the rush job would involve additional expense.

As usual the drop wasn't arranged beforehand. Witchy buyers trusted no one; they would call again to see if everything was ready, and the meet would be arranged to mutual advantage, giving Treacher time enough to reach his car and roll if he intended to collect. He might be watched, between times, though he hadn't caught them at it yet, and doubted that he ever would.

Emerging from the shower, Mickey snagged a towel and started scrubbing at his face, his hair. The chest was next, and he was working on the family jewels before he noticed that he had a visitor.

The big man studied him impassively from his position near the bathroom door. The pistol in his hand was fitted with a silencer and aimed at Mickey's groin.

"What the hell—"

"We need to have a little talk about your customers."

"Says who?"

The automatic waggled at him, raising gooseflesh on his arms.

"It's in your own best interest."

"Yeah, I see that now."

"I'm looking for a special buyer."

"Oh?"

"No junkies. Nothing in the business trade."

"That shaves it down."

"A little magic, maybe. Black should do it."

Shit.

"You've got me, pal. I really couldn't say—"

"Your prayers. Or else a simple answer. Take your pick."

"That kind of question makes a lot of people nervous. Someone could get hurt."

"I'm looking at him."

"Yeah, okay." The dealer had begun to tremble, reading his obituary in the tall man's eyes. "What is it that you need?"

"A name."

"They don't use names. Now wait! I know that sounds like bullshit, but they don't. Not safe enough, okay? Street names, maybe. It's the best I can do."

"I'm listening."

"Okay." He swallowed hard and prayed the guy would take them out first, or die in the attempt, before he could reveal Mickey's treachery. "A guy called Scratch is s'posed to be the pickup man. I don't know when or where. They've got a thing about security, you know?"

"You have the merchandise on hand?"

"In there." Dejected, Mickey pointed past the tall man, toward his bedroom.

"After you."

Still naked, Treacher fetched the Baggies from their hiding place inside the walk-in closet, took them into the bathroom with the automatic following his every move.

"Go on," the big guy said.

"You're going to piss somebody off."

"I'll risk it."

"Yeah."

Mickey grimaced as he emptied out his stash and flushed the toilet, watching thirteen thousand dollars disappear.

"If I were you, I'd think about a short vacation."

"Funny how the great minds think alike."

Except that it would be a *long* vacation, and it would take him far away. Assuming there was any place to hide.

"If Scratch calls back—"

"Forget it, man. I'm permanently out to lunch."

"In case." The big guy seemed to have a problem understanding negatives. "A little something for your customers, to tide them over."

Reaching out, he placed a shiny object in the dealer's hand. Some kind of medal, like a target, with the bull's-eye made up of concentric rings.

"Hey, isn't this some kind of Army thing?"

"Some kind." The big guy was already backing toward the door. "Take care now, Mickey. You could catch your death."

Some joke.

He stood and waited for the sound of the intruder's exit, trembling harder as the front door's latch engaged. A sudden spasm gripped him, brought his breakfast up to chase the stash, and Mickey Treacher knelt before the toilet, retching in an attitude of helpless supplication. By the time he finished dressing, made arrangements with his travel agent, the intruder was about to keep his date with a retired detective.

Both of them were thinking urgently about a man called Scratch.

8

Carr talked nonstop as they approached the snarl of down-town Denver. "Basically," he said, "the structure of your basic devil cult has quite a bit in common with the KKK. Are you familiar with the Klan?"

"I was a member, once upon a time."

"What!" Carr shot him an uncertain glance. "I'm hoping that was line-of-duty."

"You were saying?"

"Mmm? Oh, yeah. All right. Your Chingons have a leader, nationwide, just like your Klansmen have a wizard, but they do their own thing when the boss man's not around. That's *all* the time, except for yearly Sabbats when the whole gang comes together for a barbecue."

"You know the leader's name?"

"Hell, yes. I knew his father's name. It's an inherited position, though I daresay Mr. Big may have some problems picking out an heir. He's gay as hell, and I've heard rumbles that he might have AIDS. It should be interesting to see what happens when he goes to meet the Master."

"Power struggle?"

"It's a possibility. You ever hear of Crowley? First name Aleister?"

"It rings a bell. I couldn't tell you anything about him."

"Back in 1915 Crowley brought his cult to North America from England. They call themselves the OTO—that's Ordo Templi Orientis: Order of the Eastern Temple. If you buy their arguments, they're all descended from the old Knights Templar, who were executed on a charge of witch-craft in the thirteenth century. Whatever, Crowley was an okay salesman, and he set up chapters of the OTO across

America and Canada before he packed it in and went back home to England. Round about the time he died, in 1940-something, there was friction in the stateside OTO. Two honchos disagreed about ascension to the throne, and when they couldn't iron the problem out by casting spells, they started getting physical. The loser had a yacht blown out from under him with dynamite before he took the hint.''

"What happened to the OTO?"

"They're still around. Their so-called Solar Lodge was rubbing shoulders with a guy named Manson for a while, in '69, before the FBI stepped in and charged a pack of them with child abuse. The leaders split for Ensenada and the others went to ground. A couple of them did hard time. I've got a list of fifty lodges here in the United States, another twenty spread around nine foreign countries.''

"Documented criminal activity?"

"Suspected. Journalists have tied them in with Manson's tribe, with Son of Sam, assorted other homicides and disappearances, but building up a case for court is like collecting sunshine in a Mason jar. You don't find witnesses—or if you do, and they agree to talk, they have a lot of accidents. Some disappear, some die, some get amnesia on the way to trial.''

"You could be running down a blueprint for the syndicate.''

"You're catching on. These cultists might be out of touch, from our perspective, but that doesn't mean they're stupid. They can read—they're big on history—and they've been learning by example, from the Mafia, the Klan, the biker gangs. Today the hard-core Satanists are dealing drugs and women, peddling pornography and laundering the money just like it was skim from Vegas. They've already had their sit-downs, formed alliances the way the ethnic bootleg mobs laid out their territories in the 1920s. And they've set up an enforcement arm to deal with witnesses, defectors, anyone who gives them any shit.''

"You mentioned that before. Black Circle?"

"Cross. Black Cross. Satanic symbolism mixed with business, get it? Members of the Cross are hard-core killers who have proved themselves through human sacrifice and independent contracts for their covens. If a local cult's connected with the Chingon network, they can drop a dime and have a hit team on the road in hours. Naturally a monetary 'offering' is called for, in advance.''

"You're sounding like a script for *Boris Karloff Meets Meyer Lansky*."

Carr responded with a barking laugh. "You're too damned close for comfort. That's *exactly* what it sounds like, and the past eight months or so I've seen some indications that the syndicate *is* dealing with the cults. We've known about a biker-cult connection since the sixties; now the dope and kiddie porn your cultists sell is being gobbled up by wholesale dealers for the mob. The Satanists are in the food chain, Mike. They mean to eat us up, and I, for one, suspect they have a decent chance."

"And you've got nothing that will stand in court?"

"I told you, they've been studying. Intimidation-wise, these goons have practice out the ass. Hell, witches have been scaring people shitless since the dawn of time. Compared to them the Mafia's a new kid on the block. Now you've got witches dealing dope, backed up by others using automatic weapons, silencers, plastique. It doesn't matter whether you believe in them or not. Dead's dead."

"And if the Chingons fall?"

Carr shrugged. "Who knows? The members of the Mafia commission have been sentenced to a hundred years a piece. Did that wipe out the syndicate? I do know that the Chingon network is the skeleton, the glue that holds it all together. Take that glue away, break down the skeleton, it's got to have some impact."

"Granted. Did you have a starting point in mind?"

"It's funny you should ask." Carr spied a parking space on Colfax, two blocks south of City Park, and curbed the dark sedan. It was a short hike back.

"What's up?" Bolan asked.

Carr smiled. "The surest source of information is the horse's mouth. We're going to see a witch."

THE SHOP WAS SMALL and cluttered, but its stock had been arranged by someone with an eye for order. Items hadn't been displayed haphazardly. Along one wall a clothing rack was hung with floor-length robes in several colors, white and red predominating. Books on the occult were neatly stacked on shelves that ran from floor-to-ceiling, authors slotted alphabetically. The large glass cases, filled with candles, charms and amulets, were polished to a mirror sheen. Behind the counter jars and bottles filled with powders, herbs and liquids were displayed by color groupings, like a magic rainbow painted on the wall.

The shop seemed unattended, but a tinkling bell above the door announced their entry. It was answered by a pleasant female voice that emanated from behind a beaded curtain, screening off a door that Bolan thought must open on a stock room.

"Be right there."

Another moment and the curtain parted to reveal a woman in her early thirties, tall and dark, with glossy hair that grazed her buttocks. She was dressed in something like a shift, the clinging fabric showing off her trim, athletic figure to its best advantage. Bolan was immediately captivated by her face—the porcelain complexion, almond eyes that seemed to carry sparks of fire within their depths. She glanced at Bolan briefly, then at Carr, and cracked a dazzling smile.

"Dear Amos!"

"How are you, Cass?"

"I'm well. And you?"

"I'm hanging in. Cassandra Poole, Mike Blanski. Mike and I are working on a job together."

"Ah."

Her hand was soft and warm. He let it go reluctantly.

Carr smiled. "I told him I was taking him to meet a witch."

"And you expected someone...older, shall we say? With hairy warts?"

"You live and learn."

"Perhaps." Her eyes bored into Bolan, probing, and he thought the bare suggestion of a shadow passed across her face. "Some live. Some learn."

"I should have warned you, Mike. Cass has a knack for reading minds, so keep it clean."

"You're talking nonsense, Amos."

"Oh?"

"I don't read minds. Nobody does." She turned the magic eyes on Bolan once again. "Let's say I'm...sensitive to certain emanations."

"Sensitive? My corns are sensitive. You've got a gift."

She changed the subject, cutting Amos off. "A job, you said. What sort of job?"

The light went out behind the ex-cop's smile. "We're taking on the Black Cross and the Chingons."

"Amos—"

"Hey, I know. I'm crazy, right? What else is new?"

"Have you explained the risks to Mr. Blanski?"

"Course I have. He knows the score."

"I wonder."

"Cass, the reason why we're here—"

"You want my help."

"We're after information. Nothing else. I wouldn't have you risk a thing."

"I run a risk by speaking to you, Amos. Every word we say from this point on is dangerous."

"Okay, forget it. I don't want to cause you any problems."

"Spare me the theatrics, Amos. You're perfectly aware that I cannot refuse you."

"Cass, you don't owe me a thing."

"There are responsibilities beyond ourselves."

"I don't know what you mean."

"You sly old badger. Tell me what you wish to know."

Carr glanced in the direction of the beaded curtain and the room beyond. "We're alone?"

"Of course."

"Okay, I had to ask. There was a homicide last night—"

"A girl, Mount Olivet. I know."

"You call that 'sensitive'?"

"News travels."

"Yeah. Well, if you know that much, I guess you'll know about the others I've been following cross-country."

"Rumors, nothing more."

"You know about Apocalypse and Lucian Slate." It didn't come out sounding like a question, but Cassandra nodded all the same. Her face was set, intense.

"I'm tracking a connection," Carr went on. "I'd bet my life these sacrifices tie in with the tour somehow. That means a link with Slate, the Chingon network, Children of the Flame—the whole damned ball of wax."

"And if your suppositions are correct?"

"I mean to bust them, one way or another. High and wide. No matter what it takes."

"You're chasing an obsession, Amos."

"Maybe. What the hell, it keeps me off the streets."

"If only that was true."

"You're sounding like a mother, Cass."

"A friend."

"Okay. What can you tell me?"

"Very little, I'm afraid. There have been movements, rumors. Nothing firm."

"I'll take whatever I can get."

She frowned, and even that looked good. "A local group, the Coven of the Ram, was forced to join the network several months ago. They weren't invited, understand. They were inducted. The alternatives were said to be unpleasant."

"So they're down to drafting converts now?" Carr turned to Bolan with a wink. "That fits your syndicate analogy. They're ringing in the independents, one for all and all for number one."

"I don't have any proof," Cassandra told him.

"Never mind." Carr seemed to have a sudden inspiration. "Listen, Cass, I'd like to ask a favor."

"What? Another one?"

"Touché. I've got some people I should see, but they're a little skittish, follow me? An unfamiliar face shows up, they get amnesia. I was wondering..."

"If I could show your friend around and brief him on the local scene?"

"I'm telling you, the lady reads my mind!"

"Perhaps because your mind's an open book."

"So, how about it?"

She was smiling cautiously. "We haven't heard from Mr. Blanski yet. He may resent the notion of a baby-sitter."

Bolan answered with a shrug, immediately conscious of the pulse that hammered in his temples. "I'm not the resentful type."

"Okay, it's settled." Carr was grinning like a football coach whose team has scored the winning touchdown. "We'll regroup for supper, right? The meal's on me."

"I'll have to get somebody in to watch the shop."

"Hey, listen, if it's too much trouble—"

"No," she answered quickly, eyes avoiding Bolan's gaze for once. "It might be interesting. A small adventure."

"Just be careful, eh?"

"I'm always careful, Amos." She retreated through the beaded curtain. In another moment they could hear her talking on the telephone.

"We're in," Carr whispered. "Cass knows everything that happens with the cults around this town. She's got it all down cold."

"And where will you be?" Bolan asked.

"I'll be around. I've got a few informants of my own, some markers I can call. I'll meet you back at the motel. Let's call it sevenish, okay?"

"I wouldn't want civilians in the cross fire," Bolan said.

"Don't worry. Cass is no civilian. Anyway, you're doing basic homework. She knows all the questions, and she knows who *not* to ask."

"I hope you're right."

"Me too." And with a wink the guy was gone.

As ALWAYS, Cass had tried to minimize the issue of her sensitivity with Amos. In the presence of a stranger it was never wise to let yourself be seen and understood in every detail. Strangers could be dangerous. Sometimes they didn't even have to try.

For all of that, her sensitivity was known among the circle of her chosen friends, accepted if it wasn't fully understood. Cassandra's people took such things for granted, as a blessing, and they never seemed to question the mechanics of the gift. Nor did they recognize the other side, which sometimes made the blessing seem a curse.

When she was very small, Cassandra had been good at finding things when others gave the items up as lost. Her instinct for recovering the car keys, toys and coins, the odd stray puppy, had endeared her to her family and neighbors, but the talent had begun to show its darker side around the time she entered school. In class, and later in her home, Cass realized that she could recognize a lie without a shred of independent evidence, by simply glancing at the person who had spoken it, or by touching him or her if it was practical to do so. On the first occasion when she caught her father in a lie—and later, when she recognized that he was cheating on her mother—Cass had felt betrayed.

Her parents hadn't been religious people, and she sought an explanation for her gift—along with the means of losing it—alone. The fundamentalists had preached to her about the dangers of accepting messages from hell, and Cass had recognized their lack of understanding at a glance. The more enlightened Christian orders were inclined to speculate on such phenomena as ESP, avoiding serious investigation with the platitude that anything was possible, through God. The academics had her look at playing cards and guess how many times a quarter, tossed aloft, would come up heads or tails. And it was all a waste of time.

She found the Old Religion quite by accident, through conversation with a friend in junior college. Cass had been astounded to discover that her classmate was a self-proclaimed practitioner of witchcraft. For a moment she was certain that her search had bottomed out, her quest for answers bogging down in fringe religions where eccentrics looked for cosmic answers in a maze of drugs and ritual. Instead Cass found that she was dealing with a strong young woman, totally secure in her environment and within herself. The invitation to attend a coven meeting had been cautiously accepted. One year later, after passing through prescribed initiation rites, she had become a full-fledged witch.

The Old Religion was not circumscribed by rules and regulations, dos and don'ts. The single overriding key was harmony—with nature, the environment, other humans and within one's self. The "magic" practiced by her coven placed less emphasis on hexes, alchemy and love charms than on opening the soul to Nature and her daily miracles. If anyone around the Denver area was turning princes into frogs, Cass hadn't seen it yet.

There was a darker side, of course, as in all things. As Christians had their Inquisition and the Muslim world its endless holy wars, so members of the Old Religion had their own bad apples to contend with. Some were more intrigued by power and its uses than by harmony with Nature and their fellow man. For others, the adoption of a "quaint" religion offered a convenient cover for indulgence in narcotics, violent, twisted sex, brutality. A few, the truly dark ones, seemed to reach beyond themselves and tap a well of evil that was everywhere around them, waiting to be utilized.

Cass feared them, though they posed no clear and present danger to her personally. She might change that by helping Amos, but she seemed to have no choice. Beyond her fear, there lurked a sense of duty that wouldn't permit her to remain aloof. If there was something she could do to save a life, to help the young ones find their way, she had to make the effort.

Carr's companion troubled her, as well. He didn't frighten her, but when she took his hand, Cass had received a garbled image fraught with pain and violence. She couldn't say with any certainty if she was looking into Blanski's past or future. It was possible that violence lay behind him *and* before. In any case, his eyes spoke eloquently of the suffering that he had witnessed in his life.

They also told Cass that he wanted her, the way a small boy passing by a candy store may crave the chocolates in the window, just beyond his reach. He posed no threat—she recognized that much on sight—and it was flattering to see the hunger in his eyes, but she would have to watch herself. Their fleeting contact had inspired an embryonic hunger of her own, and she wouldn't allow herself to be involved with someone who might very well be gone—or dead—tomorrow.

There was blood on Michael Blanski's hands, but Cass didn't believe he was an evil man. She sensed an old wound, never fully healed, that had compelled him to react with violence, and his first reaction somehow had become a personal crusade. He might have been a soldier or policeman; Amos hadn't mentioned occupations, but she knew he wouldn't bring a cleric or an academic into battle with the Children of the Flame.

She thought about the Chingon network briefly, changing tacks before the bestial images could soil her mind completely. Too much evil there. If Amos thought that he could break the network by himself, Cass feared that he was very much mistaken. As for Blanski—

She was interrupted by the jingling of the bell out front. It would be Sandra, come to watch the shop. Cass sorted through the items in her bag, made certain she had everything she might need and shouldered through the beaded curtain with a smile.

"Thanks a million, Sandy."

"My pleasure." She was checking out the tall man, smiling to herself with a flagrant prurience.

"Lock up at six?"

"Will do." As Cass moved past her, Sandra winked and said, "Good luck."

The sudden color in her cheeks made Cass uncomfortable. She had no chance to respond as Blanski turned to face her with a cautious smile. The hunger in his eyes was now tempered by something she didn't immediately recognize.

"All set?" he asked.

"If you are."

"Well, I didn't bring my crucifix."

She laughed. "Relax, I've got a spare. Besides, they only come out at night." But that, Cassandra thought, wasn't precisely true.

9

"In nomine Dei nostri Satanas Luciferi excelsi!"

Clay had learned to keep his eyes closed when they prayed. It added to the mystery and helped him catch the mood, communing with the Master one-on-one. Of late he'd begun to understand how Holy Rollers seemed to "get the spirit" when their ministers cried out in tongues. He wondered how they would have liked *his* spirit, and the mental image made him smile.

He didn't mind the frequent prayers so much these days, the way he had at first. It took some time for him to understand that everything—success included—had its price. His life was finally on track, and if he had to spend a daily hour on his knees to keep things rolling, he would do it gladly. Clay knew that you weren't supposed to look a gift horse in the mouth.

Especially one that just might eat you alive.

He'd been skeptical at first—about the Master, the devotions, all of it. When Slate had offered his prescription for a turnaround, designed to save a fading band from rock-and-roll oblivion, Clay thought that someone must be having one last laugh at his expense. He needed proof before he would believe, and it hadn't been long in coming.

Neither of their first two albums—what he thought of now as products from the "old days"—had compiled impressive sales statistics. They did well enough on tour, but the fact was, *any* metal band could draw a crowd these days, and they'd never seen the ground swell of support that marked a band en route to stardom. They were drifting, plain and simple, with an agent who was running out of lame excuses for their third-rate bookings, a producer who declined to accept phone calls when they rang him up collect.

The change, when it began, had been a gradual thing. Their new approach to life and music took a while to impact on the fans, but sales had started climbing and the crowds they drew began to swell. It could have been coincidence—or so he thought, until he saw what happened in Detroit.

They'd been scheduled as the opener for DeathDreem, recognized among the faithful as an up-and-coming band with no holds barred. It wasn't great to be the opener for *anybody*, but at least their act had been connected with a more prestigious show.

That night they'd been warming up, with minutes left to go, when Baby Huey, DeathDreem's leader, shot himself a speedball in the dressing room and wound up screaming in a corner, clawing at his eyes. The doctors said his royalty checks would be delivered to the psycho ward in future, and the upshot was that DeathDreem wouldn't—couldn't—play. The audience was going ape. They started throwing things when the announcement finally came, and then Apocalypse was blazing out onstage, and in a few more moments everything was cool. They played the whole damned show without an opener, and they were great.

So Clay believed, and there'd been no looking back.

He didn't want to think about what might be gaining on him from behind.

He took the chalice, drank and passed it on.

"ABADDON AND ASTAROTH, Asmodeus and Baphomet, attend our summons!"

Johnny Beamish knew what everybody said about him when he wasn't listening. He was a little light upstairs. His elevator didn't reach the penthouse. He was playing with a short deck. He was out there where the buses didn't run.

Okay.

It wasn't any secret that he spent four years in junior high school, dropping out of senior high when it became apparent he would qualify for Medicare before he graduated. School was shit. A lot of rules and regulations thrown to-

gether by the staff to waste your time and keep you in your
seat while they were filling up your head with worthless information. When you got right down to it, who gave a shit
about the date when Christopher Columbus first discovered Canada? What fucking difference did it make if he
could punctuate a paragraph or find the hippopotamus of
a triangle?

The music was his life. Correction: *drumming* was his life.
There had been brief experiments with other instruments
when he was younger, but he barely managed reading En-
glish, let alone the swarms of printed notes with Hispanic
phrases scattered all around the page. So screw it. Johnny
Beamish played the drums, and he was doing fine.

It had been rocky for a while. The band was going straight
to hell, no matter how he kept the beat. You didn't need a
fancy-ass diploma on the wall to realize that they were
headed for the toilet in a hurry, with the lousy record sales
and shitty bookings on the road. He'd become discouraged, thought of taking off and looking for another band
that would appreciate his talent, when they got together for
a Saturday rehearsal, prior to one last tour, and Clay walked
in with Lucian Slate.

The guy was trippy, there were no two ways about it.
Something in his eyes, for starters. He could look right
through you, like your skin was cellophane and all your guts
were made of glass. It seemed like he could tell what you
were thinking, and he always had the answers waiting half
an hour before you asked the questions. Trippy.

Beamish hadn't fully understood the devil-worship bit,
but it was cool, so what the hell? If Slate could get them
bookings, boost the album sales, it wouldn't hurt old John
to wear a robe and mumble words he didn't comprehend.
Hell, he'd been repeating things he didn't understand for
years in school, but this time he was getting paid. And that
made all the difference in the world.

It grew on you, the ceremonies with their incense, candles, music in the background. Not his kind of music, but
it definitely helped to set the mood. Sometimes he half
expected Caroline Munro or Jamie Lee to drop in for a sé-
ance. *That* would be a trip, and no mistake. Like some-

thing from the late show, only Beamish would protect them when the monster came along. And they would be so grateful they'd simply have to drop their clothes and—

Johnny shook the image off and concentrated on the ritual. Slate got a little testy if he missed his cue and muffed the lines, like he suspected Beamish might be out to lunch or something. Johnny wasn't certain he believed in all that Satan stuff, but now they had an image. That was something in itself, and he didn't intend to blow it for the band when all he had to do was kneel and mumble once or twice a day. It was a piece of cake.

The blood had bothered him at first. Still, it didn't taste so bad when you got used to it, and there was something in the ceremony that made Beamish feel . . . well . . . special.

Chosen.

He couldn't have struggled through an explanation of the feeling if his life depended on it, but the good part was, he didn't have to. Everybody in the band appeared to understand, and who else was there?

Beside him, Clay was passing off the goblet as they answered Slate in unison, repeating the infernal names. It didn't make much sense to Beamish, but he found it comforting to learn that there were many gods instead of one. In Sunday school, before he got too old and gave the whole thing up, it seemed to Johnny that the world was much too large for God to cover all the bases. Someone—lots of someones—could be lost and God would never know about it. It was troubling, until the music started filling up his brain and crowded out the daily clutter he received in church and school.

These days, with many gods to choose from, Johnny thought the whole arrangement made more sense.

He took the goblet, raised it to his lips and drank. The salty taste was something he got used to, over time, but Beamish didn't think that Coke or Coors had any worries in the sales department. Out of nowhere Johnny flashed the image of a businessman on television, wiping crimson lips and griping, "Gee, I could've had a V-8."

He cracked a smile, and quickly tucked it out of sight before Slate had a chance to catch him grinning. The Master didn't go for levity when they were running down a righteous ceremony. Beamish wasn't exactly scared of Slate, but he didn't want to piss the dark man off.

It wasn't good for business.

And he had a sneaking hunch it would not be too healthy, either.

Mumbling on cue, he passed the goblet on.

"O BEELZEBUB, BEHEMOTH, Dagon and Diabolus, pay heed to these, your humble servants!"

Mike O'Neal was ready when the chalice reached his hands. He turned it slightly—he could see no point in swapping spit with Johnny Beamish—raised it to his lips and drank.

The rush was instantaneous. He still suspected Slate of spicing up the ritual with chemicals from time to time, and that was fine. The lead guitarist for Apocalypse wasn't averse to mixing pleasure with religion. Sometimes, though, he thought it was a pure rush of power he felt each time the chalice with its dark elixir passed his way. He wondered briefly where they got the blood, and whether it was USDA choice.

It was a funny thing, the way a person's mind changed over time. A couple years ago, he would have scoffed at the idea of a belief in anything he couldn't see, touch or taste. The notion of participating in religious services, whatever the denomination, would have laid him in the aisles.

Okay. Times change.

When Lucian Slate had first approached the band, with Clay's endorsement, Mike had figured it was all some kind of put-on, possibly a last-ditch gimmick to attract a few new fans. Of course, there *was* that side of it. The metal-heads ate up that devil-worship number, cleaving to the ultimate rebellion as their parents had been crazy for the Beatles, their grandparents for Elvis Presley. Satan was a selling point, but there was more involved than dollar signs.

These days O'Neal *believed*. It hadn't come upon him all at once, by any means. He took convincing, and the money in his pocket wasn't necessarily enough to turn the trick. If he was honest with himself, he knew that any band could have a turnaround, a change of luck. You couldn't take a walk in Hollywood without encountering some has-been who was trying for a comeback, and enough of them succeeded every year to keep the dream alive. When the members of KISS took off their makeup, everybody thought the band was dead, but they were back and sounding better with the war paint gone. He had been pleased when people started buying records, sure, but there were easily a hundred different explanations, none of which had anything to do with Lucifer.

It took the accident to change his mind.

Of course the D.A. had another phrase for what had happened. Vehicular homicide they called it downtown. A blood test proved that Mike was snorting primo flake within an hour of the time he missed that stop sign in Topanga, and the drugs were prima facie evidence of negligence. His public notoriety had made the prosecutor try for murder two, setting for voluntary manslaughter when they couldn't prove intent. Dark days, and for a while Mike had been certain he'd have to do some time.

Slate told him otherwise. He was advised to trust the Master, double his prayers and make damned sure his private consecration to the Prince of Darkness was sincere. With faith, all things were possible. Without it . . . well, he might as well start filling in San Quentin on those change-of-address cards.

It blew his mind when the victim's family accepted the financial settlement. He knew there was a heavy payment off the record, but if no one minded shelling out the cash, O'Neal wasn't about to rock the boat. The studio had staged a little ceremony, snapping photographs as Mike delivered a check to the bereaved, and everybody stood around all red-eyed, looking solemn. There would still be time to serve, but with the injured party pacified, an aging judge wasn't inclined to press the issue. Mike had done his time on weekdays, in the county lockup, safely isolated from the freaks who might have tried to fuck him over in a bid to earn a reputation.

And the band played on.

He had expected animosity from the survivors at the payoff ceremony—God knows they were glaring daggers at him during his arraignment. But the whole damned bunch had undergone a change of tune while he was waiting for a trial date. This time, when they met, the men of the family had looked at him with something very much like fear behind their eyes. And there had been no doubt about the woman. They were terrified.

With faith, he told himself again, all things were possible. And hallelujah, brothers.

Smiling to himself, he passed the chalice on.

"O HECATE AND LILITH, Loki, Mephistopheles and Moloch, hear our prayer!"

The goblet always made him feel a little queasy, sure, but Freddy Sykes wasn't some wimp to be scared off that easily. He took the heavy silver cup and raised it to his lips, drinking more deeply than normal to throw off the shakes and assert his control.

As the taste tried to gag him, Sykes blanked out his mind with an effort. Slate's voice was a whisper, miles distant; the words didn't seem to make sense. Freddy focused on girls, sleek and naked, the younger the better, and after a moment it helped.

Just like always.

The girls calmed him down every time. Oh, they stirred him up, too—there was always that problem—but Sykes had to cope with one thing at a time. At the moment he didn't feel much like disgracing himself in the midst of a ritual, tossing his cookies while everyone else did their bit and moved on. If he needed a crutch, that was his business, nobody else's.

He leaned on the girls.

They had called him a deviant back in L.A., when they locked his ass up on the sex charge. It could have been worse, he supposed. If the girls had been younger—eleven or twelve, say—the D.A. might well have insisted on pushing the case. As it was, two fifteen-year-olds, wiggling and giggling up there on the witness stand, helped to support Freddy's contention that he had been deceived. The best his prosecutor could promote was statutory rape, which was a damned sight better than a child-molesting rap. In jail they used the baby rapers for a combination punching bag and dart board. Freddy didn't need that crap at all.

He'd been sentenced to a term of eighteen months, with six suspended on condition that he put himself in therapy, and he had served eleven months of the remaining year before he walked. Inside, there'd been sessions with the jailhouse shrink, and Freddy had been forced to play their games with ink blots, written tests and word-association drills, the whole nine yards. He had enjoyed himself at first, and later, when the games got old, he stonewalled, letting everybody think they had a breakthrough on their hands, when he was actually marking time and waiting for the day when he could hit the streets again.

And find himself some girls.

Apocalypse had saved his life, no doubt about it. Not that Clay or any of the other boys had tried to turn his head around. They didn't seem to give a shit what Freddy did offstage, and that was cool, but they had put him in position to acquire substantial cash, and with a wad of greenbacks in his jeans, he found the girls more readily accessible, in situations far less apt to blow up in his face.

He didn't have to cruise the schoolyards anymore, for starters. There were people you could call in any major city, and the chicken was delivered to your door. Sometimes, if you were really in the mood for something heavy, you would have to take a little drive to one of the facilities that catered to "unusual" tastes. Again, most major cities had at least one such emporium, provided you could make the proper contacts.

Lucian Slate had contacts everywhere.

Sykes wasn't sure about the blood and prayers and all, but Slate had put the band on track, had lined them up for major money, and he had a knack for finding tender flesh in every town along their way. That made him Freddy's man.

He took another sip, just for the hell of it, and passed the goblet to his left.

"O PAN AND PLUTO, Set and Shiva, Thoth and Yaotzin, harken to our cry!"

The cup felt warm as Tommy Piersall took it from the bass guitarist, swirling ruby contents in the depths before he raised it to his mouth. He didn't mind the taste at all—or wouldn't have, if he had tasted anything.

The coke could do that for you if you used enough. It helped to get a little of the flaky powder on your fingertips and rub it all around your gums, a little on the tongue and—presto!—you were in the middle of a whole new sensory experience. The drawback was you couldn't taste your enchiladas for a while, but the effects were transitory and it all came back.

At least it all came back so far, but there were times when Tommy thought his food was tasting bland, and he remembered that he hadn't done the oral trick for hours, even days. A doctor could have told him he was burning out his nerves and shriveling his mucous membranes, but the lecture would have fallen on sedated ears. Tom Piersall didn't give a shit.

He dug the Lucifer routine because Slate told them that the devil loved a self-indulgent acolyte. The more you partied, slept around and snorted shit, the more you fell in line with Satan's master plan. If he had been compelled to take a quiz, the keyboard player couldn't have described that master plan in any detail, but he liked the sound of someone in divine authority who was a righteous party animal. It made the scattered pieces seem to fit.

These days, when he could easily afford the coke in larger quantities and greater purity, he thought how great it was to be a rock star in the good old U.S.A. Where else on earth could he be paid so well for doing next to nothing? Where else in the universe could he become a star?

It was amazing how the band had turned around the past two years. He didn't know if Satan was responsible, but Slate believed it, Clay apparently believed it and the others went along because you didn't piss on Lady Luck when she was smiling at you.

It was a decent life, in spite of the rehearsals and the road time. Piersall could have been worse off, and he didn't intend to throw his one and only big-time shot away. If Slate came in tomorrow and said they ought to worship Gumby for a while, it wouldn't bother Tommy in the least, as long as he could toot some shit and take the long view. Already looking forward to another hit, he passed the chalice on.

"WE CALL UPON YOU to pay heed and grant our plea!"

Slate took the goblet back from Tommy Piersall, raised it to his lips without a second thought and drained the salty contents in a single swallow. For an instant he was tempted to forget the source, the means by which their ritual elixir was acquired, but he could tolerate no weakness in himself. To purge the momentary doubt he forced himself to picture York, the others, as they did their work. It steeled his nerves and left him feeling cold inside.

He could recite the prayers by rote, without a conscious thought, and sometimes Slate examined the peculiar members of his congregation while he rattled off the roster of infernal names. Clay, on his left, wasn't a problem. Clay was sold, and it would cost him more to break away than he could readily afford. As for the others...

Beamish was a moron, plain and simple. With the emphasis on *simple*. Still, he had a soul, of sorts, and every offering was holy in the Master's sight. If Beamish had the understanding of a child, that only made him more receptive to the message at a real, gut level. He would stick because he liked the life-style, and because he had no other talents in the world.

O'Neal might once have been a problem, but the accident had left him deeply in Slate's debt. The Master's debt. He didn't need to know that York and company had visited the family of his lamented victim, cash in hand, a message on their lips. It would be wise, they counseled, to accept the money and go on about their lives, before the dear departed suddenly had company. O'Neal believed that prayer had made the difference, that Lucifer had intervened—and so he had, but in a rather different manner.

Freddy Sykes enjoyed the girls, and Slate was happy to provide them if it kept the bass guitarist happy. Sex and drugs and rock and roll. It was the message of Apocalypse, and Slate encouraged every member of the band to live the fantasy each day, all day. Depravity was just another form of living sacrifice.

For Tommy Piersall, drugs described the boundaries of his universe, and Slate was pleased to keep him flying while he served the Master well. It was the very least he could do.

No reason any of them had to know about his other dealings, on the side. They mightn't understand, might even be resentful, and he didn't feel their minds were capable of grasping all the details in the Master's battle plan. There would be angry words if Clay or any of the others knew that he was trading on their name and pocketing a handsome profit, none of which returned to feed the band.

So be it. Slate would keep his little secret to himself. His Master was the Prince of Darkness, after all. The Father of Lies. He thought that Lucifer would be delighted with the scheme, the way he played both ends against the middle to attain the ultimate result. It was a masterstroke, no pun intended.

And the notion made him smile.

10

Carr chose to work alone for two important reasons. First, he had established contacts in the underground community of cults and fringe religions who would deal with no one else. A strange face at his elbow, anyone at all, and sources would begin to wither on the vine. He needed information now, without a long, protracted chase. He didn't need to waste his precious time persuading key informants they were safe.

And second, while he trusted Cass implicitly, he wanted cold assessments of the Denver situation that hadn't been filtered through the eyes of a believer. Amos Carr, for all the flack that he'd taken from his brother officers, the press and all, was still a skeptic in his heart. It didn't faze him when old friends began to call him "Ghost Buster," inquiring whether he had captured any vampires lately. Amos knew the art of sharing laughter at his own expense, but underneath his smile the stubborn captain of police was still hard as nails.

Put simply, Amos didn't buy the supernatural. In fifty years of living he'd never seen a ghost, and he didn't expect to. Witches were another matter altogether. They existed, in the same way cops and crooks and politicians all existed. They had taken on alternative religions, life-styles; they believed in magic. But that didn't mean the magic worked.

In fairness, Carr could honestly report that he had seen a woman murdered through a voodoo curse. A *houngan* in New Orleans had informed the lady she would die within a week, and she believed him. Friends and relatives had tried to talk her out of the obsession, but it didn't take and she was dead on schedule, almost to the hour. Carr had made a study of the case at the request of local homicide detectives, and he recommended that they close their file. If anything the woman's death would have to stand as suicide. The weapon: raw hysteria.

It was *belief* that made the witches, warlocks and assorted dingbats dangerous. There were no demons from the pit, no evil spirits circling in the stratosphere. Man had enough to cope with in the 3-D world of day-to-day without believing in a pack of fairy tales.

And yet there were occasions when he still believed in hell. Not a TV evangelist's type, but rather hell on earth. In more than twenty years of law enforcement Amos Carr had seen hell many times.

He'd been treated to a taste of it that morning, in a Denver cemetery.

There were evil men abroad in Denver, in America at large. Some went on television, begging for the hard-earned dollars of their faithful viewers, money that would line their pockets, fuel their yachts and limos, hire their hookers for the weekend. Others weren't content with money. They were after blood, and anytime a life was on the line, the killers had to take priority above the common thieves.

When Carr took time to analyze the Satanists, he knew that some were pitifully sincere, attempting to discover order in their lives by taking old, established dogma, turning it around and giving it a shake to see what might fall out. A larger number were attracted by the lure of promiscuity—with drugs, with alcohol, primarily with sex—that was a major tenet of the devil-worshiper's philosophy. And then there was the true hard-core, a clique of mind-warped individuals as rigidly committed to their doctrines as a commissar in Moscow was committed to the party. They *believed*, and they would kill in furtherance of that belief. Conviction made them doubly dangerous.

Police responses to the new occult explosion had been mixed. Too many officers refused to see the problem, writing each new act of violence off as simply "drug related," "gang related" or a simple case of one more psycho punk who finally blew his top. A few went overboard the other way, becoming prisoners of what Carr liked to call the Cotton Mather Syndrome. These saw witches, Satanists, and drugged-out zombies everywhere, responding with a kind of tunnel vision which made every violent crime seem cult-related. Either way, through their indifference or obsession, too damned many cops had missed the mark.

Between the two extremes, Carr gathered facts, built solid cases, sometimes even saw them go to court. The wrap-up, nine times out of ten, would be a bargain, with the perpetrator copping to a lesser charge on the condition that his cult involvement not be laid before the jury. Carr could live with that, as long as bad guys went to jail where they belonged, but in the process members of the public weren't being educated to the danger in their midst. If anything, he thought the average citizen had been deliberately deceived.

And Amos meant to change all that in Denver, if he could. Apocalypse meant headlines nationwide, and if the band was linked with sacrificial murders, if the link could be established to the satisfaction of a judge and jury, he would have his victory. Exposure of the Chingon network would be gravy. As a hard-nosed realist, Carr didn't hope for everything at once.

The rest would come in time, unless they killed him first. He'd been living with the possibility for several years, since an informant first advised him of the Chingon net's existence. Skeptical at first, Carr had compiled a massive dossier of "disconnected" leads and bits of evidence that finally, with proper handling, combined to form a more or less coherent picture of a nationwide conspiracy. The bastards dealt in drugs, in female flesh and children, in pornography of every stripe. They also dealt in murder when it suited them, for self-protection or in furtherance of their sadistic rituals.

How many dead so far? Carr didn't even want to know. He was concerned about the living—one of whom, if he was right, wouldn't be living when the sun came up tomorrow morning. He didn't know her name, but he could see her in his mind, pale flesh exposed to brutal daylight, mutilated like the victim of an animal attack.

He had perhaps twelve hours to find the animals. And, failing that, he had tomorrow, with the opportunity of saving yet another victim. While Apocalypse remained in town he had a shot. And when they left . . .

Carr's knuckles whitened as he gripped the steering wheel. If he should fail in Denver, Amos knew that he would follow them. Forever, if he had to. He would follow them to hell to make his case, and when they met there Amos would be ready for the barbecue.

CASSANDRA POOLE was driving. Bolan studied her in profile, alternately shifting his attention to a survey of the streets. He understood that they were going to be visiting some friends of hers, associates in the pursuit of "magic," and he was expected to be unobtrusive while she handled any questioning. It seemed a fair arrangement since he had no local contacts of his own and didn't know what questions he should ask.

Except for one. "What's the attraction?" Bolan asked her after they had traveled several blocks.

"I beg your pardon?"

"Satanism. Based on everything I've heard, I would have thought it was a little dark for someone like yourself."

Her laughter took him by surprise. "You mean, what's a nice girl like me doing in a religion like this?"

"Well, if you put it that way—"

"Mr. Blanski, I'm no Satanist. There are Satanic witches, granted, but the vast majority are followers of Wicca, what we call the Old Religion. It predates your Christianity by several thousand years—and, incidentally, it also predates Satan."

"So you don't believe in Lucifer?"

"I have a strong belief in good and evil. Names are insignificant."

"But you agree with Amos? I mean that these deaths are cult related?"

"Certainly. Is that so strange? Remember Manson? Reverend Jones? The People's Temple? The atrocities are real enough."

"It's hard to picture something like this going on for years and no one knowing."

"No one *wants* to know. It's easier to pass the murders off as simple teenage violence. Gangs and drugs. Make all the preschool children out as liars so you're not compelled to face your neighbors, teachers, pastors, in a way you can't imagine. It's the ostrich option, Mr. Blanski."

"Mike."

"Our first stop is a bookstore, Mike. The owner is a friend of mine. He doesn't practice anymore—he had a bad experience, I think—but he's extremely knowledgeable in the movements of the dark side."

"Which makes you—"

"A white witch.... I believe he's got it."

"I expect a rabbit with a stopwatch any time now. This is getting weird."

"It's weird to you because it's strange. You're not familiar with the territory. I imagine I'd feel much the same investigating robberies or tapping telephones."

He wondered what, if anything, Carr might have told her to explain his presence in the hunt. "I don't do much of that," he said, and let it go.

"We're here," she told him, pulling to the curb outside a seedy-looking bookshop called the Crystal Ship. From the appearance of the neighborhood, he wondered how the owner made a living out of books at all, less the mystic-sounding volumes offered by assorted posters in the window.

"Appearances deceive," Cass said, and Bolan felt the short hairs rising on his neck.

"Pardon?"

She blushed. "I'm sorry. I had the impression that you might be thinking . . . never mind. Forgive me."

Bolan liked the flush of color in her cheeks. "No, please, go on."

"Well, I imagined you were thinking what a run-down place this is. The area and all."

"You do read minds."

"Not really." Cass was quick to change the subject. "Actually Thomas has a widespread reputation in the craft, throughout this country and in parts of Europe."

"He's the answer man?"

"I hope so."

Bolan followed her inside the store. If Cass's shop was cluttered, this was chaos. Books were alternately stacked and scattered on the floor, piled high in cardboard boxes, wedged two-deep on shelves, without an obvious attempt at alphabetical or topical arrangement. It was great for browsing, but for the shopper with a given book in mind the place would be a nightmare.

A dwarf was seated on a wooden stool, perched behind the register. His eyes lit up at the sight of Cass, and when he spoke his voice was deep, surprisingly melodious.

"Cassandra, welcome! It's been . . . what? Six months?"

"Too long."

"Indeed." His eyes were tracking Bolan now. "And who's your friend?"

"Michael Blanski, Gandalf."

Bolan shook the hand that was extended.

"Am I correct in my assumption this is not a social call?"

"We need your help. *I* need your help."

"Of course." He studied Bolan for another moment, turning back to Cass. "Go on."

"The Chingons."

Gandalf stiffened. "Be specific, please."

"I think they're here in Denver. I assume you've heard about—"

"Mount Olivet? Of course. Distasteful business."

"We have reason to believe the Children of the Flame might be involved."

"What reason?"

Bolan caught a glance from Cass. She hesitated, finally nodded.

"Carbon-copy homicides in several other cities," he informed the shop owner. "Young women, girls. We have a pattern and a link."

"Which is?"

He hesitated, wondering how far he ought to trust the man. "Let's say the deaths are following a predetermined schedule."

"Ah. Are you a music lover, Mr. Blanski?"

"When I have the time."

"And have you listened to Apocalypse?"

"Last night."

"I see." He cut a glance toward Cass, addressed them both. "There might be danger."

"We accept that."

Bolan was surprised by Cass's turn of phrase. He didn't plan to put her on the firing line.

"You have prepared yourself?"

She nodded. "Yes, as best I can."

"An unbeliever finds no sanctuary in the craft," the little man told Bolan. "How do you propose to meet the Children of the Flame?"

"I thought I might fight fire with fire," the Executioner replied.

"They are a ruthless breed, devoid of conscience and constraint."

"I know the type."

"I wonder." Gandalf frowned. "Perhaps, if you believed—"

Cass tried to bring him back on track. "Do you have any information we can use?"

"Mere rumors. Lucian Slate, as you must know, is privately connected with the movement. Now he's also a celebrity of sorts. A heady combination, Cass. It breeds ambition, avarice—the traits his Master so admires."

"And you've heard nothing of the sacrifices?"

"Nothing useful. Names are meaningless. The Children change identities the way a reptile sheds its skin. I'll wager some forget the names that they were born with."

"Motives?"

"Who can say? Perhaps another 'Helter Skelter,' mmm?"

"You must have some idea."

The little man expelled a weary sigh. "The sacrifices haven't been confined to holy days. Therefore we have a riddle. I'm inclined to think that sacrifices in such numbers indicate a special ritual of summoning, or else..."

"Go on."

"Publicity."

"Publicity?"

"The Slaughter Tour." Bolan's words were out before he had an opportunity to stop them.

Gandalf shrugged. "I wouldn't rule it out. Remember Manson and the music. Don't insist on rationality when you begin to search for motivation."

"You mentioned summoning."

"Another possibility. In that case holy days might be irrelevant. The Children would be acting on a schedule of their own, preparing for the consummation on a date unknown to any but the chosen few."

"And who would they be summoning?" the Executioner inquired.

"Why, Lucifer, of course. Who else?"

"You buy all that?"

Cass read the skepticism in Bolan's tone and frowned. "He wasn't selling anything," she said. "We asked for his opinion, and we got it."

"Right. But summoning the devil?"

"You're surprised? What else would you expect from worshipers of Satan? Everything they do is theoretically designed to pave the way for the institution of their master's undisputed reign on earth. It's the equivalent of Christians looking forward to a Second Coming, but the Chingons aren't content to sit and wait. They're taking steps to make it happen."

"Maybe."

"All right, *maybe*. You believe the other theory? That they're killing people to promote a record album?"

Blanski shrugged. "I don't know what to think right now. The whole damned thing is—"

"Weird?"

"You got it."

"Tell me, Mr. Blanski—Mike—who are you used to dealing with?"

"Assorted lowlifes. It's the mystic line behind the violence that surprises me."

"It shouldn't. Faith moves mountains. It can also move a man in strange directions."

"So I hear."

"Go back and read your history. How many wars, atrocities and revolutions have been rooted in religion."

"Granted. Still, it's hard to picture anyone in modern-day society believing they can conjure Lucifer by killing girls."

"You don't believe in evil."

"Sure I do, but not the pitchfork cloven-hoofed variety."

"It's not important how we visualize our demons. They exist."

"I thought your faith predated Satanism."

"So do good and evil. Satan is a concept—a name some people give to Evil in its purest form."

"And what does Wicca think about all this?"

"We try to live in harmony with nature and the spirits of the earth, avoiding evil when we can, cooperating with the good where possible."

"You practice magic? Hexes? Things like that?"

"We practice our religion. It is no more weird or humorous than Catholic ritual, bar mitzvahs, tent revivals."

"Hey, I wasn't poking fun."

"I know. I'm sorry."

"Skip it."

"May I ask you something?"

"Sure, if I can ask you something first."

"All right."

"Back there, with Gandalf, when you said you had prepared yourself. What did you mean?"

She kept it simple, on a level she believed he would understand. "I meant I had prepared myself for contact with the evil, if it cannot be avoided. There are certain prayers and invocations that provide a measure of protection from attack."

"You did all that before we left your shop?"

"Not all. A prayer doesn't require some special place or garment. I've been asking guidance since you came into the store."

"I see."

"My turn." She put her thoughts in order, searching for the right approach, deciding to be blunt. "Are you with the police?" she asked.

Bolan shook his head. "I'm private. Contacts put me onto Amos, and I'm checking out his problem, just in case there's something I can do."

"Such as?"

"I don't know yet."

She took a chance. "I feel that there is violence in your life."

"Sometimes." The sudden distance in his voice put Cass on guard.

"The people you are seeking live for violence, Mike. Their sacraments are blood and pain. Be careful."

"How about yourself?"

"I'm helping Amos gather information, nothing more."

"Some people might regard that as an act of war."

"I'm not a warrior."

"What's your link with Amos, Cass?"

"We're friends, I think."

"You think?"

"It's difficult to say sometimes. He's cynical, of course, an unbeliever—but he cares. He tries to help and saves lives where he can. I think he is a good man underneath the bluster."

"Does he call upon you often?"

"Only when our interests overlap. When he's in Denver I expect a call."

"We spoke with some police this morning, and they mentioned other homicides in Denver, several years ago."

"The Becker case," she told him, frowning. "No connection with the Chingons, I'm afraid. Todd Becker was a one-man coven, self-styled Satanist and sorcerer. He got the notion he could make himself immortal if he sacrificed five virgins, synchronized the phases of the moon. Detectives picked him up before he got to number four."

"He had no group behind him?"

"Only in his mind, and that was courtesy of LSD, amphetamines, you name it. By the time he started killing he was wasted all the time."

"It sounds like he was wasted in the womb."

"Exposure to the dark side can be perilous. Todd Becker was a college student, pre-med, when he started dabbling 'for fun.' It ate him alive."

"No self-control?"

"Perhaps."

"Don't tell me you believe he was possessed?"

"I don't dismiss the possibility. If so, I'd say he brought it on himself." She smiled as Blanski shifted in his seat, enjoying his discomfort. "We've got two more stops," she told him, "in the suburbs. Friends from other covens. They might have some information we can use."

"You've got a lot of witches in this town."

"I think it's something in the air." She caught him watching her and grinned. "A joke."

"I knew that." Blanski's smile was there and gone again, a fleeting thing.

"Don't worry. Witchcraft's not contagious."

"That's too bad. A decent spell or two might come in handy sometimes."

"We can work on something later." Even as she spoke Cass felt the color rising in her cheeks.

Be careful. This one was a man of violence, and his footsteps led to mortal danger. Cass could not afford to think of what might happen if she tried to follow him.

"I'm looking forward to it," Blanski said, but when she glanced at him, his face was turned in profile, studying the streets.

11

Carr was waiting in his room when they arrived. Together, Cass between them, they walked over to the coffee shop and found a booth that offered them some privacy. Cass sat on Bolan's side, with Amos opposite, and he was totally, acutely conscious of her presence, inches to his left.

"Good hunting, children?"

Bolan let Cass answer.

"I touched three of my associates," she told the former lawman. "Gandalf, Libra, Zane."

"Okay. They ought to know the score."

"That's just the problem. All of them have heard about the murders, but they have no reading on a Chignon coven in the Denver area. I can't believe all three would miss it if the group exists. I'll have to say you're dealing with a transient hunting party."

"Yeah, I was afraid of that."

"Is that a special problem?" Bolan asked.

"It means they've got no roots," Carr said. "At least no roots that we can put our fingers on. They'll be receiving orders word-of-mouth, and we don't have a hope in hell of pinning down a source."

"Sounds pretty grim."

"I won't say hopeless." Carr fell silent as the waitress brought their meals, arranged them on the table, moved away. When he resumed he spoke around a bite of breaded veal with gravy. "These guys might be mobile, but the network doesn't like its people running free. They'll have a contact, like a supervisor, close enough to monitor their act and pull the plug if things get hairy."

"And if you can find the supervisor . . ."

"Then we've found our hunters. Simple."

"I don't suppose you've got a roster of these Chingons? Any sort of list at all?"

Cass smiled, and Amos laughed out loud. "You kidding? I'd lay odds their leader doesn't even know who all his people are. They sign a contract with the Master, see—in blood, of course—and then the contract's burned, like so." He cupped his hands. "That sound familiar?"

Bolan nodded. If the ritual wasn't an imitation of the ancient Mafia initiation ceremony, it was too damned close for comfort.

"Yeah, I thought so. Anyway, it symbolizes that recruitment is a one-way ticket. Once you're in, you're *in*."

"And there've been no defectors?"

Carr looked vaguely ill. "I heard about one, once. A young guy, out in Hollywood. He got fed up and started making overtures to LAPD's criminal intelligence division. They were skeptical at first, and then he started feeding them selected goodies. Bodies here and there, that kind of thing.

"So, anyway, they finally buy his rap and set a meeting in this underground garage. The cops are early, and they're looking for this red Trans Am their man's supposed to drive. Surprise! They find it waiting for them, with their guy behind the wheel. The only problem was, somebody skinned him. Literally. He was still alive, but there was no way he could name the perpetrators. Someone took his tongue."

"Please, Amos."

"Sorry, Cass."

"I'm betting there have been no more defectors," Bolan said.

"Smart money. Pay the winner."

"Okay," Bolan said. "You've got no man inside, no information on a local coven. How are we supposed to find the contact, let alone your hunters, if we don't have anything to go on?"

"Well, there's always Slate."

"You think their contact's with the band?"

Carr shrugged. "I'm fishing. Cass?"

"It's possible. We know that Slate's connected with the upper levels of the network."

"Wait a second," Bolan interrupted her. "I've heard that twice now. But you've got no man inside the group, they keep no records and they operate in secrecy. So what's your basis of connecting Slate?"

"Surveillance," Carr responded. "Certain cops in California have been working on the Chingon net for years, since Manson and his creepy-crawlers went away. There were a few leaks in the old days. Guys picked up on drugs who shot their mouths off, this and that. They never got enough for trial, but they got names. The leader, for example. Certain cronies, up and down the family tree. It's pushing twenty years now, they've been watching members, known associates, and keeping tabs whenever possible. The system's far from foolproof, but at least we have a basic working knowledge of the group."

"Ironically," Cass said, "the Chingons might not be as secretive as they appear. Of course, their rituals are closely guarded, and they execute defectors, but the actual existence of their group has been well-known among practitioners since roughly 1967. Many Satanists—and certain Wiccans—could provide you with a censored capsule history, including names and places."

"But the cops are working in the dark?"

"Most of them never ask," she told him. "Talking to a witch is like consulting psychics when you have an unsolved murder on your hands. Most officers won't do it, period."

"Okay, so Slate is definitely tied in with the network?"

"Positively. When the founder's son took over from his late, lamented daddy, Slate was one of fifteen lucky stiffs invited to the coronation banquet. That was 1986, October. Right around the time Slate got his new job with Apocalypse."

"And if he is the contact, then the hunters will be clearing things through him?"

"At least. He may be giving them their orders."

"Damn." He turned to Cass. "Publicity?"

"How's that?" Carr looked confused.

"It's something Gandalf said," she answered. "Since the rituals don't coincide with holy days, he thought they might involve a summoning, or else they might be staged to gain publicity."

"That's what I call a damned hard sell."

"Assuming that you've got Slate pegged," the warrior said, "what then? You can't expect him to cooperate."

"We'll squeeze him if we have to, as a last resort, but first I've got some other sources that I need to tap." Carr checked his watch. "And I've got something you should listen to. We finished here?"

Carr made a show of picking up the tab, and they were back inside his room five minutes later. From his suitcase, he produced a squat transistor radio and fiddled with the dial until he had the strains of organ music loud and clear.

"Your basic local Christian channel," he announced. "Tonight they've got a special guest. Go on and have a seat. The show's about to start."

BACKSTAGE, surrounded by the members of his road crew, Jordan Braithwaite bowed his head in prayer. His hands were clenched before him, and he kept a Bible, bound in leather, tucked beneath one arm.

"And finally, our Father, we beseech thee to enlighten us and show us how your enemies may best be stricken from the earth. We pray that you will guide our hands and give us strength in this, the hour of trial. Amen."

He checked his Rolex as the choir began to sing their final hymn out front: 8:25. Beside him Arthur Trent was shuffling a few last-minute notes.

"Full house," he said, and smiled. "You'd have them standing in the aisles if we could clear it with the fire department."

"Never mind. Sufficient unto this day is the blessings we receive."

"Amen."

"Make sure the ushers circulate their buckets in the upper tier when we collect the offering. I still think some of them got lazy and missed out last night."

"I'll speak to them again."

"Make sure they understand. If anybody doesn't do his job, he won't get paid."

"Yes, sir. I'll make it clear."

"All right."

Onstage the choir was finished, and spotlights focused on the podium where he was being introduced. He waited for the first reverberation of applause before he left the wings, arms raised, the Bible brandished overhead. The gooseneck microphone reared up before him like a cobra.

"Praise the Lord!" he bellowed, and the faithful answered him in unison. "All glory be to God!"

They let him have a chorus of "Amens," and then the crowd fell silent, waiting, eager to receive the message.

"Children, I have grievous news tonight," he told them, putting just the right touch of emotion in his educated voice. "I'm sure that many of you, most of you, already know the sorry tale. A young girl from your own community was killed last night. I don't mean by accident, or in some random act of violence that we hear so much about these days. This child was *sacrificed* to *Lucifer* by individuals who made a conscious choice to serve the prince of thieves and liars.

"Did you hear me? I said she was *sacrificed*! Her heart, where love of Jesus should have dwelled, was ripped out of her body by an unclean hand. Now the police won't tell you that. The local press won't tell you that. They don't want anyone to know the details of this heinous crime, in case the public might become *alarmed*!"

He paused to let them chew that over, big hands gripping each side of the podium, his Bible spread before him.

"I believe it's time we all become alarmed," he shouted. "And I'm here to tell you, children, Satan wants your soul. He wants it so bad he can taste it. He'll do anything to win your soul away from God, and I mean anything!"

Relaxing slightly, Braithwaite sipped the glass of water that had been provided for him.

"Last night I had a word or two to say about the so-called heavy-metal concert that was playing at your local Mile High Stadium. Well, there's another one tonight, my friends. Another celebration for the Prince of Darkness right here in your Rocky Mountain city.

"Some folks think I come down just a little bit too hard on modern music, don't you know? They tell me I should live and let live. Go with the flow. Kick back and get it in the groove."

A wave of laughter rippled through the audience. Relief.

"I'm here to tell you, children, that I don't believe I've come down on this so-called modern music hard enough! I don't believe I've made my point, but there are others out there who are bound to make it for me. And I don't appreciate their help one bit, but maybe—*maybe*—if we get this point across and put this message over, then I guess there's truth in scripture when it says that all things work together for good, to them who love God."

"Amen!"

"I've spoken to you of a child who lost her life last night. I haven't told you *where* she met her enemies, the filthy unclean spirits who seduced her to her doom. She didn't meet them in her local house of worship, Lord. She didn't meet them on the street or at the shopping mall. Police won't tell you this, but I'm obliged to tell you that she met her killers at that godforsaken heavy-metal concert that was held last night within a mile of where you're sitting now. The devil came *that close* to you last night, and if you think he's slipped away to hide somewhere, you're very much mistaken."

Members of the audience were lifting up their hands and rocking in their seats, a few of them already muttering in tongues. The preacher dropped his voice a decibel or two and brought them back and forth.

"We need to be on guard each minute of the day and night against the wiles of Satan, people. He will never rest from his attempts to undermine our faith, destroy our peace of mind, and bring us low before the sight of God. His agents may be legion, and their weapons fierce, but Christians who agree to put their faith in Jesus Christ need have no fear."

Another pause. Another sip of water while they waited for the up-side of his message. Braithwaite wasn't ready to release them yet.

"I look around sometimes, my children, and I wonder what this great, God-fearing nation has become. I'll tell you one thing, with the leaders we've got in power today, the nation *should* be fearing God, because his righteous anger will not be forgotten and his hand will not be stayed on Judgment Day!"

"Amen!"

"The Lord is weighing souls tonight, and when he's finished with the dead of ages past, it will be time for him to visit earth again and judge the living. Are you ready? Can your heart withstand inspection, children? Have you exercised your duties faithfully tonight?"

The ringing silence told him they were chewing on it, and he gave them several seconds of discomfort, on the house.

"There's one thing you can do for God tonight, and that's to spread his word. Now some of you may say you don't possess the skills, the courage, to go out and witness on a daily basis. That's all right. Your calling may be somewhere else. But you can still support the spreading of His message, and the war against this filthy, godless rock and roll that claims our children's lives, their very souls. You can do something to defeat the foul purveyors of this murder music!"

"Yes, Lord!"

"Preach it, brother!"

"You can dig down deep tonight and let your conscience be your guide. Let love for Jesus guide your hand as you begin to weigh your offering tonight. Before you try to cheat the Lord and save a penny here, remember that poor child who lost her life last night. We pray she didn't lose her soul! In any case, we still have other children waiting to be rescued, saved by Jesus, and the only way that He can reach their hearts tonight is through a dedicated, vital ministry. Do you believe me, children?"

"Yes, Lord!"

"Yes!"

"Amen!"

"All right, then, children, you know what to do. And when those ushers come around in just a moment, don't let Satan whisper in your ear. Be generous, as God was generous with you on Calvary. For He so loved the world, that He gave his only begotten son! Can you do any less tonight?''

CARR SWITCHED OFF the radio. "So, is he charming or what?"

"The 'or what' has my vote," Bolan said. "What's the point?"

"Maybe nothing." Carr shrugged. "Could be chance, I suppose, that the past few months Braithwaite's been speaking in each town Apocalypse played. Every time there's a murder, he's there to make hay while the sun shines. I guess it's coincidence."

"Doubtful," the soldier replied. "But you know that already. The odds are he's dogging their tracks for publicity, using the crimes to put over his message."

"Could be." Carr seemed skeptical. "But then there's this."

Snapping open a briefcase, he pulled out a legal-length photostat, passing it over to Bolan. A glance showed the page to be crowded with printouts of phone records, several of which had been outlined in red.

"Braithwaite's phone bill for April through June," Carr explained. "I believe I neglected to tell you I also run backgrounds on various cult groups aside from the Satanists. Faith healers, 'love prophets,' con men who rip off the crippled and elderly. Anyway, Braithwaite was named in a beef out of Louisville. Someone who thought he had healed him of cancer discovered the tumors were still going strong. That was *after* the preacher soaked up the guy's savings and scrammed. So I'm checking him out for the locals, a spare-time pursuit, and I came up with this."

"And the number you've marked?"

"It's a head shop in Frisco."

"So what?"

Carr produced yet another sheet, crowded with numbers, the same one illumined in red, fourteen times in three months.

"And these bills?"

"Lucian Slate's."

"Tell me more."

"There's no more to be told. I've checked into the shop, but I can't tie its owner with Chingons or Braithwaite. That just means he's careful, okay? But I'm betting my pension the place is a drop. They might even have hookups for conference calls. Hell, who can say?"

"And you think Braithwaite works for the Chingons?"

Carr frowned. "I don't know what to think. Hell, the cult might be working for *him*. All I know is, it stinks to high heaven. You heard the guy's sermon. You think he'd be calling some head shop an average of three times a month?"

Bolan shrugged. "Preaching's one thing, and living's another. Remember Swaggart? Jim and Tammy? Hell, remember Billy Sunday? Ministers with moral lapses are a dime a dozen, Amos."

"Granted. But I'm interested in this one, and I'd like to know why he had Lucian Slate keep calling San Francisco on the same damned days."

Another glance showed Bolan he was right. The pattern never varied. Braithwaite placed a morning call on April 26, and Slate called later in the day. Then, two or three days later, Braithwaite dialed again. To get his answer? Seeking confirmation of instructions? Simply killing time?

The Executioner had no way of discovering the answer, but he was increasingly unable to accept a tidy explanation. In Bolan's heart, he knew that Braithwaite wasn't simply reaching out to touch a salesgirl who had caught his eye.

"You've checked the staff?"

"No tie-in. Drifters, aging hippies. No one with a link to Braithwaite."

"And the calls from Braithwaite? Is it possible that someone else was dialing?"

"That's his private billing, not the ministry's. The preacher's solo act, my friend. No wife, no kids, no pets. He likes to travel light."

"You've checked his background?" Cass inquired. It was the first time she had spoken since the radio began to blare its sermon on the sins of rock and roll.

"The best I can. He's got no rap sheet. Never even had a traffic ticket as far as I can tell. That means he's either awfully straight or mighty careful. Legend has it that he got the calling at a tent revival on his thirteenth birthday. He's been preaching ever since, in one way or another, and it's been his only source of income for the better part of twenty years."

"Ordained?"

"By the United Church of Christ Our Savior, 1969. He worked their pulpits for about five years, and then he had a falling out with leaders of the group. No details, sorry. He's been on his own since late '74, traveling coast-to-coast. Discovered radio in 1975 and television in '78. I understand his weekly sermons and the various crusades are broadcast over something like two hundred channels. He's a household name, of sorts."

"And you believe he's running scams?"

"I know he is. The bastard salts his audience with phony cripples he can 'heal' to keep the suckers lining up around the block. Since 1980 he's been going on the air two nights a week to preach about the joys of giving money. Nothing else—no sermon, scripture, anything. He has one text, describing how the Lord will multiply your offerings a hundred times when he returns your blessings, and he uses that to milk the faithful. I've got tapes of Braithwaite telling people they can ask God for a car, a job, a brand-new house—but first, of course, they have to send in specified amounts to his crusade. A thousand dollars is the average."

"People fall for that?"

"I'd say. He did twelve million five last year in tax-free revenue. And that's not bad, considering he as no church, per se, no missionaries in the field, no programs for the poor and needy. Any overhead is staff and air time. Like I said, he travels light."

"Assuming that he's sharp enough to build his act around Apocalypse and take advantage of the murders, why should he make contact with the Satanists? What have the Chingons got to offer Braithwaite?"

"There you've got me." Amos winked at Cass. "I flunked Mind Reading 101."

"I've told you, Amos—"

"Right, you're sensitive. I know."

"You piss me off sometimes."

"It's one of my endearing qualities."

The Executioner cut through their banter. "What's your thinking on an angle of attack?"

"I've got a few more markers I can call. I may turn up a piece of useful information yet. And Cass—"

"Has other things to do," she interrupted him. "I have a service to prepare for."

"What, tonight?" Carr beamed. "That's perfect. Is it closed? Could Blanski tag along as an observer? Maybe help him get the feel of things a little?"

Bolan glanced at Cass, imagining a tinge of color in her cheeks. "I'd have to call around and get approval from the other members."

"Listen, if it's too much trouble—"

"No." She seemed to have her mind made up. "I'll call. Where are you staying?"

Amos answered for him. "Here. That is, the room next door." He smiled at Bolan's curious expression. "Never fear. Hal's picking up the tab."

"Terrific."

"Right," Cass said. "I'll be in touch. An hour or so."

When she had left them, Bolan turned to Amos Carr. "What's this about a service?" he inquired. "It seems to me we're wasting time."

"Not wasting, son, investing. Hell, who knows? You might learn something if you don't watch out."

12

The hunter liked to take his time. It didn't pay to rush selection of a subject. In the long run, time invested at the outset of a hunt would be rewarded in the kill. It was the way things worked in life—and death.

His name was Owen York, a fact not subject to the "proof" of files and dossiers. His fingerprints weren't catalogued in any policing agency, and while he had been photographed in youth, a modern viewer of those fading snapshots would find precious little similarity between the image and the flesh. He paid no tax and kept no fixed address. He had no telephone, and he received no mail. He stood outside of organized society the way a window-shopper stands outside of a department store, amused by the distortion of his own reflection in the glass.

The vanishing of Owen York had been a conscious effort; nothing in his life was left to chance. At sixteen years of age he'd abandoned home and family forever, dropping out of school by the expedient of simply not reporting for his Monday-morning classes. It had been the year of love and flowers to the north, in San Francisco, where the fabled Haight-Ashbury intersection beckoned like a magnet and the sage gurus of LSD invited all comers to "Tune in, turn on, drop out." It was the Age of Aquarius, replete with promises of peace and understanding. Love was in, and hate was out.

Behind the flowers and the rhetoric, however, other messages were being broadcast in the Haight. Their troubadour was Charlie Manson, with his quirky songs and tribe of willing females, but you didn't need diplomas on the wall to realize that Manson was a mouthpiece rather than a brain. His "conversations" with the Beatles were delusionary, strictly off the wall, but he had contacts, and for Owen York, the men behind the scenes were fascinating, awe-inspiring. He began to haunt their councils, hanging on their every word as if it was the gospel.

Which, in fact, it was.

Later, as he gained experience and leaders of the movement came to trust him, York was favored with assignments of his own. Elimination of defectors was a top priority. Few members lost their nerve, but one could be enough to bring the movement down, and so each traitor had to be exterminated, his or her elimination serving as an object lesson to the faithful and the world at large.

Since Manson's day the movement had been publicly "exposed" by certain journalists, reluctantly investigated by a handful of detectives in New York and California, but the Master's work hadn't been seriously hindered in the process. Newsmen couldn't go to press with names unless they had their flanks protected from a crushing libel suit, and thus far they had nothing they could take to court. A rumor here, a crazed "confession" there—in either case, undoubtedly inspired by drugs or paranoia. Owen York and others like him made certain that the evidence remained elusive, the potential sources silent.

Dealing with police was problematic. Aside from isolated cases—as in Utah, where an undercover officer had recently been made to disappear—direct assaults upon the badge were actively discouraged. It was easier to touch a witness, make a piece of evidence evaporate, than to engage a whole police department in guerrilla warfare. A detective, stripped of sources, normally lost interest in a case and moved along to other items on his crowded docket. They relied upon informers for the most part, and discouraging informers had become York's specialty.

Each time he thought about the old days in Manhattan, York experienced a sweet pang of nostalgia. Hunting in the neon darkness, one hand on the Bulldog .44 as he approached a darkened car, the lovers grappling inside while steamy windows blinded them to Death's approach. If Owen concentrated he could almost hear the sharp reports of gunfire, battered back and forth between the brownstones on an empty street.

Good times. But times were changing; the movement was growing and prospering. There were new objectives now, and York commanded other troops, as he had once been subject to command. He muscled dealers now and then, intimidated witnesses or made them disappear, enforced the Master's dictates with a zeal that made him legendary in the movement. He'd never missed a target, never failed to get results. Commitment and efficiency had won him the assignment that engaged his full attention now, and so far they were dead on schedule.

More precisely, their selected prey was dead on schedule, and he meant to keep it that way, everything according to the master plan.

This evening he had exercised his option to select the girl himself. His choice didn't imply dissatisfaction with the work his comrades had performed thus far. He simply missed the hunt and sought to reaffirm—if any proof was necessary for the others, for himself—that he still had the magic touch.

Selection of the proper target was essential. York invested time and care, bypassing dozens, hundreds who didn't possess that certain flair, the raw vitality he needed for the ritual. Onstage the warm-up band was thrashing through its final number, but he still had time.

His patience was rewarded moments later, as he found the perfect gift for Lucifer. York's smile was hungry as he closed the gap between them, brushing others rudely to the side.

"Hey, man, watch out!" a glassy-eyed urchin snapped behind him. York reversed directions, caught the piss-ant by his throat and flexed his talons.

"What did you say?"

"Forget it, man! It's cool!"

"That's what I thought you said."

York dropped the weasel on his ass and turned back toward the girl. The hungry smile never left his face.

MARLA SHARP WAS growing restless, waiting for Apocalypse. The warm-up band was fair, but she'd come to hear

Clay Deatheridge, and no one else would do. For Clay she'd engaged in yet another of the endless battles with her wid- owed mother, finally storming out to catch her ride before she could be grounded, both sides conscious of the fact that she would still attend the concert, either way.

In fairness, Marla's mother wasn't one of those fanatics who believed that listening to rock and roll would send you straight to hell. The murder had her worried. Murders, rather, for the *Post* had run an article about how girls were getting killed in every town Apocalypse had visited the past few weeks. It frightened Marla, too, but underneath the fear she felt excitement. Marla loved Apocalypse, loved Clay especially, and if there was an element of danger in attend- ing the performance . . . well, that simply made the trip a grand adventure. Marla wasn't suicidal, but the confidence of youth assured her she was safe. Even assuming that the maniac would strike twice in one town—which the paper said he had not done before—the odds against his finding her were astronomical.

Besides, there was safety in numbers.

Marla had come to the concert with three of her girl- friends, and no one, no matter how crazy, would try to take four girls at once. Glancing back through the crowd, Marla wished they would hurry. The opening act was completing its set, and Clay's first song was always the strongest. She hoped it would be "Love and Pain."

It was Sarah's idea, this ridiculous last-minute run on the snack bar. No doubt she would have to stop off at the bath- room beforehand, with Alix and Deb playing tagalong. Marla had shined it on, letting them go. For the price of her ticket, she meant to see Clay and the band, not a mob scene of head-bangers lined up for Pepsi and popcorn.

The tall man collided with Marla in passing and knocked her off balance. He snaked out an arm to keep her from falling, all smiles as he made his apologies.

"Jesus, I'm sorry. Are you okay? I can't believe I'm that clumsy."

"Forget it."

"No, really. I get in a rush, with the hassles backstage, and sometimes I don't look where I'm going."

"Backstage? Are you part of the crew?"

"PR work, this and that. I step in when the roadies get rowdy, you might say."

She laughed. "That must take up a lot of your time."

"I get breathers at Christmas and Easter. Hey, listen, I feel like I owe you one. What about after the show?"

"What about it?"

"We're having a party, the band and some friends. I can bring who I want."

"Are you serious?"

"Sure. Wanna come?"

Marla thought about Sarah and Alix and Deb. "I'm with friends."

"Well . . ."

"Three girlfriends," she added on impulse.

He smiled. "What the heck. More the merrier, right?"

"Wow, you mean it?"

"Why not? I mean, that is, assuming your friends don't object."

"Oh, they won't," Marla told him. "Believe me, they'd die to meet Clay and the rest of the guys."

He was grinning. "That's perfect. One problem, though. I have to split in about half an hour to get things set up for the party, you know?"

Marla frowned, made her mind up. A party with Clay was worth missing the end of the show, absolutely. The others could follow her lead, or she'd go by herself.

"That's okay," she informed him. "As soon as they're back with the snacks, we'll be ready."

"Terrific." He frowned. "It occurs to me, we haven't been introduced. You are . . . ?"

"Marla."

"Hi, Marla. I'm Scratch." They shook hands, and she giggled. "Okay, Marla, here's what you do . . ."

AMOS CARR PARKED his wheels on the street and walked back to the shop. It was closed, but a light was still burning in back, and he knocked on the door. Once again, when he got no response, he checked out empty sidewalks in either direction.

No enemies here.

The pursuit had been taking its toll, he decided. The nerves were the first thing to go. Paranoia sets in, and the first thing you know you'll be checking the closet for witches before you can turn out the lights. It was humorous, all things considered. And yet . . .

An old slogan came back to him, dusty with age. Something out of the sixties, he thought. He'd seen it on a poster somewhere.

Just because you're paranoid, it doesn't mean that no one's out to get you.

Right.

Off hand, the former captain of police could think of ten or fifteen groups that would be thrilled to see him dead.

There was movement in the shop, and Amos tensed before he recognized his contact. Arnold was the kind of guy you wouldn't look at twice if you were stuck together in an elevator going nowhere. Nondescript. A zero. But his mind was razor keen, and he possessed a photographic memory for faces, names and numbers, bits of conversation overheard in passing. Arnold's brain was like a sponge, and Amos thought that it was time to give the sponge a squeeze.

"You're late," his contact said, looking disgruntled as he closed and locked the door.

"So what? You going somewhere?"

"Hey, I've got a life. You're not the only one's got things to do."

"I'm sorry, Arnold."

"Skip it. Coffee?"

"Straight?"

"What else?"

"Okay."

The storeroom had a hot plate, folding table, chairs. Carr didn't see a bed, but Arnold could have stashed a queen-size in among the stacks of cardboard cartons. Half of them were stamped with labels bearing foreign languages and cryptic symbols.

"Business must be good."

"I'm getting by. You want it black?"

"That's fine."

They settled at the table, facing each other.

"So?"

"I'm working on the Chingons, Arnold."

"Yeah? What else is new?"

"I need a handle."

"Settle for advice. Go home. Go anywhere. Forget it, will you? Mess around in this, you could get hurt."

"They're hurting people now. They're hurting kids."

"You figure you can stop them?"

"I can try."

"Good luck."

"I don't need luck. I need a handle."

"Yeah? What makes you think I can help you?"

"An elephant never forgets."

"Elephants make easy targets, Amos."

"No one gets your name from me."

"They've got their methods."

"How's the family, Arnold?"

"Fine. They're fine."

Three years had passed since Carr had first laid eyes on Arnold, during his investigation of an Arizona coven linked with drugs and child pornography. The kid was fed up with his "brothers," looking for an out, and Carr had helped him find it. Later, when indictments were returned and members of the cult had started talking vengeance, Carr pulled strings to get his family settled out of state. In Denver, Arnold had perversely kept in touch with members of the underground, relaying information back to Carr from time to time.

"I need a handle on the Children of the Flame."

"The hunters? Man, you don't ask much."

"I'll take whatever I can get."

"You know they operate disposal teams?"

Carr nodded. "Tell me something new."

"How new is new? Eight weeks ago they iced a kid in Phoenix. He was running drugs across the border, skimming off the top. Case closed."

"I'm following the Slaughter Tour."

"Well, shit."

"They're killing girls."

"I *know* that, man!"

"I want the who and why."

"Forget the why. Who needs a reason? Girls are there, somebody's got to kill them, right?"

"Not good enough. The Children don't do anything without a reason."

Arnold shook his head. "You're talking reasons? They get off on killing people, man. You know that."

"Motive, Arnold."

"All I have are rumbles."

"Go ahead. I'm listening."

"The network has an interest in the band. You're onto that?"

Carr nodded.

"Okay. The rumor is, they've found a way to make it pay off twice."

"How's that?"

"Apparently it's need-to-know. I ask and all I hear is that they're playing both ends off against the middle. That make sense to you?"

"It might. I still need names."

"Good luck. These fuckers all use family names, you know? Remember Charlie's girls? You pick up names like Squeaky, Moon Dog, who knows what. They don't mean shit."

"It's more than what I've got."

"Okay. The ramrod is supposed to be a guy called Scratch. He's been around forever. Since the sixties."

Amos scowled. "That old?"

"Go figure." Arnold cracked a sour smile. "They say he's iced a lot of people. I mean *lots*, okay?"

"I hear you."

"Some of this is bullshit, maybe. I don't know."

"Keep talking."

Arnold shrugged. "You buy the rap, they'll tell you that he used to hang around with Manson. Maybe he was in New York a while ago, when guns were going off. They say he set the Black Cross up himself, to deal with leaks and obstacles."

"A guy like that should have a heavy record."

"Street talk says he's *very* careful. Shooters come and go, but Scratch goes on forever."

"Bullshit."

"Hey, you asked."

"You said he was the ramrod. Who's his backup?"

Arnold shook his head. "Nobody knows."

"*Somebody* knows."

"I guess you'd better ask them, man."

"I might."

"It's been nice knowing you."

"Such confidence."

"You're up against a fucking army. Confidence won't help. You need an army of your own."

"I'm working on it."

"One more for the road?"

"No, thanks."

He hesitated on the doorstep, scribbled the motel's number on a business card and handed it to Arnold. "Just in case."

"Take care, man."

Amos felt the young man's eyes on him as he back-tracked to his car. His mind was racing, trying to assimilate the sketchy information he had received.

A guy called Scratch? No riddle there. It was an ancient nickname for the devil, dating back at least two centuries. The bastards had a sense of humor, anyway.

And they were "playing both ends off against the middle." What the hell did that mean?

Amos had a hunch, but he'd have to pin it down. If his suspicions were correct...

He made his mind a blank and concentrated on his driving.

13

"What do you call this service?"

"Eshbat." Cass was driving once again, her high beams boring tunnels in the darkness as they left the city lights behind them. "It coincides with the full moon each month, and incorporates special objectives. Tonight we will ask for protection."

"From what?"

She was frowning. "From those whom you seek."

"Do they frighten you?"

"Madness is always disturbing. In this case the madness is coupled with evil. They frighten me, yes."

They drove on for a short time in silence, the road climbing gently, before Cass addressed him again.

"Understand that the eshbat is normally closed to outsiders. My brothers and sisters agree to your presence, accepting my own guarantee of your conduct."

"I'll try to behave," Bolan said.

"It's no laughing matter. Our service will surely be strange to you. It is critical that you observe without speaking. There must be no break in the flow of our worship. No sacrilege may be permitted."

"You won't know I'm there."

"Yes we will. One or two of our brothers expressed their concern that your presence may silence our guides."

"Come again?"

"We rely upon spirits to guide us and carry our prayers during worship. Some feel that an outsider's presence may drive them away and prevent us from making a contact."

"If this is a problem—"

"I've counseled them," Cass interrupted. "I have every confidence we will succeed. If a problem arises, we'll deal with it then."

"You have pull in the coven?"

"A bit. I'm in charge."

"Does that make you a priestess?"

"Flamenca. The concept of priests has no meaning in Wicca."

"And spells?"

"Incantations. We act in accordance with nature, as moved by our guides. If you're looking for dolls full of pins, I suggest you try voodoo."

"Forgive me if all this seems . . . strange."

"What is your faith?"

He smiled. "I'm not sure if I have one."

"You must. Every soul needs its shelter from harm."

Bolan studied the night, dark trees blurring together outside. They were five or six miles out of town now, still climbing.

"How long?" Bolan asked.

"Not much farther." It was a mile, give or take, before Cass slowed and turned off the highway. The new road was gravel; she followed its course for about two hundred yards before parking outside of an A-frame surrounded by trees. Lights were showing inside, and a half-dozen cars were parked off to one side.

"Are we late?"

"Right on time," she assured him. "I meant what I said, Mike. Whatever you see, you must not interfere."

"I'm the soul of discretion."

"I hope so." The night breeze was warm as they stepped from the car. Moonlight painted the trees with a rich silver gloss. "We'll be working outside," Cass informed him. "It's better, when weather allows. In the winter we don't have much choice."

She knocked softly, waiting for the sound of footsteps from inside. The door swung open to reveal a youthful, fair-haired man attired in flowing robes. He studied Bolan with a cautious eye, then turned to Cass and kissed her on the cheek.

"Merry met and blessed be."

The soldier followed her inside and found himself surrounded by a dozen pairs of watchful eyes. With Cass, the coven numbered thirteen souls.

"Our guest is Michael," she informed the others. "He requests our blessing and support in conflict with the sons of darkness." Moving on around the circle, he was introduced to individuals with chosen names like Raven, Ariadne, Thor, and he shook hands with each in turn. That done, Cass left him for a moment, disappearing into an adjacent room. When she returned, she had exchanged her street clothes for a robe that matched the others, save in color. Hers was red, the others white.

"I have informed our guest of the requirements and restrictions for his observation. He has sworn that nothing seen or heard tonight shall pass his lips. So mote it be."

"So mote it be," the others answered her in unison.

"Is all prepared?"

The young man, introduced as Victor, nodded. "All is done, within the limits of my power."

"Excellent. Let us proceed."

Cass led the way through sliding doors directly opposite the entrance, followed by her coreligionists, with Bolan bringing up the rear. Behind the A-frame, level ground had been plucked clean of grass, swept clear of stones. A cheery flame was leaping in the fire pit to their right, while logs and tinder, stacked to form a bonfire, waited in the middle of the open ground, unkindled. Bolan saw the earth was covered with a sprinkling of something that resembled salt. Concentric rings of sulfur had been laid out on the open ground, the fire-in-waiting at their center. Each was broken at a single point, resembling a gate, and candles fitted out with tall glass chimneys were positioned at the compass points. Between the middle and the outer rings, the circle's architect had spread a layer of aromatic herbs.

"Sit here," Cass ordered, pointing Bolan toward a wooden bench that stood against the back wall of the A-frame. Silently he did as he was told.

"Prepare yourselves," she told the others, and before the soldier had a chance to wonder what she meant, Cass shed her robe, revealing naked beauty underneath. She stepped out of her sandals, moving gracefully in the direction of the broken circle, moonlight painting dappled light and shadow on her splendid body. Bolan noted that she held a silver dagger in one hand.

Around him other members of the coven, male and female, were discarding robes and kicking off their footwear, palming daggers of their own as they joined Cass inside the circle. Victor, last to enter, took a firebrand from the pit and handed it to Cass, retreating to his own place in the ring of flesh as she bent down to light the fire. That done, she filled her hand with sulfur from a tidy pile beside the bonfire, moving back toward Bolan, ignoring him completely as she closed off the open circles one by one.

Inside, the members of the coven had arranged themselves with male and female alternating, right around the ring, but Bolan concentrated on their leader as she took her place beside the fire, her dagger raised. In profile, with the flames in front of her, the moonlight cold behind, she offered the impression of a wood nymph, glimpsed by dreaming eyes.

Outside the circle Bolan strained his ears to catch her words as Cass began to speak.

"Be joyful and acclaim the Spirit."

Members of the coven answered her in unison. "Praise him and glorify him always."

"O Spirit, we are naked in your sight. Our minds and bodies are unclothed. Protect them, and send to us what you will."

Cass used her athame—the sacred blade—to sketch a Celtic cross before her, in the darkness, watching as the others followed her example.

"Let us pray. Our friends who are in heaven, hallowed be your names. God's kingdom come. God's will be done on earth as it is in heaven. Give us today our daily bread. Forgive us our weaknesses as we forgive those who wrong us. Help us to resist temptation, and deliver us from evil."

She could feel the warmth of fire against her thighs and stomach, while her back felt cool, in striking contrast. With her eyes closed, Cass addressed the group.

"Protect yourselves."

Around her, members of the coven circled counterclockwise, scattering more herbs—verain and rue, rosemary, sage and anise—in the outer circle, chanting as they made their rounds.

"Spirits of evil, you may not cross this line. Spirits of good, come to us."

Cass turned in profile to the fire, acutely conscious of Mike Blanski watching from the shadows, eyes staring at her body. With a will she pushed the thought away.

"All spirits above and below us," she cried, "hear now my warning. If any be evil or malicious, you will be trapped by our magic and made to work. If you are not afraid, stay. If you are frightened, leave us now and keep your peace."

The members of the coven answered her in unison. "Evil spirits above and below us, go or forever hold your peace."

Cass scooped up a handful of sulfur and sprinkled it over the flames, stepping back a pace as it flared with a puff of malodorous smoke.

"Evil spirits, see how the sulfur burns." She opened her arms to the darkness. "If you cross this line, you will surely burn. Spirit guides, we will not harm you. Come in peace and friendship."

She raised her athame to heaven, the assembled members of the coven doing likewise.

"See, O evil spirits, how sharp are our sacred blades. We place them upright so that they will cut you, be you deep in earth or high up in the heavens."

On her cue the others faced toward outer darkness, laying down their knives, the sharp sides of their blades arranged to face the consecrated ring of sulfur. With a single voice they joined her chant.

"Evil spirits, if the sulfur does not burn you now, the herbs will sicken you to death. Our blades will surely cut you. You are not at liberty to cross this line. Our spirit guides, we will not harm you. Come in peace and friendship."

Cass turned her face to the eastern candle, kneeling as the members of her coven prayed in unison.

"Spirits of the east, behold this guiding light. Come with the rising sun and moon to visit us."

She rose and moved a quarter turn around the circle, kneeling once again before the southern candle.

"Spirits of the south," they chanted over her, "behold this guiding light. Come to us from the fiery heat of the sun."

Cass stood, continued on around the ring to kneel before the western candle.

"Spirits of the west, behold our guiding light. Do not follow the sun and moon, but rather come to visit us."

She finished off the circuit, kneeling at the north.

"Spirits of the north, behold this guiding light. Forsake the cold, and join us in its warmth tonight."

Around the inner circle members of the coven joined their hands as Cass stepped closer to the bonfire.

"Heavens above and earth below, as shown by these your signs, send us your spirits now."

"Benevolent spirits," they answered in unison, "come to us now. Guide us and protect us in your wisdom. Malicious and unguided spirits, leave us now or hold your peace forever. We now seal our temple against all comers."

Cass raised her arms to heaven, trembling.

"We ask that the power of this circle be directed toward protection of our coven and our guest tonight. Evil spirits, remain at bay. Only capture and enslavement awaits you here. Be gone! Return no more!"

"Be gone!" the others echoed. "And return no more!"

Silence fell on the clearing as Cass and the others stood rigid, arms raised, their minds melded as one. In a moment, the breathless sensation departed. Cass opened her eyes.

"Let us rest."

Advancing to the inner circle, Cass leaned down and used the knife edge of her hand to scrape a two-foot gateway clean. The process was repeated for the middle and outer circles, opening a clear path to the world outside the magic ring. It wouldn't matter if their incantations were effective; nothing evil would have strength enough to violate the circle.

At the moment, though, she had a very different problem on her mind. She moved toward Bolan, while the others, pairing off, dispersed into the darkened woods behind her. Now she stood before him, startled as she realized that she was trembling.

"I don't have a partner for the next phase of the ceremony," she informed him. "Will you help me?"

"If I can." He took her hand, surprised to find it almost feverishly warm, and followed her in the direction of the nearby trees. Cass picked her robe up on the way, but didn't slip it on.

"The final portion of our service is most serious," she told him as they moved across a stretch of open lawn. "Success depends on concentration, clarity of mind and purpose. In our rest break we attempt to deal with tension and eliminate the physical distractions that might otherwise defeat us."

"You feel tense? Distracted?"

Cass was smiling. "At the moment, yes."

"That's funny, so do I."

They found a clearing just inside the trees, where moonlight reached them in a mottled pattern, broken up by leaves and needles. Someone had been busy spreading pine boughs on the forest floor to make a bed of sorts. Cass briefly turned her back to Bolan, twirling her robe like a matador's cape, draping it over the boughs like a blanket. She swiveled to face him again.

Bolan shed his jacket, and she stepped back, startled at first sight of the Beretta in its shoulder rigging. Cass reached out to touch it, drew her hand away once more.

"Such violence."

"Not tonight," he promised, peeling off the harness, laying it aside.

They kissed, and he crushed her against him, his big hands exploring her warm, velvet flesh. He cupped her buttocks, lifting her, while Cass attacked the buttons of his shirt with nimble fingers. In a moment he could feel her firm breasts pressed against his skin, and she attacked his belt with mounting desperation, moaning when she fumbled on the first attempt.

He pushed her hands away and dropped his slacks, rewarded as the hands came back and found him, smooth and practiced. "Easy," Bolan cautioned her. "I'd like to stay distracted for a while."

She pulled him down beside her on the makeshift bed, and Bolan kissed her deeply, moving on from lips and throat to tease her nipples, nibbling across the soft plane of her stomach to the downy junction of her thighs. Cass caught her breath and raised her hips to greet him, gasping as he brought her swiftly to a shuddering release.

He mounted her before she could recover from the first explosion, driving deeply. Her ankles locked behind him, sharp nails digging into Bolan's shoulders, Cass began to match his rhythm.

The moment was too powerful to last. Bolan tried to withdraw, but Cass caught him, held him fast inside her as the world dissolved around them, spinning into darkness laced with fire.

"That's some technique for relaxation," Bolan said, when he could catch his breath.

"I find it useful," Cass replied, and kissed him softly, lingering.

"I guess we should be getting back."

"We still have time."

He smiled. "That's good, because I still have one or two anxieties we haven't dealt with yet."

"I'm glad."

RETURNING TO THE MAGIC CIRCLE, Cass held Bolan's hand. She wore the scarlet robe, tied loosely in front. Her feet were bare.

A number of the others had returned already, and they waited for the rest, each couple speaking softly, tenderly, with no attempt to kindle fresh desire. When all had assembled, Cass stepped back inside the circle, leaving on her robe this time. The others followed suit, and she went through the motions of sealing the ring behind them. As they all joined hands, she stood beside the fire and raised her athame.

"We thank you, guides, for protecting our temple. We now reverently reenter so that we can praise and be guided by the Spirit."

Stooping to retrieve a handful of green oleander and holly, she dropped the leaves into the fire.

"Guides above, protect us while we pray. Employ these fumes to help you in your work." Turning from the flames, she addressed the coven at large. "Prepare to raise the cone of power."

On her cue the others responded in unison. "We pray you, God, make strong our thoughts, within us and without. Make strong our thoughts. Enable us to do your work."

Eyes closed, Cass concentrated on the mental image of a white and shining cone, ascending from their circle toward the heavens, luminous with power, beckoning the spirits of the night. She held the image for approximately sixty seconds, drawing power from it, feeling those around her as they individually surrendered to the force.

"We pray you, Spirit, to assist us in resistance of our enemies. Their darkness threatens to destroy our harmony with you, with Nature, with the universal source. Befriend us now, and strengthen us against attack. Your power, lend to Michael Blanski. Make him strong and resolute in contrast to our common adversary. Add your strength to his and see him safely through to victory."

Cass opened her eyes, a fleeting image of the powercone remaining with her as she circled once around the fire, intoning, "Thank you for your help, O Spirit. Come to us when once the moon is full again. Go now, and rest content. We thank our guides for their protection and enlightenment. We pray you will assist us in the coming month, God, we joyfully thank you for your bounty and your blessing. Good night, and blessed be."

Once more she broke the circle, standing back this time to let the others exit first. None of them spoke to Bolan as they moved back toward the A-frame and the wine that would be waiting for them there. Cass joined him, found her sandals and slipped them on.

"What now?"

"The coven spends some time in fellowship and meditation. Basically we're finished. Guidance has been asked for and received."

"You got an answer, then?"

"Of course."

"Which was?"

"In concrete terms, be cautious."

"That's some radical advice."

She felt a sudden twinge of irritation. "What were you expecting? Trumpets? Lightning? A celestial call to arms?"

He looked contrite. "I'm sorry."

Cass allowed her mood to soften, thinking of their time together in the forest. "Never mind," she said. "I can't expect an unbeliever to accept our ways on faith."

"Oh, I have faith, all right."

"In that?" She glanced at Bolan's jacket, where the hidden pistol hung beneath his arm.

"It hasn't failed me yet."

"You might have need of other strength before your mission is completed."

"A prediction?"

"Just a feeling." Glancing toward the A-frame, Cass frowned. "I can't invite you in for our discussion, but I won't be long. No more than half an hour."

"I'll be fine." He smiled. "It's warm out."

"Yes, it is." She hesitated. "When we're done, I'll take you home."

"Where's home?"

"I mean to the motel."

He wore a look of disappointment.

Grappling with her own emotions, Cass turned back to join the others. They had crucial business to discuss, not least of which would be the coven's role in giving aid to Mike and Amos Carr. Her vote would count no more than any other in the final balloting, but Cass already knew that she couldn't let go.

Not yet.

She had too much invested in the struggle, as it was.

She had too much to lose.

14

From the beginning Jordan Braithwaite knew the meeting mightn't be a good idea. A man in his position, in the public eye, couldn't afford to give the wrong impression. Or, in this case, the *right* impression. If the truth was known...

He shrugged, as if the simple gesture could dismiss his deep anxieties. So many things could still go wrong, but he wouldn't allow himself to concentrate on failure. He'd come too far, invested too much of himself, to see the effort wasted now. He was a man of destiny, anointed with a mission, and he meant to take advantage of the means available—whatever they might be—to guarantee success.

The Englewood motel had been selected as a kind of neutral ground, with darkness covering his late arrival, making him secure against the threat of prying eyes. There was an outside chance, of course, that he might still encounter someone from the congregation of his crusade, but he'd have to take the risk. When all was said and done, he had no choice.

The drive from his hotel to Englewood had taken fifteen minutes. Time enough to think en route and ponder his alternatives. As if there were alternatives. As if he had a choice.

In fact his options had been exercised some two years earlier, when he was struggling to get his television ministry in gear, beset by tribulations all around. In those days it was difficult to pick up a paper or turn on the television without discovering another scandal in the church. Loose women. Drugs and homosexuality. Pornography. Political chicanery. A touch of plain old-fashioned larceny. No sooner was one ministry demolished than another was revealed to stand on feet of clay. There seemed to be no end in sight, and for a time his faith had wavered, threatened to desert him. Braithwaite felt that he was crying in the wilderness and no one cared.

In time, of course, the scandals had receded, public curiosity had shifted back to motion picture stars and politicians, offering the church a chance to heal itself. For Jordan Braithwaite, the demise of ranking television pastors was a blessing in disguise. It offered new arrivals on the scene an opportunity to grow, expand, maneuver for position in an industry where competition was as fierce as any found on Wall Street. Christian viewers might be pious as the day was long, but there were limitations on their physical ability to give. They needed motivation and direction, someone who could show them how to spend their hard-earned dollars wisely for the Lord.

Abundant Grace had been the answer. Focusing on Bible texts that emphasized God's generosity in doling out rewards for gifts of love, accentuating money as a source of blessings rather than a mere appendix to the service, Jordan Braithwaite had begun to prosper. It became apparent that his followers, his flock, were hungry for a new direction, someone who could turn their lives around and set them on a road to new success in this life, rather than the world beyond Death's door. Surprising numbers of the faithful hungered to believe that their donations, with an added twist of prayer, could land them a new job or a different house, eliminate their ills or put a new car in the driveway. Pushing it, he had begun to specify amounts, imagining his sheep as they sat watching in their dens and living rooms, experimenting with the buttons he'd have to push to get results.

Some angles of attack were fairly safe. If Braithwaite shook his finger at the camera and prophesied that someone in the viewing audience had cancer, heart disease, arthritis, he was fairly certain of a contact. When he called for offerings, inviting them to stand before the television set and feel God's power coursing through their bodies, many of them would respond. If only one or two experienced a brief cessation of their suffering, and if they wrote to thank him afterward, it kept the ball in play. If others found the job they'd been praying for, or got some unexpected money in the mail, so much the better. Everything was grist for Braithwaite's mill.

The pastor was a pragmatist, but he wasn't entirely cynical. He used professionals at public healing rallies to ensure that others saw the power of the Lord in action, but employment of a shill or two didn't imply a lack of personal belief on Braithwaite's part. He knew the power was real, had felt it flowing through his hands and into withered bodies. He'd seen God's work firsthand, and he had faith.

But, at the same time, he believed in covering his bets.

The Lord helps those who help themselves. Amen.

More recently he'd been haunted by a vision of America in moral ruins. Things were bad enough already, but the spirit of the Lord had offered him a glimpse of days to come, when economic failure, crime, disease and drug addiction pulled God's nation down into the mire of degradation. Welfare rip-offs, teenage pregnancy, destruction of the country's moral fiber through assaults upon its youth. The specter of a pact with godless communism gave him nightmares, and the background music of those hellish dreams was always rock and roll.

Unlike so many of his brethren in the TV pulpit, Braithwaite knew precisely what was called for to reduce the current trend and save America. God's nation needed leadership, and never mind the arguments about a separation of church and state. The founding fathers of America had all been godly men and Christians—with the possible exception of Ben Franklin, who had joined the Hellfire Club in England and was known to have a taste for teenage girls—and Braithwaite knew that none of them had seriously contemplated a society that relegated God to the position of dusty good-luck charm. The authors of the Constitution had been pious men, believers in the Word, and the condition of America today would have them spinning in their graves, if they hadn't gone back to dust long since.

America was ripe for reformation, but she needed leadership, and it was clear that neither of the mainstream parties could produce a candidate or platform cleaving to the message of the Lord. New voices were required, new insights, with a brand-new vision of America-to-be. If no one else would lead the movement, Jordan Braithwaite was compelled to intervene.

The voice of God had told him so. Repeatedly.

In fact, his move was gathering momentum. He was on his way.

Ahead of him the motel's neon sign winked on and off in greeting. There appeared to be No Vacancy, but Braithwaite wasn't checking in. He'd already been provided with the number of a room, and he'd find it for himself, without disturbing anyone inside the office. Braithwaite saw no reason why their rest should be disrupted, why they ought to see his face.

The motel was a T-shaped structure, with the office, registration desk and coffee shop up front, the rooms stretched out behind, surrounded by a parking lot. He drove around the building twice, from end to end, examining the other cars for any sign of lurking spies, a television crew or pack of yellow journalists that might have strayed off course and settled in to kill some time. Exposure was the one thing Braithwaite didn't need just now, and he'd rabbit at the first sign of a camera or notebook.

Convinced the parking lot was safe, he concentrated on the room his second time around. Ground floor; sufficient distance from the all-night coffee shop and office. Light was showing through the curtains, other windows dark on either side. They might have cameras in adjacent rooms, he thought. It would be like the press to stake out a motel and spring from hiding to surprise him as he left his car.

He parked and killed the engine, studying the darkened rooms. One had a small Do Not Disturb sign hanging from the doorknob, while the other had a vacant parking space in front. The neon sign had said No Vacancy, but Braithwaite knew of no law forcing motel guests to park their cars within a given distance of their doors.

A worm of apprehension wriggled in his stomach and he shifted in his seat, removed his keys from the ignition.

Having come this far, the pastor had no choice. He had to go ahead.

The night was warm. He tried to keep it casual as he crossed the blacktop, stood outside the door to number 27, rapping softly. He was braced to fight or flee at any sign of danger to himself, his mission, feeling terribly exposed and vulnerable to his enemies.

A moment passed and someone turned the television down inside. The safety chain was disengaged. Another moment, dragging on forever, as the door was opened and he glimpsed the mocking, too-familiar smile.

"Good evening, Reverend. Please come in."

THE PASTOR LOOKED like hell, an interesting simile that brought a smile to Lucian Slate's lips. "Rough night?"

Suspicion flared in Braithwaite's eyes. "Why do you ask?"

"You look . . . a little weary."

"Mmm. It's traveling so much. I'm fine."

"I hope so."

Slate was perfectly sincere in his expression of concern. He didn't care a damn for Jordan Braithwaite, but he had no wish to kill the golden goose before its time.

The preacher found a vinyl-covered chair and settled into it, the cushions hissing underneath his weight. "All right, you called this meeting. What's so damned important that we have to sneak around like this?"

"Your language, pastor!"

"Never mind. I asked you something."

"Would you rather that we met in public?"

"I would rather that we didn't meet at all. I think you know that, Slate."

"Alas. From time to time, life has its little disappointments."

"What *is* it?"

"I'm concerned about the quality of service you've been getting for your money, Jordan. Has the work been . . . satisfactory?"

Beneath the pastor's sun-lamp tan, a creeping pallor made itself apparent, working downward from his hair line. Slate was fascinated by the change. It looked as if someone had pulled the reverend's plug, allowing several pints of blood to trickle down the drain.

When Braithwaite spoke again, his voice was distant, feather light. "I'm not complaining."

"No. Except, of course, from the pulpit. Which is as it should be."

"Now, Slate—"

"And the turnout? I'm told your revivals are packing them in."

"I've been blessed with a healthy response from the people, it's true."

"How's the bankroll these days?"

"We've been meeting expenses."

"And then some, I wager. A marvelous country, America. All of that money, tax free, for the prophets of doom and destruction."

"I don't have the time for this, Slate. If you just called me here to insult me—"

"By no means." Slate's frown was constructed of genuine plastic. "I value our friendship too much. I've been counting on future endeavors together."

"Such as?"

"I've been thinking of politics lately. Have you?"

Braithwaite stiffened, recovered too late to disguise the reaction. "I don't understand."

"Don't you? Well, I've been thinking. A man with your image, your audience, ought to be sharing his wisdom with every American, shaping their lives day-to-day."

"It takes time."

"For a minister, yes. For a candidate..."

"Slate, I don't know—"

"Briggs and Carver," he said with a smile. "Do the names sound familiar?"

"I think—"

"They take polls, I believe. Any subject, all parts of the country. They're not up with Gallup or Harris, just yet, but they're young. I have hopes."

Braithwaite glared at him. "So?"

"So, the gentlemen mentioned have lately completed *your* poll of selected conservative Christians, including a question or two about Washington. Do they believe that a well-known evangelist should be elected to office? How do they really feel about the separation of church and state in today's corrupt society?"

The pastor's eyes were boring into Slate's. "You're spying on me, dammit."

"I prefer to think of it as guarding an investment."

"What investment? *I've* been paying *you*."

"That's true, of course. But we've invested time, incurred substantial risk. It would be foolish to ignore the obvious potential of our situation. And, whatever we may be, I promise you we are not fools."

"I hired your men to do a job."

"Which they have done, and which they will continue doing, as you need them. In the future, though, we must anticipate a variation in the terms of our agreement."

"So. You want more money?"

"Not at all. The opposite, in fact."

The pastor looked confused. "Explain yourself."

"In future, any service that we may perform on your behalf should be considered as a contribution to the cause. No price tags, Jordan."

"I don't understand."

"Come now. A future President of the United States should never be naive."

"If you're suggesting—"

"I'm suggesting what we both know to be true. Without our special contributions, you might still be playing circus tents and flying coach around the Bible Belt. We've given you the focus, the momentum. Your competitors are scrambling in the dust, reduced to hanging on your coattails."

"You exaggerate your own importance, Slate. I built the television network on my own, without a bit of help from you or anybody else. My ministry—"

"Depends for its vitality upon a clear and present danger," Slate advised him, interrupting brusquely. "Lose your enemy, your issue, and I'll wager that you lose a major portion of your flock, as well.''

"I doubt that."

"Do you really? Shall we put my theory to the test? A severance of all connections, to begin immediately?"

"Slate—"

"Of course there's still the matter of exposure."

"What?"

"Your public might be interested to know that you've been dealing with the devil, as it were."

"You wouldn't dare."

"Of course the various particulars might be obscured, but there are tapes of conversations, canceled checks made out to holding companies. In business I believe it's called 'the whole nine yards.'"

"You can't expose me, Slate. You'll hang yourself."

"I beg to differ. If you think about it, you'll recall we've never met. The fact is, I'm not here at all. I'm dining with a group of famous witnesses in one of Denver's finer restaurants. As for the phone calls, checks and other trivia, my people are prepared to sacrifice a few subordinates. Are you prepared to sacrifice yourself?"

"I had a solemn guarantee our dealings would be confidential."

Slate threw back his head and laughed out loud, enjoying Braithwaite's consternation. "My, how quickly they forget. My master is the Father of Lies, if you recall. Your words, not mine."

"God's words."

"Whatever. Now that we've been introduced, let's cut the crap."

"What do you want?"

"A chance to be of service. You desire the Oval Office. We believe there might be profit in supporting your campaign."

"What kind of profit?"

"Who can say? We're gambling. Another sin, but what the hell. Who's counting?"

"Come the judgment day—"

"We'll all shout hallelujah. In the meantime, I prefer the status quo. You go on preaching, pastor, and my people will continue their, ah, contributions to the cause."

"Suppose I blow the whistle? What's to stop me?"

"Common sense, if nothing else. *We* have the evidence, the tapes—whatever. All you have to peddle is a story from the late-night creature feature. You'll become a laughing-stock."

The pastor seemed to shrivel. Slate was amused to see the glint of tears in Braithwaite's eyes. The holier they were . . .

"You'll burn in hell for this."

"In fact," Slate told him pleasantly, "I'm counting on it."

THE RENTED CHEVY'S dashboard clock told Arthur Trent that nearly half an hour had elapsed since the Reverend Mr. Braithwaite disappeared inside the motel room. A lot could happen in the space of thirty minutes. Scandal. Ruination. Doom.

A baked-on scowl was carving ruts in Arthur's face. His mind's eye fed him images of flashbulbs, minicams and microphones. A ministry dissected and destroyed on *60 Minutes, Nightline, 20/20*. Film at eleven.

It galled him that Braithwaite would risk everything they'd worked for together, the gains they'd made in the battle for souls. Trent was conscious of physical need. He had urges himself on occasion, but Braithwaite was smart enough—*should* have been, rather—to minimize risks with a little discretion. The seedy motel was a perfect location for a media ambush, and Trent clenched his teeth at the thought of his mentor on trial in the press.

It wasn't disappointment so much as raw anger that troubled him now. Five years in televangelism had demol-ished his illusions, but the months with Jordan Braithwaite had been . . . different. Never mind the shills at public heal-ings, or the women who occasionally helped the pastor to relieve the tension and fatigue of long weeks on the road. Their Lord would willingly forgive the latter sin; as to the former, it was merely window dressing for the service, scarcely sin at all.

Discretion was the key. In Trent's mind sexual liaisons were a relatively minor problem. The peril lay in jeopardizing other souls through poor example, risking scandal that would drive uncounted thousands from the Truth. If other souls were lost through Jordan Braithwaite's negligence, his own would surely be at risk.

And Trent's?

He thought about it and decided he could best serve God by serving Jordan Braithwaite and the thousands, millions of devoted followers who hung on Braithwaite's every word. God's word. If he protected Braithwaite from the world—and from himself, where possible—Trent would have earned his just reward.

Suspicion was aroused when Braithwaite took a phone call at the auditorium, emerging from his dressing room with worry lines around his eyes, a deep frown on his face. He'd deflected Arthur's tactful questions, citing strain, fatigue, but Trent had seen the man in all his moods and knew when Jordan was concerned.

Or frightened.

It had taken nerve to follow Braithwaite, weaving through the late-night traffic, praying he wouldn't be seen. In fact the pastor had scarcely paid attention to his driving, drifting once or twice in such a way that casual observers might have called him drunk. Trent knew his mind was elsewhere, and despite the risks involved, he felt a smidgen of relief when Braithwaite pulled into the motel parking lot, proceeding to a designated room. Trent had secured himself a parking place, prepared to stand the watch for snooping journalists and let it go at that.

Until a man had answered Jordan's knock.

It never crossed his mind that Braithwaite might be having an unnatural affair. For all of his repression, his attempts at self-control, the pastor liked his ladies fairly young and definitely straight.

Some other reason for the covert meeting, then, and Arthur thought at once of blackmail. Someone had obtained incriminating information—from a woman, possibly, or one of Braithwaite's "cripples"—and was offering to keep it quiet in return for cash. It was the only explanation that made sense.

And blackmail never ended. Trent was wise enough to know that once an enemy discovered weaknesses, a chance for easy profit, he would never let the matter drop. Unlike a kidnap case, where ransom payments bought a hostage's release, incriminating knowledge couldn't be returned. Surrender of a document, a tape or photographic negative wouldn't eliminate the threat. In time there would be other copies, dubbings, reprints, coupled with demands for further payments, new concessions. To eliminate the threat, decisive action was required.

The door to number 27 opened, spilling light across the pavement. Trent hunched down behind the steering wheel and watched as Braithwaite turned to make some parting comment, hastily retreating to his car. The pastor's aide-de-camp sat motionless as Braithwaite pulled away. His business now was with the man inside that room.

Trent's hand was on the door latch, he was primed to move, the plan still forming in his mind, when the lights went off in number 27. Several seconds passed before a tall, dark man emerged and closed the door behind him, moving toward a car parked three doors down. He slid behind the wheel, backed out and headed for the street.

Afraid to waste an opportunity that mightn't come again, Trent cranked the Chevy's engine into life and followed. He had no idea where they were going, no clear thought of what he meant to do when they arrived. He only knew the enemy had shown himself, and Trent couldn't afford to let him get away.

The small procession rolled through darkness made surrealistic by the intermittent bursts of neon, back toward downtown Denver.

15

"Are you sure this is the right way?"

"Sure I'm sure." York smiled, enjoying the deception, smiling in the face of Marla Sharp's suspicion. He'd never taken four girls down at once, and he was doing it alone. Almost alone. It was a heady trip.

Behind him Snake and Jagger were trailing in a second car, in case the girls got hinky and started bailing out. York had no fear of that, but it was best to take precautions. One mistake would give the pigs their handle, and he didn't plan to make that one mistake his own.

Two of Marla's friends were giggling in the back, but one—the little redhead—seemed to have an eye for scenery. York had no doubt that she was checking out the landmarks, street signs, trying to make sense of their winding course. She muttered something to herself as York cut through a corner of the Wheat Ridge suburb, entering Arvada.

"What's the matter, Alix, aren't you having fun?"

"Don't mind her," Marla said. "She's always gloomy."

"I am not!"

"So cut us all some slack. We're going to a party, not a funeral."

The redhead pouted. "I thought we were going somewhere nice."

York kept his smile in place. "Relax. You'll love it."

"In Arvada? All the really nice clubs are downtown."

"And that's the problem," York informed her. "Number one, the band members can't show their faces in a club downtown without some kind of mob scene, dig it? At a party you're supposed to loosen up, relax, not sign a couple thousand autographs before you get a chance to have a brewski. Number two, unless you girls are older than you look—and I mean *older*—none of you could get inside the clubs downtown without some first-rate fake ID. Okay?"

"The clubs out here still check ID."

"Which is precisely why we won't be going to a club."

"No club?" The gigglers looked confused. York thought the question came from Sarah, but he wasn't sure.

"Sit tight. You'll see."

"Hey, I know where we are." The redhead pointed toward a massive structure on their right, the Ridge State Home and Training School, where hundreds of delinquent youths were housed. "My brother's best friend spent the summer there two years ago."

The place reminded Owen of a factory. "So, how'd he like it?"

"It was creepy. He could see this cemetery from his window."

"Coming up."

York tapped the brakes and cranked the steering wheel hard right, proceeding through the open wrought-iron gates.

"Hey!" The redhead sounded worried now. "What's this?"

"The perfect place for party animals to get down, undisturbed," he told her. "You all know how the boys are, right. I mean, about their spooks and all? They like a little privacy, a little atmosphere."

"I think it's cool," the brunette giggler said.

Her blond companion nodded. "So do I."

"There's someone back there."

"Back where, Alix?"

"There." She pointed to the trailing headlights. "Someone's following."

"Well, sure they are. You didn't think the five of us were going to party by ourselves? I'm flattered, girls, but really—"

That broke up the gigglers, and he let it go, concentrating on the narrow blacktop circuit as he neared their destination, flicking off the headlights, coasting to a stop. Behind them Snake and Jagger parked and killed their lights.

He couldn't see the fire from here, which suited York just
fine. He didn't want some insomniac at juvey hall to witness the proceedings and start bawling for his keepers. Still,
the close proximity of captive boys inspired York, adding
flavor to the scene.

"It's dark."

"That's brilliant, Alix." Marla rolled her eyes at York in
mute apology.

"Hey, who are these guys?"

"Snake and Jagger, meet the girls. That's Alix, Sarah,
Debbie. This is Marla." As he spoke the last girl's name,
York slid an arm around her shoulders, felt her shiver in re-
sponse.

"This way, ladies."

York led them off between the headstones, noting that the
gigglers had fallen silent. Snake fell in beside him as they
walked.

"The watchman cool?"

"Like ice," Snake told him, grinning.

"Fine."

"You sure about this thing?"

"I'm sure."

They topped a rise, and now the dark lawn fell away before them in a natural depression, like a shallow crater,
possibly one hundred feet across. Its gently sloping sides
were marked with gravestones. In its center leaping flames
completed the impression of a meteoric landing or a recent
shell burst.

Zero and the others had their robes on, moving purposefully around the fire in preparation for the ritual. York felt
his pulse begin to quicken.

"Here we are."

Another moment put them all at fireside, where the extra
robes were provided for Snake and Jagger. York wrapped up
the introductions.

"Ladies, this is Zero, Hacker, Felix, Thorn."

He scooped up his own robe and slipped it on.

"Don't we get any costumes?" Marla asked.

"You won't be needing them." He glanced around the
circle, saw the others moving into place behind the girls.

Two men for each of Marla's friends, with Snake behind their guest of honor. Waiting.

York produced the pistol—a Colt Woodsman .22—and smiled.

"Let's party."

Marla saw the gun and knew it had to be a joke. She couldn't cope if he was serious, for God's sake. It would be too radical. Too weird.

And suddenly she wished that she was safely home in bed. Somehow she found her voice. "That isn't very funny."

"Well," Scratch said, "the real laughs come a little later."

"I think you should take us home now."

"Sorry. That's impossible."

Alix bolted, but the two men standing just behind her caught her easily. In seconds Debbie and Sarah both were pinned, as well. The pistol, meanwhile, held a bead on Marla's chest. She didn't dare to move.

Afraid to hear the answer, Marla asked the question anyway. "What do you want?"

"Oh, nothing much. Your souls."

"You're joking, right?"

"I've never been more serious."

"Is this some kind of *Candid Camera* thing?"

"Try *This Is Your Life*."

"I don't get it."

"You will."

Marla braced herself and took a step backward, colliding with muscle and bone. A strong arm looped around her throat, lifting her feet off the ground when she tried to kick at her captor.

"Gently, Snake. Let her breathe."

She collapsed on the grass, felt it cool on her face. There were beating drums in her ears, and it took her a moment to realize that she was hearing her heart beat. Boots came into focus, inches from her face, as fingers tangled in her hair and hauled her painfully erect. Scratch met her frightened gaze, the muzzle of his weapon wedged beneath her chin.

"Our guests of honor need a little something to help them relax. Will you do the honors, Snake?"

Marla heard Alix protesting, her sharp voice receding in seconds until she was muttering softly. Debbie was sobbing and cursing before they got through with her, whimpering afterward, childlike and small. Sarah took it in silence; for all Marla knew, she was dead on her feet.

"You don't mind sharing needles, I hope," Scratch was saying, his breath warm and stale in her face. "I'm afraid we weren't counting on so many guests."

She stiffened, prepared for the brief stinging pain in her arm, but the weightless sensation that followed was totally unexpected. She felt herself drifting again, like before, but without the sensation of drowning.

She knew there was danger here, terrible danger, but suddenly Marla discovered she no longer cared.

And not caring was worse than the fear.

THE STANLEY PLAZA HOTEL was on Sherman Street, downtown, a short block from the State Office Building. Arthur Trent tailed his man into the parking lot, finding a space for himself near the street while his quarry used the valet service, tipping a uniformed attendant and surrendering his keys. It was a race, but Trent pushed through the tall revolving doors in time to see the dark man ambling toward the bank of elevators. From the general direction of his track, it was apparent he'd stopped off at the registration desk before proceeding.

Trent knew he could never catch up now, and what would be the point, in any case? A confrontation in the elevator? Fisticuffs between the twelfth and thirteenth floors? It was ridiculous.

Before he made another move Trent had to learn the dark man's name. He wore a studied, casual air as he approached the registration desk, the youngish clerk all smiles, prepared to serve him.

"Welcome to the Stanley Plaza. May I help you, sir?"

Trent flashed a sheepish smile. "I know this sounds ridiculous, but I believe I know that man." He cocked his thumb in the direction of the elevators. "If I'm right, we served together in the military. You know how it is. I thought I might invite him out for drinks and talk about old times.''

"Yes, sir?" The clerk was clearly puzzled by this line of patter.

"Well, you see, the problem is I can't recall his name. We all had nicknames in the service, and . . ." He stopped himself before we went too far, appending too much detail to the lie. "Well, anyway, I'm hoping you can spare me the embarrassment of looking like a total ass."

"How's that, sir?" Caution in the smile this time.

"If you could let me have his name. . . ."

"I'm sorry, sir. House rules, you understand. We make an effort to respect our patron's privacy."

"Of course, and that's commendable." He palmed a twenty-dollar bill. "If only I had some alternative . . ."

The twenty disappeared.

"I guess it won't hurt anything this once. He's Lucian Slate."

"That's it!" Trent found the name familiar, but he couldn't place it at the moment. "Thanks a million."

"Funny you'd forget *his* name."

"Why's that?"

"Well, sir, I mean, his being famous."

"Is he?"

"Are you kidding? I mean, yes, sir."

"Famous how?"

"He's with the band."

Something stirred at the back of Arthur's mind and the short hairs stood on his neck. "Which band is that?"

The desk clerk looked bemused. "Apocalypse. They're staying here. They always stay here when they play in Denver."

"Ah, I see."

"You mustn't be a music lover."

"I'm not," he replied, "but if a friend's involved, I just might take an interest. Thanks again."

"Thank *you*, sir."

Trent felt dizzy as he backtracked to his car. Of course the name had seemed familiar. Jordan Braithwaite must have spoken it a hundred times, but Arthur's days and nights had been consumed with the mechanics of producing a crusade and keeping Braithwaite on the air. He heard the pastor's sermons on a daily basis, but he rarely listened anymore.

At once his blackmail notion was demolished. What could Lucian Slate, the occult mentor of Apocalypse, hold over Jordan Braithwaite's head? The men were mortal enemies—at least in Braithwaite's view—but to the best of Arthur's knowledge, they'd never met before tonight.

His knowledge, obviously, was the problem. Charged with managing the Braithwaite road show and his television network, Trent now found that he was working in the dark. For all he knew, the "mortal enemies" were old acquaintances. Slate might have something—anything—on Braithwaite; information gathered through his spies in seedy dives around the country.

Trent reined in his runaway imagination as he slid behind the steering wheel. He was committed to Abundant Grace, and Jordan Braithwaite's personal crusade to put the nation back on track. It sickened him to think of Braithwaite dabbling in sin, but it was worse to think of trivial mistakes returning constantly to haunt the minister, dredged up by servants of the Anti-Christ and turned to their advantage.

He would have to act, and swiftly. Braithwaite must be spared at any cost, and Trent decided to proceed without enlightening the pastor to his plan. In fact it would be premature to dignify his jumbled, racing thoughts with any label such as *plan* or *scheme*. He had a few ideas, but they rattled around inside his skull like ricochets, still lacking clear direction.

Never mind. He had to move before Slate could sabotage the Braithwaite ministry. If nothing else he had to buy some time in which to think and form a rudimentary, coherent strategy.

Trent drove four blocks before he found a small convenience store with pay phones bolted to the wall outside. He dialed the Stanley Plaza, tried belatedly to change his voice and asked for Lucian Slate.

"Hello?"

"Good evening. Mr. Slate?"

"That's right."

"We need to talk."

THE ROUGH ROPES chafing at her wrists and ankles were a blessing in disguise for Alix Price. They helped to clear the fog a little, giving her a point of focus in the haze that chemicals had spun around her conscious thoughts.

The shot had clearly been some kind of tranquilizer. She hadn't blacked out, but it had ceased to matter when they hauled her to the van and bound her with hands behind her back, a length of twine connecting tethered wrists to hobbled ankles.

Lying on her side, the carpeting like prickly grass against her cheek, she tried to focus on the others. Deb and Sarah had somehow been bound together back-to-back, and Alix had a momentary flash of thankfulness that she'd been the odd one out. At least this way she had a chance.

For what?

To get away.

Before her conscious mind could issue the command, her hands were working on the knots. It wasn't easy—she could barely reach, for starters—but her fingernails were long and pointed. She'd taken lots of flack at home about the style, but Mom and Dad would sing a different tune if they could see her now.

Oh, sure. They'd sing a different tune, all right. They'd whip her butt for taking rides with strangers, and they'd ground her for about a thousand years.

All things considered, at the moment grounding didn't look so bad.

She hadn't understood the tall man's rap about their souls, but it was obvious the whole damned crew was wired on something. Maybe speed, or PCP. They'd been tuning in Apocalypse so long that all the spooky witchcraft nonsense must have taken root somehow.

Alix knew she was in trouble, and she also knew there wasn't any cavalry about to save the day. Her instincts told her that if any of them walked away from this one, they'd have to buckle down and do it on their own.

Which kept her digging at the knots, despite the chafing at her wrists, the burning protest from her fingernails. Pain helped. It didn't matter if her nails were broken to the quick, as long as she could free herself in time.

"Hey, Sarah? Deb?"

No answer.

Sarah Cliver, facing Alix, had her eyes closed. She was either dead or dreaming, and it came to Alix that her captors mightn't always use the proper dosage for sedating hostages. If they were feeling hassled, who could say they might not shoot an accidental overdose?

She tried to focus in on Sarah's T-shirt and the breasts that sometimes made her jealous. Was she breathing? Alix thought so. Yes. Unconscious then, and that left Debbie.

"It's Alix, Debbie. Can you hear me?"

"Unnh."

A start.

"I need you, Deb. Wake up, okay?"

"Too dizzy."

"Listen to me, Deb. We've got to get these ropes off. Do you understand?"

"Too tight. Too dizzy."

"Dammit, Debbie! Answer me!"

Silence, once again.

Alone with pain and anger, learning terror, Alix concentrated on her fingernails, unraveling the ties that bind.

AS ALWAYS, York was last to wash his hands when they were finished. Afterward he poured the plastic bucket's murky contents on the fire and smelled its ashes steaming. She'd been a virgin after all.

"What happened to the night man?"

Felix pointed in the general direction of the gates. "They have a guard shack, near the mausoleum. We left him there."

York frowned. "We'll clean it up before we leave."

"How come?"

He turned on an arctic smile. "Because I said so, little brother. And because a mystery may serve our purpose better than a second body."

"Huh? Oh, right. I didn't think."

"That's why I'm here."

Snake helped him pack the instruments. "I'm still not sure about this other thing."

"I'm sure."

"Four girls together. Man, that's going to raise some hell."

"No pun intended?"

"You know what I'm saying, Scratch."

"I've thought it through. It's perfect. We need one more here, and two for Vegas."

"Lots of girls in Vegas."

"This is better. Half the risk is trolling. This way we eliminate the problem."

"Hauling meat across state lines is federal business."

"Worried?"

"No, just thinking."

"Save your strength. I've got it covered. Anyway, we want publicity."

"I'd just as soon not see my name in headlines."

"Follow orders. Do your job. You'll have no problem."

"Sure. Okay."

York stood and took the tool kit with him, pausing to survey the scene. At length he satisfied himself that nothing was forgotten, nothing left behind by accident. The girl, of course, was meant to stay.

Snake's doubts were an annoyance, and he wondered if the other members of his team were having second thoughts. Handpicked to carry out this mission, they'd been the best available. That wasn't saying much, in terms of genius, but each possessed raw courage in sufficient quantities to carry out his job on cue. York wouldn't let himself begin to worry yet. If cracks appeared he would respond with necessary measures.

Everyone was equally expendable, where service to the Master was concerned.

Meanwhile they could forsake the hunting for a bit. Tomorrow none of them would have to show their faces at the concert, thereby narrowing the odds that any spaced-out fans or homicide detectives might start putting two and two together. York had all the fresh meat he would need.

Let Thorn and Felix dump the watchman. It was their mess; they could clean it up. Tonight—this morning, rather—York would let himself relax. One of the spares might keep him occupied until he felt the urge for sleep. And then again, perhaps all three.

He felt a sudden hunger as he started for the van.

16

Bolan used a pay phone for the call. He had a fair idea that Hal Brognola's office lines would be secure, but there was no point taking chances. Hal, presumably, would know he was in Denver; anybody managing to trace the call would strike a dead end at a small convenience store two miles from his motel.

"Hello?"

"Good morning."

"Striker, what an unexpected pleasure."

"Is your line secure?"

"We swept it yesterday. And yours?"

"It's relative. I'm on the town."

"Okay. How's tricks? You find the bogeyman?" If Brognola was joking the amusement didn't surface in his voice.

"I've seen some interesting things." He thought of Cass at once, and pushed the image out of mind before his body could respond. "Right now the only thing I'm sure of is that someone's killing girls."

"What else is new?"

The soldier frowned. "Are you familiar with the theories of our mutual acquaintance?"

"More or less. I haven't made a detailed study, but he seems sincere."

"I'm interested in some background on the group he's chasing."

"What was that again—the Klingons?"

"*Ching*ons." Bolan's fleeting smile was there and gone. "It seems incredible they aren't on file, if even half of what he says is true."

"I thought the same," the big Fed agreed, shifting papers at the far end of the line. "I did some checking on my own. The Bureau has a file of sorts, but mostly it's a lot of interviews with 'sources of unknown reliability.' Somebody's cousin claims they know a guy who knows a member of the cult. Somebody else has friends who saw a snuff film, but they've all been out of touch for years, and now he can't recall the 'good friend's' name. That kind of crap."

"Sounds pretty thin."

"Remember, this was breaking back around the time that Manson and his honeys took their fall. J. Edgar had his sights set on the Berrigans, the Panthers, SDS—you name it. He was taking heat at Orangeburg, on the Kennedy and King assassinations, and the last thing anybody wanted was a scandal on the FBI investigating some religious group. That doesn't mean they didn't look. It only means they didn't look too hard."

"And after Hoover?"

"New priorities, new business. Cult-related crimes are normally a local kind of thing. Some kid gets whacked while half a dozen of his classmates watch. Whatever. Any evidence of interstate activity would probably be tied to drugs, and so far DEA has all that it can handle with the regulars."

"And in the meantime no one moves. Is VICAP working on the homicides, at least?"

"Sure thing—as much as eight men nationwide can work on anything. Our friend has filled out spec sheets on the crimes to date, and Quantico agrees the probability is high of one or more perps doing all of them, across the board."

"I was afraid of that."

"You're having problems?"

"So far I've been killing time and listening to horror stories. If our friend has any kind of solid handle on this thing, he's kept it to himself."

"Well, like I said before, no guarantee the case would fly."

"The trouble is, it flies in all directions. We've got one dead girl, in case you haven't heard. Our friend expects a couple more before the troops move on. Meanwhile I'm hearing music that could fry your brain and touring the head shops, going nowhere fast.''

"The FBI and boo-coo locals say your contact knows his business, but it's still your call. You want to pack it in, feel free. It was a long shot, anyway. My feelings won't be hurt.''

"Not yet. I want to run a couple names for background, anything at all.''

"Let's have them.''

"Number one is Lucian Slate.''

"Okay.''

"And number two is Jordan Braithwaite.''

"Not the TV preacher?''

"That's affirmative.''

"Is he in this?''

"I'm hoping you'll tell me.''

"I hate these church things.''

"Welcome to the club.''

"All right. That's it?''

"For now. How long?''

"Let's call it noon, your time.''

"I'll be in touch.''

Bolan cradled the receiver, trotted to his rented car. As he cranked the engine over, the warrior reached out distractedly and tuned the radio to find a local all-news station. As it was, he caught the bored announcer in the final moments of his headline piece.

"... discovery this morning of a second mutilated victim in a local cemetery. Homicide detectives have no leads, but their investigation is continuing. Authorities refused to comment on the rumored link between the murders and appearances in Denver of the heavy-metal band Apocalypse.''

HARRIS FIENHOLD KNEW he had a problem when the bell rang, signaling a customer out front. He had to hustle, knowing that the younger ones would steal you blind unless you watched them every second, but his apprehension quickened as he recognized Cassandra Poole.

"Hello, Cass.''

"Harris. How's the business?''

"Fair. And yours?"

"About the same."

In fact his business in the past few months had ranged from poor to terrible, but he expected an improvement in the next few weeks. He told Cassandra none of this, because they weren't friends. He was surprised to see her, and surprise was a first cousin of suspicion.

"So, what brings you out this way? Run short on henbane?"

She returned his smile with perfect courtesy. "In fact," she said, "I hope you might be able to supply me with some information."

"Ah. Specifically?"

"I'm looking for some background on the Chingon network. More specifically, a local tie-in."

Fienhold's breakfast did a lazy barrel roll inside his stomach, but he held the plastic smile with grim determination.

"Local? Cass, you know that's California craziness. You're talking La-La Land, not Rocky Mountain high."

Her fetching smile had disappeared, and she was frowning now, all business. She was nice to look at; Harris had to give her that.

"I have a feeling there may be a local chapter in the works," she told him.

"Any special reason?"

"I suppose you know about the murders?"

"Ghastly business. But I don't see—"

"I believe there's a connection. If I'm right . . ." She hesitated, started over. "Look, I know we don't see eye-to-eye on application of the arts. I can respect your views, but this is something else entirely. This is . . ."

"Evil?"

"Yes."

"I do believe you're frightened, Cass."

"I'm not concerned about myself."

"Of course. The famous altruism."

"Harris—"

He feigned repentance. "That was cheap. I'm sorry."

"Never mind. I didn't want to come here, but I thought if you knew anything..."

"I understand. My sympathies, of course, lie with the dark side of the power, but there are limits, even so. I've been concerned about the murders."

"You agree they're sacrificial?"

"Almost certainly. I don't believe, however, that they indicate a local coven of the Children has been organized."

"It's possible."

"I'm sure I would have heard. A whisper. Something."

"And you haven't?"

Cass was looking through him with those piercing eyes. He wondered for an instant if there might be any substance to her reputation as a seer.

"Unfortunately, not a rumble."

"Well, I'm sorry I disturbed you, Harris, but I had to ask."

"Think nothing of it." She was moving toward the door, but he could not resist a parting shot. "Oh, Cass?"

She hesitated, turned.

"If you're right, perhaps you ought to be concerned. About yourself, I mean."

"I'll see you later, Harris."

"Looking forward to it."

Fienhold watched her cross outside the picture window of his shop, examining her profile for a moment, thankful when she disappeared. He felt a sudden urge to rush outside, make certain that she wasn't lingering around the corner, spying on him.

Foolishness, he thought. Besides, there was no time.

Behind him, rustling curtains whispered of a new arrival. Fienhold turned to find Snake watching him, and forced a smile.

"So, how'd I do?"

"Not bad." Snake drifted toward the window, studying the street outside. "How well do you know this bitch?"

He shrugged, the gesture wasted on Snake's back. "I know her."

"Good. *I* want to know her, Harris. Teach me."

Fienhold thought about it for a moment, took a breath and told the hunter everything he knew about Cassandra Poole.

AN HOUR LATER, after three more stops, Cass still couldn't shake the feeling of uneasiness that lingered from her talk with Harris Fienhold. He was hiding something—she had felt it in the waves of apprehension that disturbed his normal aura—but she couldn't put her finger on the lie. He might have seemed defensive in the face of any questioning, considering their clash of ideologies and personalities. It didn't have to mean the Chingons were involved.

She really had no grudge against the dark practitioners. Whatever faults Cass had, religious bigotry wasn't among them. She'd coexisted peacefully with voodoo *houngans*, Satanists, black witches, followers of Santeria, even while considering them all misguided in their handling of the Power. As a witch she recognized the dangers of a forcible attempt to standardize beliefs. With Harris Fienhold, though, the feelings she experienced were different. Strange.

They had encountered each other, for the first time, seven years before. A friend had introduced them at a gathering designed to mark the vernal equinox. On shaking hands with Harris, Cass had been immediately stricken by the aura of corruption that surrounded him. His soul was decadent, corrupt, and while she gathered no impressions of involvement in specific crime, Cass almost felt that he was waiting, marking time until the perfect opportunity arrived.

And had it come?

Cass took a breath and held it, pulling in the reins on her imagination. Fienhold viewed her as an adversary—possibly an enemy—but there was nothing to connect him with the Chingon network. Nothing but the feeling that she tried in vain to shake.

His parting words came back to Cass. "Perhaps you ought to be concerned. About yourself, I mean."

A threat?

She was prepared to deal with any supernatural attacks, but if the Chingons were involved, there might be danger of a more substantial nature. Cass didn't believe that Fienhold would attempt to harm her on his own. If others were involved, however, anything might happen.

Unavoidably her thoughts were drawn to Michael Blanski. *He* would be in danger if their mutual suspicions were correct. An unbeliever, he couldn't prepare himself against the spiritual and psychological assaults in which their adversaries specialized.

Recalling their tempestuous encounter, Cass still felt ambivalent about her strong reaction to the man. He was a stranger, in the strict sense of the word, although Cass felt she knew enough about him in an hour's time to trust him with her life. He was a violent man, yet capable of sensitivity, gentleness. The violence that dogged his tracks had been, in some ways, forced upon her. He had suffered grievous losses and survived, a stronger man, still plagued by waking nightmares, bitter memories.

That there was danger in associating with the man, Cass had no doubt. She recognized the fact that he attracted violence like a human magnet, drawing lethal adversaries from a distance. Mayhem, past and future, streaked his aura with the crimson stain of fresh-drawn blood. This man had killed, and many times at that. She couldn't estimate the number of his victims, but she sensed, intuitively, that her choice of terms was imprecise.

In retrospect she thought that the individuals Mike Blanski had dispatched to other planes wouldn't be weighed as "victims" on the universal scale. Instinctively she knew his targets hadn't been the innocent and helpless. Rather, he had killed as soldiers kill, in open combat with a designated enemy. His prey might not "deserve" their fate, in abstract terms, but they had brought it on themselves.

Somehow the Chingons had become his target, drawing Amos Carr one fateful step beyond his normal role as an investigator and adviser to police. There would be blood, this time, unless Cass missed her guess.

There had been blood already.

Two young girls were dead, and news reports suggested that there might be others missing. Cass hadn't absorbed the details, but she felt the tension like a weight upon her soul.

Raw violence, once unleashed, might escalate until it reached the point of no return.

It would be relatively easy now for Cass to separate herself from the crusade. She had complied with Carr's requests, for friendship's sake, and owed him nothing more. The interlude with Blanski was an aberration, nothing in the nature of a permanent relationship. Both men would understand she had a life to lead. It wasn't *her* crusade.

And, then again, perhaps it was.

The very core of her belief, for all of its antiquity and emphasis on harmony with Nature, dealt with endless struggle. Abstract Good triumphant over timeless Evil. Cass could no more turn her back on those beliefs than she could voluntarily stop breathing.

It was simple, then. While Carr and Blanski were in town—another day or two, she thought—Cass would continue seeking information, passing it along. When they departed, following their adversaries to another hunting ground, she would attempt to put the problem out of mind.

The tiny parking lot behind her shop was empty, except for Sandy's old VW. Cass came in through the back, and was about to speak when she heard other voices in the shop.

A customer.

The sudden wave of apprehension took her by surprise. She froze, spent several heartbeats sorting out her various emotional reactions, finally moving toward the beaded curtain for a look.

The man was moderately handsome, somewhere in his later twenties. Blond hair fell across the collar of the long black duster that hung well below his knees. At first glance Cass mistook the garment for a cloak, and thought he must be uncomfortably warm.

"I'm sorry," she heard Sandy telling him, "but we don't keep the *Necronomicon* in stock."

"Why not?" His voice was deep and silken smooth.

"We haven't had a call for it in ages."

"Could you get a copy for me?"

"That would have to be a special order."

"Fine."

"For that you'd have to see the owner."

"Is she in?"

Cass felt her hackles rise. How did this stranger know the owner of the shop was female?

"No, I'm sorry. Not just now."

"Okay. When *can* I see her?"

Sandy hesitated, taking stock. "That's hard to say."

Good girl.

"I'd really hate to take my business elsewhere."

"Thank you. If you'd care to leave your name?"

The blonde considered it, deciding in the negative. "No point, I guess. She doesn't know me anyway."

He drifted toward the door, paused, glanced back at Sandy, then in the direction of the beaded curtain. Cass imagined he could see her, knowing even as the thought took shape that she was being paranoid.

"I'll keep in touch," he said. And he was gone.

Cassandra wondered why the simple comment, made in passing, sounded so much like a threat.

LUCIAN SLATE and Owen York kept pace with each other through the bright spring greenery of Barnum Park. Across the lake, York caught a glimpse of young men tossing Frisbees back and forth. He wondered why they weren't in school.

"We have a problem," Slate informed him, smiling at a luscious woman who passed them, jogging in the opposite direction.

"So you mentioned on the phone."

"I got a call last night, from Arthur Trent."

"Don't know the man," York said.

"No reason why you should. He works for Jordan Braithwaite."

"Ah."

"I met with him this morning over breakfast."

"So?"

"He knows about our deal. Enough, at any rate, to cause some nasty speculation if he blows the whistle."

"Pay him off."

"No good. The man's a true believer. All he wants is to 'preserve the ministry'—and, incidentally, the great man's shot at public office. Cash won't do it, I'm afraid."

"I'll need an address and description."

"Done."

The slip of paper passed from Slate to York without a break in stride.

"We've got another problem," he informed his contact as they made their way around the north end of the lake. "Two problems, actually."

"I'm listening."

"A local witch is asking questions. So is Amos Carr."

Slate cursed beneath his breath. "I thought we'd seen the last of him with the Toledo diggings."

"He's a bulldog," York replied. "He won't give up. You should have let me take him then."

"It wasn't necessary."

"Now?"

Slate thought about it. "Now," he said at last, "I think the nosy bastard might be in our way."

"I'll give the word."

"About this witch—"

"She talked to Fienhold."

"And?"

"He shined her on, but I don't see her giving up that easily."

"All right, but try to find out what she knows. If she's been talking . . ."

"I'll take care of it."

"And make it clean."

"No problem."

Slate had something on his mind, besides the snoopers. York fell silent, letting him come around to it in his own way and time.

"I'm curious about the news this morning."

"Oh?"

"I gather several girls are missing."

"Three, to be exact."

"And an employee of the cemetery?"

York could feel his patience wearing thin. "My people whacked the watchman on their own initiative. I couldn't pull a resurrection, so I did the next best thing and made him disappear. The chances are they'll find him in a month or two. Meanwhile, we've got a suspect drawing off the heat."

"I'm more concerned about the girls."

"Don't be. Your friendly fuzz are looking for the watchman. He was black, in case the papers didn't say. A little racial tension always stirs things up."

"Why so many?"

"Let's say it was a challenge."

"What about the heat?"

"This time tomorrow we'll be in Vegas."

"Dammit, Scratch—"

"Don't fret so much. It gives you worry lines."

Slate's eyes were boring into him. It made York want to laugh out loud.

"I won't have everything we've worked for jeopardized by arrogance."

York stopped to face him in the middle of the path. "I do my job," he said. "If you've got someone who can do it better, bring him on."

Slate's smile was frosty. "None of us are indispensable. Remember that."

"Remember *this*," York whispered, handing him a Polaroid shot of the previous night's work before he stalked away. Without a backward glance, he knew that Slate was staring at the photograph, engrossed, perhaps a trifle sickened by its detail, trembling where he stood.

Sometimes, York knew, he pushed more than he should. The network might dispose of him one day, if he presumed too much. The prospect didn't terrify him as it might have, years ago. With so much seen and done, mere death inspired no awe. The Master would be waiting for him when he fell, with secret pleasures to reward His faithful servant.

In the meantime, though, York still had work to do. Three meddlers: Amos Carr, the woman, Arthur Trent. Each case required a different approach, but he was equal to the challenge.

Slate wouldn't attempt to pull his plug before the contracts were fulfilled, and once the job was done, he would be too impressed with York's efficiency to press the issue. Still, there was the possibility that he might nurse a grudge, attempt to undermine York's standing with the leadership. In that case he would have to be eliminated.

"None of us are indispensable. Remember that."

Slate's words. They might come back to haunt him.

York smiled and made his way out of the park.

The hunt was on.

17

Success came hard to Arthur Trent, while unadulterated triumph rarely came at all. His closest brush with greatness, thus far, had been his acceptance as the roving aide-decamp of Jordan Braithwaite, serving as a combination manager and troubleshooter for the overworked evangelist. In Braithwaite's shadow, Arthur felt secure, protected. Safe.

At least he had. Until that morning.

Lucian Slate hadn't agreed to meet with him immediately. It was late, of course, and there was other business to be done, but mention of the Braithwaite name had gotten Trent an audience at 6:00 a.m. He passed a restless night, all hope of sleep abandoned as he grappled with his fears and dark suspicions.

In the end, their meeting had been civil, almost cordial. Slate had smiled expansively across the table of their booth in a suburban coffee shop, consuming scrambled eggs and bacon while he spoke. The meeting, Trent observed, had been an overture of peace on Slate's part, an attempt to mediate the frequency and fire of Braithwaite's public blasts against Apocalypse. Unfortunately Braithwaite had always been stern, unsympathetic. He would certainly refuse to water down his sermons, or divert their trust in any way.

It had been reassuring, for a moment, but it soon became apparent Slate was lying through his teeth. His plastic smile, the answers smacking of a brief rehearsal, the apparent grace with which he willingly accepted failure. It was all too pat, and obviously none of it was true.

Trent would have known as much if Slate had been a perfect liar—which he certainly wasn't. The truth had also been inscribed on Jordan Braithwaite's face as he'd furtively departed the motel. The pastor's look hadn't been that of someone who has met the enemy and forced him to retreat. Indeed, if anything, it had been Braithwaite who was running, harried, scowling at the news he had received.

He dared not challenge Slate directly, thereby possibly compelling him to take some action that would damage Braithwaite's ministry. Trent realized the man had a hold on Braithwaite, somehow, but he couldn't logically expect their enemy to spell it out and thereby give himself away. The secret would be something to unravel, piece by piece, if there was time. Or he could try another angle of attack.

He could attempt to pry the truth from Jordan Braithwaite.

Grudgingly Trent had allowed himself to be "persuaded," outwardly surrendering his doubts, submitting to his adversary's charm. The man was slick, no question there, and Arthur wondered if his mentor and employer had been similarly charmed, seduced into a situation where he could be compromised, manipulated.

It was possible that Slate had told the truth about the purpose of their meeting. Braithwaite's publicized attacks on heavy-metal music—with particular attention to Apocalypse—reportedly was cutting into tape and record sales. The specter of congressional investigations had encouraged several companies to label albums with a warning of explicit lyrics, and a few displayed the lyrics on their album covers, granting parents the prerogative of censoring the music that was brought into their home. If Braithwaite's drive had pinched the pocketbooks of certain music fat cats, Arthur Trent was glad to hear it. He could also understand why Lucian Slate, the "spiritual adviser" for Apocalypse, might fear the termination of his cushy job if things went sour in the record stores.

So much for motive. Method was the problem plaguing Trent. No matter how he racked his brain, he couldn't figure out the hold that Slate, or any of his rock-and-roll fraternity, might have on Jordan Braithwaite. Arthur realized that he could learn that only from the man himself.

At length, pretending to be mollified, Trent took his leave of Slate, but not before the man played his trump card.

"There's no reason you should tell your boss we had this little chat," Slate said. "He's won, I've lost. Besides, he might suspect you're spying on him."

There it was. The problem in a nutshell. If he *did* his job, there was a decent chance that Arthur Trent might *lose* his job. If he confronted Braithwaite with his knowledge of the midnight meeting, Trent would come off sounding like a busybody, someone who didn't trust Braithwaite to control his private life. If, on the other hand, he kept his mouth shut, there might still be countless problems unresolved. And, worse, Slate might reveal the substance of their conversation on his own, to breed suspicion in the ministry.

Trent had no choice. His conscience wouldn't let him rest until he knew the truth, did everything he could to save the man he idolized. If Jordan Braithwaite had a problem, it was Arthur's problem, too. They would confront the enemy together, stand united with their faces toward the storm, and they would ride it out.

Unless, of course, the revelation of his spying got Trent fired. It was a possibility he couldn't dismiss without a second thought. He had seen others exiled from the ministry for less, some private indiscretion that didn't reflect upon their trust in Braithwaite's mission. Trent might easily be branded as a traitor, scorned for checking up on Braithwaite after hours. Never mind that Jordan's movements clearly *needed* checking. Doubt was heresy, and modern heretics, while safe from stoning and the stake, were still excluded from the flock.

With all of that in mind, Trent had no choice. His silence would be tantamount to acquiescence in conspiracy, while speaking out—although it might destroy him personally—stood at least a chance of saving Jordan Braithwaite.

Arthur would approach the pastor privately with his suspicions, observations, explanations of his own behavior. Braithwaite would be spared adverse publicity at any cost. If he decided to dispose of Trent, instead of coming clean, there would be other options to consider.

Arthur's coffee had gone cold, but he'd already drunk enough to turn his stomach sour. Leaving money on the table, he retreated to a pay phone in the Spartan lobby of the restaurant where he had killed the last two hours, picking over lunch and sorting out his options. Dropping in a coin, he reached the hotel desk and had his call put through to Jordan's room.

"Hello?"

"It's Arthur."

"Yes, good morning, Arthur."

"Sir, we need to talk."

"Is there a problem, son?"

"Yes, sir. It's urgent, I'm afraid."

The pastor sounded curious, not yet concerned. "I'm listening."

"I don't believe we should discuss this on the telephone."

"That serious? All right then. Are you in your room?"

"No, but I can meet you in a quarter of an hour, if that's convenient."

"Fine. I'll see you then."

He cradled the receiver, conscious of a sudden, nervous pressure in his groin. Another moment wouldn't matter now. Distracted by his brooding thoughts, Trent headed for the rest room.

MICHAEL SHIRKY, known as Snake among his fellow hunters, paid his tab, bought gum from a machine and waited for the young man to complete his phone call in the lobby. He could take his target in the parking lot, provided there were no eyewitnesses. If necessary Shirky was prepared to follow him awhile and find the perfect killing ground.

He didn't know the man he was supposed to murder. Scratch had called him dangerous, an enemy, and that was good enough for Shirky. Killing was a pastime he enjoyed; the motives, by and large, were insignificant.

The young man made an easy target, so caught up in private reverie that he was blind to those around him. Shirky had been waiting in his hotel lobby, could have dropped him there. But he was supposed to trail the mark and find another place to do his job, away from the hotel.

No problem.

Shirky's target had driven aimlessly through Denver for the better part of half an hour, finally picking out a restaurant and ordering a lunch he scarcely touched. Two hours passed in tedium, while Shirky tried to make his burger last and nurse his double-chocolate milk shake through a total meltdown. He was running out of ways to stall, afraid the waitress might remember both of them as sluggish eaters, when his pigeon made the move.

He couldn't overhear the conversation, but his mark looked worried. That was fine with Shirky. Any problems on the target's mind would help distract him, keep his guard down at the crucial moment. As he reached his car, slid in behind the steering wheel, he would be helpless. It was perfect.

Cradling the telephone receiver, Shirky's target turned in the direction of the tall glass doors, thought better of it, doubled back in the direction of the men's room. No one else had entered in the past few moments. Thinking fast, aware that he could call it off if there were any problems, Shirky followed.

Tile and porcelain. The smell of disinfectant. Urinals and sinks along one wall, the toilet stalls directly opposite. Two doors stood open, one was closed. Inside the middle stall his target stood to urinate, the bashful type, his slacks and shoes identifiable beneath the door.

They were alone.

Snake drew the Walther automatic, palmed its silencer and mated them with fluid, practiced movements. It would help, and he desired to take no chances. Moving past the sinks, he cranked each faucet open, water splashing in his wake. He caught the hot-air drier with an elbow, bringing it to life, and flushed the several urinals in turn. Behind him, startled by the sudden noise, his target hesitated, losing track and sprinkling the tile.

Shirky heard a muffled curse and crossed the room in three long strides, to the nearest empty stall. He stepped up on the toilet seat and kicked the stainless-steel lever, as one might the starter of a motorcycle. A gushing whirlpool opened at his feet, and he reached across the top of the partition, leveling his Walther at a pair of blinking eyes.

His target had no time to react. The first round drilled his hairline, punching out a fist-sized exit wound. The slack jaw opened, yawning in the face of death, and Shirky put a second round between those ovaled lips. Before his target settled in a corner of the stall, legs folded awkwardly beneath him, Shirky had the silencer detached, his weapon holstered and was moving toward the door.

He didn't bother wiping down the faucets to eradicate his fingerprints. A thousand men must use the rest room every day, and Shirky's prints weren't on file in any case. If someone ultimately traced his thumbprint to an ancient California driver's license, they would still be miles from proving murder, and by then he'd be gone.

The hunt was winding down in Denver, but he still had work to do before they hit the road.

THE TELEPHONE was jangling as Amos closed the door behind him, shrugging off his coat. He snared it as he settled on the mattress, loosening his tie.

"Hello?"

"I need to speak with Amos Carr." The voice was ageless, male, assertive.

"What about?"

"I understand you're looking for a contact with the Children."

"That depends. Which children?"

"Don't play games. I haven't got the time."

Carr frowned. "Who am I talking to?"

"Let's say I have an inside track. My contact might be interested in talking."

"Yeah?"

"For a price."

"I'm on a budget."

"You have sponsors."

"I'm afraid you're misinformed."

The caller hesitated. "Price can be negotiated."

"Possibly. I'd have to know exactly what I'm buying."

"That's no problem. My connection knows the Children inside out. He knows which closets have the skeletons."

"I'd have to check out a sample of the information before we get around to talking dollars."

"That can be arranged."

"I'll have to meet your source." Carr knew that he was pushing, but he didn't have a thing to lose.

The line was silent for a moment. "I don't know," the caller said at last. "There could be risks involved."

"I understand the problem," Carr replied, "but frankly, I've got no damned use for hearsay filtered through a go-between."

"You ask a lot."

"I didn't make the call."

"I'll have to ask and call you back. How's half an hour?"

"I'll be here."

"We'll be in touch."

He cradled the receiver and allowed himself to breathe. His hands were trembling; the burgers he'd recently consumed were rumbling in his gut.

A pair of eyes inside the Children of the Flame could bring the house down. He had dreamed of such a break for months, believing it would never come his way. And now...

Carr hesitated, sorting out the pros and cons. The caller said he *had* an inside contact, which implied that he wasn't a member of the Children. Secrecy was paramount within the Chingon network, and if properly preserved, there should have been no outside contacts, no one who could point his finger at a member with complete assurance. Still, Carr realized security was never absolute. The tightest clique sprang leaks, in time, and even one leak might be fatal.

On the other hand it had the makings of a classic setup. Tantalizing information, something that the seller knew his mark couldn't resist. A meeting in some isolated spot, where heavies lay concealed and waiting.

At a glance the caller's obvious reluctance to arrange a meet would seem to mitigate against a trap, but it could all be window dressing, an Academy Award performance guaranteed to make Carr taste the bait.

If so, the bastard could have saved himself the trouble. Amos knew that he couldn't afford to pass, regardless of the odds against the contact bearing fruit. It was a chance, however slim, and he'd never know unless he checked it out. If he was wrong and the connection proved legitimate, he'd be sitting on a gold mine of prospective evidence. Enough, perhaps, to head off future crimes and put old perpetrators in a cell, where they belonged.

And if his instinct was correct? The call a phony?

He would either get another call, or he wouldn't. If no one called him back, the problem solved itself. If, on the other hand, a meeting was arranged, he meant to be prepared.

In thirteen years of plainclothes law enforcement work, the snub-nosed .38 revolver had become a virtual extension of himself, its weight familiar on his hip. He'd been forced to fire it twice at human beings in the line of duty, neither incident resulting in a death. Carr knew he had the nerve to kill, but it hadn't been necessary. Now it might be.

These days the weapon traveled mostly in his luggage, seldom carried on the street unless he had a reason to believe he was in danger. Frowning, Carr removed the Smith & Wesson from his suitcase, checked its load and clipped the holster on his belt.

While waiting for the callback he debated whether he should get in touch with Blanski. Backup would be helpful if the meet went sour—if there was a meet—but Carr decided he should wait and see. A busy line might spook the caller, make him think that Carr was talking to the police. Conversely, putting Blanski on alert would be a waste of time unless there was a contact to be made.

The call came twenty minutes later.

"Carr?"

"Right here."

"My man agrees to meet you, but it has to be this afternoon."

"Just tell me where and when."

"One hour. Outside of Denver Coliseum. You know the place?"

"I'll find it."

"Come alone."

"How else?"

The line went dead, and Carr immediately dialed the registration office, asking for a patch to Blanski's room. Carr sat through seven rings before he gave it up and lowered the receiver.

Come alone.

He had no choice, apparently, with Blanski chasing contacts of his own. Carr phoned the office back and left a message, briefing Blanski on his destination, praying that the clerk would not forget or file the message under *U* for useless crap.

There was a map of Denver in his car, and he'd find the coliseum on his own. It never hurt to show up early for a meet with strangers, scoping out ground that might become a battlefield.

Carr only hoped that it wouldn't become a killing ground.

BOLAN DRAINED HIS COFFEE CUP and asked, "How long have you been interested in witchcraft?"

"Wicca," Cass corrected him. "I started out by reading books about the subject, out of curiosity, in high school. Full commitment takes more time."

"Your family must have been . . . concerned."

"Hysterical," she said, and smiled. "Their only concept of a witch was drawn from fairy tales and late-night movies. When they saw nobody was about to burn me at the stake, they came around."

The waitress brought their check, and Bolan left a rumpled wad of bills in payment.

"I'd feel better if you weren't involved in this."

"Too late. Anyway, you needn't be concerned about last night. We aren't engaged or anything like that. You have no chivalrous commitment."

Bolan shook his head. "That's not the point. I've seen these people work."

"And so have I. Well . . . pictures, anyway. Believe me, I know what I'm doing."

"So you won't consider taking a vacation, just until the weather clears a little?"

"No." She made a point of glancing at her watch. "In fact, I've used my lunch break up. If you're all finished..."

Bolan rose and followed her outside. The afternoon was bright and warm, belying any threat of dark, archaic evil. For an instant, he was tempted to imagine that the whole experience in Denver—Cass included—was a strange, surrealistic dream.

"You coming?"

"Yes."

The diner was a short block from her shop, where Bolan's car was parked against the curb. He scanned the sidewalks automatically, alert for enemies.

"It must be terrible," Cass said.

"What's that?" he asked her, taken by surprise.

"To live this way. Trust no one."

Once again he felt the prickly sensation of awareness that, somehow, she'd picked up at least his general train of thought.

"I make exceptions," Bolan told her, and he let it go at that.

They reached the shop and separated, Cass responding to his question with the information that, of course, she would be free for dinner. Amos was invited, if he cared to join them for an early evening.

As Bolan put the rental car in motion, he was troubled. He could lay no claim to psychic powers, but experience had taught him to rely upon his instincts. They were talking to him now, in whispers, but he read the message loud and clear.

The too-familiar voice was telling him that there was danger on the streets, and the very air he breathed. A lurking menace, waiting to explode in Bolan's face, devour everything he touched.

So be it.

Bolan only hoped his peril wouldn't rub off on the innocents around him.

"WHO IS THAT fucking guy?"

"Who cares?" Thorn slid a hand inside his denim jacket,

feeling for the Bowie knife he wore inverted in a shoulder sling. "Scratch wants the girl. No extra baggage."

Felix obviously had his doubts. "I know that, man. But listen. What if he's a cop? She might've spilled her guts already. We might have to take him out."

Across the street, the tall man, object of their mutual concern, had separated from their target. She went back inside the shop, while he retreated to his car and got in. He spent a moment sitting at the curb, and Thorn was getting worried when he finally cranked the engine over, pulled away.

"Forget about it, man. You don't go whacking cops because they make you nervous. Too much heat. Scratch wants the girl, that's what we give him."

"Maybe we should call."

"And tell him what? The bitch had lunch with some guy, and he walked her back? Big fucking deal."

"All right, let's take her then."

"Sit tight. She's still got company."

Ten restless minutes passed before the other woman, short and blond, emerged. She hesitated in the doorway, saying something to their target, finally moving off along the sidewalk, northbound.

Thorn had been concerned that they'd have to deal with customers, but none of the infrequent pedestrians appeared to give the shop a second glance. Its merchandise was specialized, and curiosity would long since have abandoned those who passed the storefront on a daily basis, moving to and from the jobs that kept them busy nine-to-five.

"Okay." Thorn checked the knife again, made sure that he could reach it easily. He took a pistol from the glove compartment, tucking it inside his belt, a last resort in case of interference. "Give me five, then pull around behind and come in through the back. We'll take her out that way and save a lot of hassle on the street."

"You got it."

Thorn was out and moving, thankful for the mirrored shades that kept the Colorado sun from shriveling his eyes. A creature of the night by preference, he functioned less ef-

ficiently in daylight and was conscious of his limitations.
Still, it ought to be an easy job. No sweat.

The shop was cool inside. A tiny bell announced his entry, and the mark glanced up from dusting a display case.
There was hesitation in her smile as he approached the
counter.

"Can I help you?"

"I've been looking for a copy of the *Necronomicon*."

"I'm sorry, we don't carry that in stock."

"I know," he told her, pleased to see the smile turn up-
side down. "I came in earlier today. The other lady told me
that I'd have to see the owner about a special order."

"I'm the owner," she informed him, trying to be tactful.
"I apologize for any inconvenience, but the truth is, we
don't deal in information or materials associated with the
black side of the arts."

He feigned surprise. "Why's that?"

"A personal concern. I can refer you to another shop that
carries everything you'll need."

"I'm disappointed."

"Oh?"

"Well, I mean, I was hoping you could help me. I prefer
to do my business with attractive women."

"As I said—"

The back door whispered open then closed. She heard it,
glancing toward the beaded curtain, where a shadow mo-
mentarily turned into Felix, smiling at the startled woman.

Even cornered, she was cool. "Who are you?"

"We're you new best friends," Thorn told her, grinning
as he drew his jacket back to show the pistol in his belt. "We
brought your invitation to a little party."

"I'm not going anywhere with you," she said defiantly.

His smile remained in place. "You wanna bet?"

18

By one o'clock the minister was growing nervous. Trent had never disappeared like this before, and Jordan Braithwaite didn't like it. There were far too many details, petty problems to be dealt with on the final night of a crusade. Had everyone received their checks or promises of same? Did the collections tally? Were arrangements finalized for proper lodging at their next stop down the road?

Although he once had handled everything himself, these days the pastor left such chores to Arthur. Trent had shown an aptitude for trivia; he thrived on paperwork and payrolls, troubleshooting for the ministry in matters of logistics, finance, personnel. He dealt, in short, with all the details that kept Jordan Braithwaite on the road.

The pastor checked his watch and scowled. Two hours late and there was still no answer from the young man's room. As if he didn't have enough to think about already.

It had all been simple once, before TV and national crusades. In those days Braithwaite understood his mission, knew that he was capable of dealing with the problems that arose. A man of God, he fell back on his faith when times were hard. Today...

He didn't even want to think about the ultimatum Slate had handed to him during their meeting. Braithwaite knew that he'd built the trap himself, constructing it from raw ambition, lust for power and authority, conviction that his word—and his alone—could save the country in its time of trial. Ambition still remained, and his commitment to the word, but they had lost their sparkle, and he knew that everything he'd worked for might be snatched away from him at any time.

There was a noose around his neck, and Lucian Slate was carrying the end of the rope. Just now it pleased the dark man to provide a little slack, allowing Braithwaite room to breathe. Tomorrow, or the next day, he might change his mind.

Exposure was the absolute worst-case scenario. Forget about your girlie scandals and misuse of church collections. This was murder, multiplied across the landscape, executed by the hosts of hell on a commission from a man of God. Cosmetic press releases wouldn't cleanse the blood from Braithwaite's hands, and if a few long-suffering members of his flock eventually forgave him, there was still the government to deal with.

Dreams of Washington, the Oval Office, were supplanted by the image of a prison cell, and Braithwaite felt his lunch begin to curdle in his stomach. He was up and searching for the Alka-Seltzer when a firm knock sounded on his door.

He let himself relax a little, careful not to smile. He'd be forced to reprimand the boy for tardiness, but he'd keep it short, displaying proper magnanimity.

"You're late," he said, the words already on his lips before he realized that the two men on his threshold were strangers. They were dressed conservatively and studied his face without emotion. On his left, the taller of the two produced a wallet, flipped it open to reveal a badge.

"Police," he said by way of introduction. "I'm Lieutenant Grant. My partner, Sergeant Miller."

"Yes? How may I help you?" Apprehension nearly stole his voice. He felt the noose begin to tighten, choking off his wind.

"Jordan Braithwaite?"

"I'm Reverend Braithwaite, yes."

"May we come in?"

"Of course, I beg your pardon." Giving ground, he saw them in and closed the door behind them, pocketing his hands to hide the fact that they were trembling. "Please, sit down."

They took the chairs that flanked a cocktail table, leaving Braithwaite with a corner of the unmade bed. He chose to stand, although his legs had suddenly adopted the consistency of lead.

"Is there a problem?" he inquired.

The lieutenant answered with a question of his own. "Are you familiar with a man named Arthur Trent?"

"Of course. He works for me." A ray of hope lanced through the gloomy clouds. Let it be Arthur, please, instead of something worse. "I hope he's not in any sort of trouble."

"Has he been with you at all today?"

The pastor shook his head. There was a chance he mightn't have to lie. "I haven't seen him since last night," he told them. "We spoke this morning briefly, on the telephone."

"What did he talk about?"

"We had a date to meet for lunch, some business talk. In fact he never came at all, and I've been quite concerned. If Arthur's had an accident—"

"He's dead," the sergeant told him bluntly.

"What?" For just a heartbeat Braithwaite thought his legs might fold, but he maintained control. "I mean...what happened? He was always such a careful driver."

"Arthur Trent was murdered, Reverend." The lieutenant was studying his face for obvious reactions. Braithwaite didn't have to feign surprise.

"I'm sorry. I don't understand. What happened? When?"

"This morning," Grant's companion answered. "In the rest room of a coffee shop. Somebody blew his brains out in a toilet stall."

"Dear God!"

"Did Trent have any enemies?" Grant's voice betrayed no vestige of emotion. "Anyone who might have wished him harm?"

"If so, he never shared the fact with me. Perhaps it was a robbery."

The sergeant shook his head. "Not likely. There was money in his pocket. It looks professional."

"You mean it was deliberate? Arthur was... assassinated?"

"It's a possibility," Lieutenant Grant replied. "What sort of business were you scheduled to discuss at lunch?"

Trent had been cryptic on the telephone, but Braithwaite glossed it over. "We are flying to Las Vegas in the morning. There were—are—various arrangements to be made."

"Where will you be staying in Las Vegas?"

"At the Hilton, I believe."

"Did Trent have any next of kin?"

"His parents are deceased. I think there was a sister, somewhere in the east. New York, New Jersey—somewhere. I could check."

"Please do. Someone will need to claim the body when we're finished."

"Certainly. If there's a problem, the crusades will handle any funeral expenses."

The detectives rose together, Grant depositing a business card beside the telephone. "If you should think of anything at all, my number's here. We would appreciate a call."

"Of course, but I'm afraid I don't have anything to add. As far as I know, everyone was fond of Arthur."

"In that case," Grant responded, "someone has a funny way of showing their affection."

"We'll be in touch," his partner added, "if we have any further questions."

"Yes, I understand."

Alone once more, he pictured Arthur slumped beside a public toilet, lifeless. *Someone blew his brains out.* Braithwaite made it to the bathroom just in time as nausea took over.

Recovering, a washcloth plastered to his face, he tried to make some sense of the disaster. Arthur *had* no enemies, unless...

The truth struck Braithwaite like a hammer blow between the eyes, and for a moment he was terrified. Hot anger followed close behind the fear, and by the time it started burning in his cheeks, his hand was on the telephone.

THE DENVER COLISEUM was deserted. Amos circled it once before he nosed his car into the parking lot. His nameless contact hadn't specified a meeting place, but Carr would make himself available. He parked within a stone's throw of the ticket office, killed the engine, drew his .38 and placed it on the seat beside him. Opening the glove compartment, he retrieved a local map and spread it out to hide the gun.

No point in taking chances. If the meeting was a setup, as he half suspected, Carr had done his best to be prepared. It would've done no good to notify police about the call; they had their hands full as it was, and private operators were intruders, plain and simple. He could wait until hell froze before Detectives Grant and Miller offered to assist him with his case.

Carr understood the mind-set. He'd been in their position, overworked and understaffed, convinced that civil- ized society was subdivided into "us" and "them"—with "us" restricted to the men in blue. Cops spent their leisure time together, sometimes took vacations with their part- ners, anything to keep a hostile world at bay.

Ex-cops might rank a notch or two above civilians on the evolutionary scale, but they were still outsiders, exiled by retirement to a netherworld that working lawmen viewed with apprehension and resentment. Ex-cops "had it made" after they "pulled the pin." And if they didn't have it made, the fact of failure gave their comrades greater cause for fear, convincing them there might be a life beyond the job.

He checked his watch: five minutes to the hour mark. Carr scanned the parking lot, an asphalt desert scarred by painted hash marks. With a game in progress, it would be a sea of chrome and steel. Off-season, it was simply barren blacktop, flat and featureless. He felt exposed, a beetle perched on a wall with nowhere to hide in the event of dan- ger.

At the far end of the lot a station wagon pulled in off the street and angled toward him, cutting over empty rows of parking spaces in a sharp diagonal. The driver stopped some fifty yards in front of Amos, with his engine running, mak- ing no move to advance. When Carr sat still the new ar- rivals—two that he could see—exchanged some comment, and the passenger got out to stand beside their car.

He was a younger man, of average height, with hair that spilled around his collar, covering his ears. His eyes were hidden by a pair of aviator's glasses, but his hands were empty, and he wore no jacket that could easily conceal a weapon.

Which meant nothing.

Less than nothing.

There could be a piece beside him, on the vacant seat. His wheelman could be sitting with an M-16 or God knows what concealed beneath the dashboard. There could be a gunner in the back, crouched down and waiting for a target to reveal itself.

He had to move. Despite a nagging fear, his sense that everything about the meet was wrong, he hadn't come this far to shine it on and drive away without attempting contact. Scooping up the snubby .38, he slipped it in a pocket of his coat.

A sudden breeze surprised him, snapping at his coattails. He was forcefully reminded of *High Noon* as he began to cross the open blacktop, moving toward the station wagon. His contact moved out slowly, shuffling his feet and killing time. Carr felt the guy's reluctance, heard the jangling of an alarm inside his skull before he heard the other sound.

Behind him. Gaining fast.

Another car had slipped in from the rear, unnoticed, keeping to the shadow of the coliseum, and it was closing on him, the engine growling as the driver found his target. In the fraction of a second left to conscious thought, Carr saw his "contact" fading back in the direction of the station wagon, turning. Amos palmed his .38 and would have tried to peg the bastard, but the juggernaut was less than fifty feet away and he was out of time.

He sidestepped, felt the wind of doom rush past him as he lost his balance, going down on one knee. Without a backward glance he struggled to his feet and struck off for the rental car. Behind him he could hear the screech of rubber, and his mind's eye let him see the hit car cranking through a turn. The wheelman would be lining up his target now, prepared for contact on his second pass.

Carr heard death coming at him, threw himself across the rental's hood. Too late his enemy corrected, sliding broadside into jarring impact with the stationary vehicle. Acting on reflex, moving with agility he didn't know he had, Carr twisted on his perch and fired once at the driver. Blood exploded from the target's shoulder, but he stood on the accelerator, powering away from there before Carr had a chance to place another round.

Aware of danger on his flank, he swiveled, rolling off the rental's fender, landing in a crouch. His "contact" had retrieved a shotgun from the car, and now he squeezed off blind, his first blast peppering the car, one pellet stinging Amos in the thigh.

Returning fire, Carr snapped off three quick rounds and saw his adversary stagger, but the gunner was either wearing a vest, or he simply didn't give a shit. Advancing like some kind of Rambo clone, he fired twice more as Amos grappled with the door and hauled himself behind the wheel.

The second round hit home, with buckshot pellets hammering the open door and half a dozen punching through to flay Carr's hip. He slumped across the seat, felt hot blood seeping through his trousers, dizziness encroaching on the realm of logic. Fumbling with the ignition keys, he dropped them, saw them bounce and disappear beneath the driver's seat.

No time.

If he had any hope at all, it lay in coolness and precision—neither trait a hallmark of his usual performance under fire. His life depended on reaction time and accuracy. Any lapse from here on out, and he was dead.

The gunner reached his door and pulled it open, taking painful pressure off Carr's ankles. Leaning in, Carr's adversary saw that he was still alive and jacked another round into the shotgun's chamber.

"Nighty-night, you stupid bastard," he said.

Carr made his move, feet lashing out to catch the scattergun and force its muzzle upward, buckshot meant for him exploding through the window as the gunner fired on reflex. Bringing up the .38, Carr used his last two rounds at point-blank range, the aviator shades imploding as his target toppled backward, out of sight.

He heard another screech of tires, retreating, and he knew the driver of the station wagon had decided on discretion as the better part of valor.

Funny, Amos thought as consciousness began to fade, he could have taken me. He could have—

REMOVAL OF THE BLINDFOLD left Cass blinking in the sudden glare of artificial light. The world was on its side—or, rather, she was, curled up on a dirty blanket, concrete underneath, her ankles hobbled, hands bound tight behind her back. In front of her the denim legs of her abductors rose like tree trunks, and she refused to meet their eyes.

"I figure the accommodations aren't so hot," the taller of her two assailants said, "but, anyway, you'll like the company. Tonight one of you gets to be a star." He knelt before her, cupped one breast and flexed his fingers in a lingering caress. "I hope its you."

They left her then, ascending stairs she could recognize by sound, although they lay beyond her line of sight. Those stairs, the temperature and cinderblock construction told Cass she was lying in a basement, trussed up like a hog for slaughter.

Company. One of you gets to be a star.

She took a chance. "Is someone there?"

"Hey, keep it down," a younger female voice replied. "They'll hear you."

Digging with her heels, assisted by the sliding blanket, Cass executed an awkward half turn, surprised to find herself facing three teenage girls. One, a slender redhead, had worked her way into a seated posture, with her back against the wall; her two companions both lay on their sides, one facing Cass, the other with her back turned.

"Who are you?" the redhead asked.

"My name's Cassandra."

"I'm Alix, this is Sarah, and Debbie's the wallflower."

"How long have you been here?"

"Since last night. These assholes bagged us at the concert."

"Us, and Marla," Sarah said. Her voice was tremulous, stretched tight with terror.

"Marla?"

"She isn't with us anymore," Alix said grimly.

The cold finality of the pronouncement sent a chill down Cass's spine. She had to ask. "What happened?"

Alix shrugged. "They locked us in the van, but Marla never made it. From the way they talked I figure she wound up just like that girl the night before, you know?"

Cass knew all right. Her captor's gloating words came back to haunt her. *One of you gets to be a star.* She had no doubt about the nature of that "star" performance, or the fact that it would be a lethal one-night stand.

"We can't just wait for them to kill us."

"I'm ahead of you on that one," Alix told her, leaning forward slightly, stretching out her hands in front of her. A rope was looped around one wrist; the other end swung free.

"I had the last knot halfway finished when they brought you down. I didn't think they'd be out bagging people in broad daylight."

As she spoke the girl attacked her ankle bindings, cursing as the knots resisted her initial overtures and further chipped her broken fingernails.

Cass watched her for a moment, then began to scan the basement for another exit, any sign of implements that could be used as weapons. At the far end of the chamber, near the stairs, a tool bench stood against the wall, its surface littered with assorted objects she couldn't identify from where she lay. There might be something...

Alix had her legs free. She rose and spent a moment working on her balance, glancing back and forth between Cass and her friends, finally tottering toward the one called Sarah.

Cass could wait. They weren't going anywhere just yet, and it was hours until dark. There should be time enough to choose her weapon, find her vantage point, await an opportunity to strike. And in the meantime she would have a chance to ponder the decision that might change her life, deciding whether she could kill another human being.

BOLAN CLOSED THE DOOR to his motel room, locked it tight behind him and moved toward the bathroom. He was halfway there before his eye was captured by the bedside telephone, its flashing message light demanding his attention. Frowning, Bolan dialed the registration desk.

"You have a message for me?"

"Just a moment, sir." The line filled up with elevator music while the girl signed off to check. She came back a moment later. "Yes, sir. A Mr. Carr called in at half past twelve to say that he was meeting with an unknown variable at the Denver Coliseum." She paused. "Does that make sense?"

"Unfortunately, yes."

He cradled the receiver, cursing underneath his breath. It must have come up while he was at lunch with Cass. A call, perhaps, inviting Amos to a one-on-one. The lure would be information on the Chingons, and the only question left was whether it would be legitimate. The way things seemed to stand in Denver at the moment, Bolan wasn't betting on a straight exchange.

The soldier checked his watch. Some ninety minutes had elapsed since Carr deposited his message with the operator. Bolan knew it was an easy fifteen-minute drive from where he sat to the coliseum, and that left ample time for anything to happen. If someone had a trap laid out for Amos, he could easily be dead by now.

Bolan had no choice. He had to check it out, and if the worst scenario was realized, if he arrived too late, there'd be other angles of attack. A more direct approach, perhaps, than Amos had been willing to employ.

His mind was racing into overdrive, and Bolan let it idle for a moment, logic catching up to raw emotion. There would be time enough for fury once his targets were identified and isolated, when the possibility of lethal errors was eliminated. Strategy and steam mixed poorly, at their best.

The coliseum first. He could find out if Carr was there, if he was still alive, and any other moves would be determined by the answers to those basic questions.

The rapping on his door brought Bolan to his feet, the sleek Beretta in his hand. He crossed the room in four long strides, switched hands to hold the pistol in his left.

The detective, Grant, stood scowling on his doorstep. "Want to take a ride?" he asked.

"Where to?"

"Presbyterian Hospital. They're checking your buddy into emergency. He had himself a little accident."

19

"What happened?" Bolan asked when they were on the road. Grant drove with only half his mind on traffic, shooting frequent glances at his passenger.

"He hasn't told us much. Some kind of setup is the way we have it figured. Someone calls and sets a meeting to exchange some information. Carr shows up and guns are waiting. End of story. A retired cop ought to know better."

"How badly was he hit?"

"I couldn't say. He took a couple of the shooters out, if that's a consolation. The responding officers found one dead at the scene, and traffic got another one, six blocks away. They thought he was a drunk at first, the way he piled his car into a traffic signal. Turns out that the car was hot, and he was cold. Internal bleeding from a single round. It took some luck to get that far."

"And he's connected?"

"Sure as shit. Your buddy says he shot two perps, for openers, and this stiff's car is all banged up along the driver's side. I'm betting that the paint chips match Carr's rental, where he took a broadside hit."

"Who were they?"

"Damned if I know. Neither one was carrying ID. We're checking registration on a shotgun, sending prints to Washington, the usual routine, but there's a fifty-fifty chance we'll come up empty."

"Oh? Why's that?"

"These guys were young, okay? And something tells me neither one of them was in the service as a volunteer. If they were popped as juveniles somewhere, the records will be sealed. If either one of them applied for a driver's license, the chances are it was a state where thumbprints aren't required—and if they were, we'll have to wait on a computer scan of single prints."

"I follow," Bolan told him grudgingly. "It's cold."

"Not necessarily, but, yeah, I'd say it's definitely chilly, any way you slice it."

Two black-and-white units were parked outside the emergency entrance at Presbyterian Hospital. Grant parked his unmarked cruiser behind one of them, and both men went inside. They found Carr in a treatment room, with an IV in his arm, dispensing plasma, while an intern probed the ragged buckshot wounds along his flank. The intern was about to ask them to leave when Grant displayed his shield.

"Your patient going to make it, Doc?"

"I'd say so, but he won't be sitting pretty for a while." Delighted with his turn of phrase, the intern chuckled to himself. "No sitting pretty. That's not bad."

"We need to get some answers," Grant informed the medic-cum-comedian.

"No problem. I'll be working with a local anesthetic for the most part."

"That's the problem, Doc. Too many ears."

"I beg your pardon?"

"We'll need privacy."

"May I remind you this is still a hospital. It is *not* a sanitary annex of the station house."

"Point taken. And may I remind you that this man might have information about two, possibly four homicides in this city during the past forty-eight hours? Will you leave us alone for five minutes, or do I ring up your supervisor for a little chat?"

The intern met Grant's level gaze. "Five minutes," he replied. "One second longer and you'll get a busy signal when you make that call."

The curtain rattled shut behind him, leaving them alone with Amos Carr. The cop looked smaller in his dressing gown, hair mussed, his bare legs pale. At least his eyes were clear, and Bolan saw no trace of the distracted out-to-lunch expression that accompanied shock.

"How are you feeling, Amos?"

"Like I just invented hemorrhoids." He glared at Grant. "Have you identified the hitters yet?"

"Not yet."

"Goddammit!"

Grant pulled up a stool and sat. "What took you to the coliseum?"

"A call. Guy promised me a source inside the network, and I took the bait like any wet-behind-the-ears rookie."

"You had to know it was a setup."

"Didn't matter. I've been waiting seven years to get a whiff of something like an inside source. No way to pass it up."

"I don't suppose you recognized the shooters?"

Amos shook his head. "They're not in my files, no."

Grant rose. "I don't suppose you've got a carry permit for the .38?"

"I think I left it in my other pants."

"I figured. Denver doesn't seem to be a healthy place for you. When you get everything patched up, you might consider moving on."

"Is that an order?"

"It's a strong suggestion. I don't need another stiff this week, okay?"

"I'll think about it."

Grant slipped through the curtain, but the wounded man caught Bolan's wrist before he could retreat. With surprising strength for a man in his condition, Amos pulled him close.

"Warn Cass," he whispered. "Bastards could have followed me, for all I know."

A spark of apprehension flared in Bolan's mind. "I will," he promised. When the intern made his reappearance, he put on a show of brisk efficiency. "Five minutes," he declared. "Show's over."

"Tell her!" Amos pressed, and Bolan nodded as he pulled the curtain shut behind him.

Grant was waiting just outside, a frown etched deep into his face. "Okay, let's have it."

"I don't follow."

"Bullshit. I've got two girls dead, three missing, two punks full of holes and one ex-cop who damn near got his ass shot off. I don't have time to dance the two-step with a glory hound from Washington. He told you something, and I want it. Now."

"He told me to be careful, Sergeant."

"That's lieutenant."

"Ah."

"'Be careful'? That was it? Suppose I don't believe you?"

"Then I'd say you've got a problem."

"Wrong. If any smartass tries a grandstand play in my town, *he*'s the one with problems."

"I'll keep that in mind."

"You do that, Mr. Blanski." Grant snapped his fingers to get the attention of a pair of uniforms and ordered them to drive Bolan back to his motel. The ride was slow and silent. He chafed at the brief delay of traffic signals, wondering if Amos was correct about a threat to Cass. She had been asking questions, making waves; there was a possibility she'd attract unwelcome notice from the enemy, draw lightning to herself.

As Amos Carr had done.

As Bolan was about to do.

"YOU DIDN'T HAVE to kill him," Jordan Braithwaite snapped. He didn't trust himself to look at Slate directly, concentrating on the storefronts sliding past outside the tinted windows of the limousine. A sliding pane prevented any word they spoke from reaching to the driver's ears.

"And what would you have done?"

"I would have handled it."

"Oh, really? He was trailing you around the city like a watchdog, spying on your every move. You didn't even notice you were being spied on."

"Arthur would have come to me."

"The point is that he came to *me*. The whelp was looking for a fight. He found it."

"How will I explain this to the press?"

"You'll think of something." Slate was smiling at him, looking smug. "A little effort and you just might get some decent mileage on the deal. A man of God, cut down by enemies of your crusade. Sounds like a story guaranteed to keep those fat donations rolling in.''

"It's not about the money, Slate."

"Of course not. It's the *power*. Money, all the other trappings, are devices, means to an end."

Braithwaite shifted uneasily in his seat, hating the man who sat beside him. ''You don't understand.''

"I understand perfectly. We're not so very different. Ambitious men, compelled to deal with underlings who cannot share our vision."

"Never mind the amateur analysis. You've killed a trusted friend of mine and brought detectives to my doorstep."

"You'll survive. The sympathy alone will counter any minimal embarrassment you might experience. Relax."

"I've had enough of this." The words lay on his tongue like ashes.

"Have you? That's unfortunate, because it isn't finished yet."

"I'm not prepared to play your sick games any longer."

"Sorry, pastor, but you're in the game. No substitutions, no time-outs. In fact, it might be more precise to say you *are* the game."

"You can't imagine that I'll help you now."

"No matter. I intend to keep on helping you. The fact that you might not desire my help is totally irrelevant."

The preacher recognized his options, couldn't bring himself to threaten Slate with the police, much less carry out the threat. Exposure meant humiliation, prison, ultimate destruction of his dream. For all the guilt he carried over Trent, the others, Braithwaite couldn't—wouldn't—see his dream go up in flames.

He tried a different tack. "I don't believe the sacrifices should continue. I have adequate momentum now. The band provides enough publicity to carry the crusade. I want the killing stopped."

"The ritual of sacrifice wasn't initiated for your benefit. It's a venerable practice, absolutely independent of our personal arrangements. Your Old Testament supplies the precedent, with Abraham and Isaac."

"Don't quote scripture to me, Slate. I want the killing stopped!"

"*You* want?" Slate's laughter was harsh and mocking. "Please correct me if I'm wrong, but I believe that's how this whole thing started, *Reverend*, with your rather weighty list of wants and needs."

Defeated, Braithwaite clung to silence as his only sanctuary, drawing back inside his shell. He loathed Slate, hated everything that they'd done together. Worse, he'd begun to hate himself.

But not enough to throw his dream away. Not yet.

The limousine rolled on through Rocky Mountain sunshine as a hint of purple dusk began to bruise the sky. The pastor didn't care where they were going. All his highways seemed to have a single destination now, and there could be no turning back.

CASS FLEXED HER FINGERS, bringing life and circulation back into her hands. The slender rope had marked her wrists and ankles, but the angry welts would fade in time, assuming she survived. For now escape was the priority, and as she rose on wobbly legs Cass knew precisely what she had to do.

For openers she made a circuit of the basement, searching for a window, anything that could provide them with an exit other than the door that was at the top of the dusty wooden stairs.

She climbed the stairs on tiptoes, tensing as she realized squeaking steps might betray her to her enemies. Cass had no concrete notion of what she'd do if her abductors had been negligent enough to leave the door unlocked. Unarmed, she was defenseless, and there might be guards outside the door, prepared to spring on her as she stepped across the threshold.

Trembling fingers tried the knob and found it locked. Retreating, Cass was almost thankful, conscious of the fact that she hadn't prepared herself for any confrontation with the enemy.

Below her, Alix and Sarah sat with their backs against the wall, ropes tucked out of sight, ready to reassume their trussed-up posture if their captors reappeared. The third girl, Debbie, lay huddled with her face averted from the light. Alix had released her from her bonds, but in the absence of any response, her ropes had been replaced, the knots remaining loose enough for Debbie to free herself when necessary.

"We have to arm ourselves," Cass said, the concept of a violent struggle alien to her beliefs. "When they come back we'll have to fight."

"Damn straight." The fiery redhead rose and joined her as she turned in the direction of a makeshift bench that stood beneath the stairs.

The workbench had apparently been overlooked by their abductors. There were tools that might be used as weapons in a pinch. A hammer. Two long screwdrivers. A chisel with a ragged edge. A heavy file. The plane and hacksaw were of no apparent use unless they tried to cut the door open, and Cass wasn't prepared to take that risk with firearms waiting on the other side.

Repulsed by the idea of stabbing anyone, she was relieved when Alix took the chisel and one of the screwdrivers for herself, weighing each in her hand for balance and comfort. Cass took the hammer, surprised by its weight, turning back toward the others.

"I'll give this to Sarah," Alix told her, indicating the screwdriver. "It's better than nothing, I guess."

"What about Debbie?"

"I don't mean to sound brutal and uncaring, but we've got to face facts. Forget her. She's vegged."

It was true. From the moment Cass entered the basement, the girl had said nothing, done nothing to indicate rational thought. She ignored spoken questions, lay still when her bonds were untied and replaced. From appearances, Debbie might well have been dead.

"Was she hurt? Did she see something?"

"Nope. We got hypos, you know, when they grabbed us, but nothing too heavy. It just made you goofy, like ludes. Nothing major."

"She might have some kind of allergic reaction."

Cass frowned. If the girl was unable to move on her own, she would hamper their bid to escape. She would have to be carried or left to their enemies, neither one a prospect inclined to promote peace of mind.

They would do what they had to, she told herself. All the logistics were hazy, and Debbie was the least of their problems. Escape from the basement was first on the list, followed closely by flight from the building and evasion of capture outside, should they make it that far. Cass had no idea of their location, except that it must be in Denver or one of the suburbs; beyond that, they might have been caged on the moon.

She returned to her place and sat down next to Alix, retrieving the ropes that had bound her and keeping them close by her side. At the sound of a key in the lock, she could take her expected position in seconds. When one of their captors came close, tried to lift her...

Then what?

Her religion was purposefully vague on the subject of killing. No blood sacrifice was required, and while Wiccans were taught to seek peace with the forces of nature, some still dined on meat, fish and foul. They weren't automatically pacifists, loath as they were to inflict harm on their fellows. Defense of the self was a personal thing, first approached on the level of spirit and mind, relegating the physical aspect to a secondary position. Still, Cass knew Wiccans who served in the military, one or two who had entered police work without surrendering their principles.

Cass knew she could fight in self-defense; as for the killing, she decided she would do whatever might be necessary to preserve herself, her fellow prisoners, from grievous harm. Her enemies were men of evil, captives of the darkness. Some might say that killing one of them would be an act of mercy.

Offering a silent prayer for strength, Cass clutched the hammer in her sweaty palms and waited for the killing hour to strike.

FOR OWEN YORK, the hunt had always been more satisfying than the kill. Selection of the prey, pursuit and capture, preparation for the ritual to come—all this imbued him with a sense of power unsurpassed by any other enterprise. The life-and-death decisions came as second nature to him now, but there was still a heady feeling of authority and dominance each time he chose a lamb for slaughter in the Master's name.

York hated it when things went wrong.

An error, even one committed by subordinates, reflected on his leadership, his strength and clarity of purpose. York couldn't afford mistakes that damaged any aspect of his reputation. Failure was an unacceptable alternative.

The mess with Amos Carr was an example. Taking down a pig-turned-private-eye was simple work, like stealing candy from a baby, but his men had blown it. Worse yet, two of his people had contrived to throw their lives away, a twenty-five percent reduction in his force inflicted at a time when things were critical and he could least afford the loss.

York felt the anger mounting as he thought of Jagger, stretched out in the morgue, with Zero on a slab close by. An easy job had blown up in their faces. In icy rage he turned on Hacker, sole survivor of the bungled escapade.

"You should have finished him." York was confident that no emotion came through in his voice.

"I wanted to, but then I figured, shit, suppose he pops me, too? They find the station wagon, trace it back—"

"That's bullshit, man. The registration's bogus and you know it. They could chase their tails forever, going nowhere."

"Fucking ay." Snake saw through Hacker's double-talk, the others, Thorn and Felix, nodding in agreement. "You got spooky, man."

"Okay, so what? I saw the bastard do for Zero. Jagger split, and now you tell me *he's* dead. What the hell was I supposed to do?"

"Your job, that's all."

"I did my job, okay? I made the call. I drove the car. All right?"

"You let the pigeon walk away."

"I still think Zero hit him."

"Right. The problem is, he didn't hit the bastard hard enough. Right now your pigeon's sitting in a private room at Presbyterian and singing for his supper."

"What's he know to sing about? He doesn't know anything."

"I'm glad you feel so confident," York told his nervous underling. "Myself, I'd like some guarantees."

"What kind of guarantees?"

"I'd like to know his mouth was shut for good."

"Okay. I'll handle it."

"You sure it's not too heavy for you, Hack?"

"I pull my weight."

"Let's see about that, man. Right now I'd say you owe us one."

"All right." Reluctance giving way to resignation. "I'll take care of it. I promise."

"I believe you, Hack. We all believe you."

"You can get his room from information," Snake suggested. "Tell them that you want to send some flowers up."

"That's good," York said. "The sympathetic touch."

"Suppose they've got him covered?" Felix asked. "You want some backup?"

"No. I made the mess. I'll clean it up myself."

"I like your style. The pig's all yours."

York let himself relax. He knew that there was nothing Carr could tell the local law, beyond a license number or description of the station wagon. He'd seen to both when Hacker came home empty, switching plates and locking up the wagon for insurance. It wouldn't be used again until they pulled up stakes to move, and even then he might decide to ditch it.

Eliminating Amos Carr was more a point of honor than necessity. The bastard was a nuisance, lecturing police departments here and there around the country, cropping up on television when you least expected him, alerting everybody and his brother to the danger posed by lurking cultists. York had seen him on the tube, and once in person, from a ringside seat, when Carr was speaking at a local auditorium in San Francisco. It was trippy, sitting in while someone ran your business down with details accurate enough to make you think he might have eyes inside the brotherhood.

It was apparent now that Carr didn't possess such inside information. He'd jumped on Hacker's bait too swiftly for a man already milking steady sources. Still, the bastard never let it rest, and he could always count on help from meddlers like the bitch downstairs. It made him laugh to think about the impotent "white" witches, huddled in their covens, praying for protection from emasculated "nature gods." In Dallas, after local teens had started sacrificing livestock, members of the Wiccan tribe had staged a public rally, casting spells to "exorcise the demons" that possessed their "poor, misguided brothers." It was all a crock of shit, but it was good for laughs.

The problems came when individuals began cooperating with the law, obtaining information on the sly and feeding it to various investigative agencies. It happened now and then, a risky business that the Black Cross hit teams were designed to cope with on a local level, weeding out informers as they surfaced. Those who were identified became examples for the rest.

York had decided that Cassandra Poole would be their parting gift to Denver, a specific object lesson for others of her kind. Eliminating Amos Carr would simply be a bonus.

20

Bolan made a drive-by, found no parking spaces open on the street and circled to the lot in back. Before he killed the rental's engine, he observed that the shop's back door was open, swinging slowly in a rising breeze.

The soldier took a moment, sidling past Cassandra's car to glance inside and press his palm against the hood. Its only trace of warmth had been imparted by the sun; the vehicle apparently hadn't been moved for hours, possibly since Cass arrived for work.

Mind racing, hoping Amos Carr had his signals crossed for once, he stood on the threshold of the shop. Instinctively he palmed the Beretta, flicking off its safety as he stepped inside.

It took a moment for his eyes to make adjustments for the dimmer artificial light. He was alone inside the combination office, lounge and storeroom, moving toward the beaded curtain and the shop beyond, attracted by a sound that he couldn't immediately identify.

The shop seemed empty at a glance, but then he caught a hint of movement on his left, behind the counter. Someone was crouching, poking through the items on display, occasionally popping up to check the windows and the empty street outside. Bolan didn't recognize the profile, but it was male; the youth appeared to be in his late teens.

Whoever he might be, the guy was working solo. Bolan spread the beaded streamers gently with his free hand, slipping through without unnecessary racket to announce his coming. He was halfway to the register before the guy discovered him and panicked, breaking for the door.

"I wouldn't," Bolan told him, letting the Beretta answer any questions. Still a few yards short of freedom, knowing he could never hope to make it, Bolan's target skidded to a shaky halt.

"I wasn't doin' nothin', man," he whined.

"In that case you'll be glad to empty your pockets. Now."

A spark of defiance lit the beady eyes. "You goin' to make me?"

"Count on it."

"Oh."

The pockets were emptied in record time, a pile of chains, charms and amulets accumulating on the counter. Money from the register lay crumpled on the side, like salad served up with a strange, unpalatable meal.

"That isn't much to die for," Bolan told him.

"What? Hey, man, you have to take me in and read my rights! You can't just shoot me down like that. I watch TV!"

"It's time to change the channel, boy. I'm not a cop."

"Oh, shit."

"You're in it. Deep. The only question now is do you sink or swim?"

"I swim okay."

"That's fine. Here's how we play the game—I ask the questions, and you tell me what I want to know. The first time I suspect you're lying to me, I take your head off. Got it?"

"Hey, I got my rights!"

He took a long stride closer to the kid, his pistol aimed directly at the pimply face. "Last rites is what you've got," he snapped, "unless you tell my everything I want to know, exactly when I want to know it. Am I getting through?"

"I hear you, man."

"That's fine. A woman runs this shop. Where is she?"

"Haven't seen her, man. No, jeez, I mean it! Place was empty when I happened by. I checked it out and went around in back, figuring they must be in the stockroom, but there's no one in the place. I ask myself, why not? A chance like that doesn't come along so often."

Bolan recognized the desperate truth of his informant's words and felt his spirits sag. "How many cars out back?" he asked.

"Just one. A blue job. I don't know the make."

"And no one in the store?"

"I woulda never come inside if there was anybody here. I ain't no Jesse James."

"You found that money in the register?"

"Where else? I didn't get a chance to look around for hidey-holes."

"No signs of anything disturbed before you got here?"

"Nothing I remember, but I wasn't paying much attention to the little things, you know?"

"You live around here?"

"Naw, in Englewood."

"Go home," the soldier told him. "If I see your skinny ass around this neighborhood again, you're worm food. Got it?"

"Sure. Hey, thanks, man."

He was gone before the autoloader found its sheath. Behind him, Bolan closed the street door, locked it, dumped the cash and other stolen items in the register before he closed the drawer. After another look around the storeroom he set the back door's automatic lock before he pulled it shut behind him.

There might be reasons, he supposed, why Cass would close down early. An emergency involving friends or family, perhaps, that summoned her away without a chance to make arrangements for a part-time substitute.

So far, so good.

But he did not believe she would run off and leave the shop unlocked, as well as unattended. Worse, he knew that in response to an emergency call, Cass wouldn't have gone on foot.

The circumstantial evidence suggested an abduction, and the thief's description of a shop with nothing out of place, crisp greenbacks waiting in the register, ruled out abduction during common robbery. It meant Cass was the target; Amos had been right.

Retreating to his car, the soldier told himself that there was still a silver lining. If the hunters simply wanted Cass eliminated, they would almost certainly have killed her in the shop instead of carting her away. Small consolation, considering the fate of others they abducted, but at least he might have time.

For what?

To shake some answers loose, for openers. He needed information, with a minimum of bullshit and delay. Already dusk was painting shadows on the pavement, darkness creeping in behind.

The Executioner had no time left to dance around with hangers-on and street informants.

He was starting at the top.

THE PRIVATE ROOM was small but comfortable, windows facing westward on the Denver skyline. From the door, Lieutenant Grant surveyed the bed, its occupant, the television mounted on the wall directly opposite.

"You're going to wear out that remote control," he said.

Carr made a sour face and flicked off the television. "We're talking Mile High City here, and the TV reception isn't worth a damn."

"You need your beauty sleep."

"It's too damned late for that. What's happening?"

"Just checking in. You change your mind about the guard?"

"Hell no. They missed their shot at me, Lieutenant."

"Nothing says they couldn't try again."

"I'm fine."

"I don't need all the flack I'm going to take if you get snuffed in Denver."

"Your concern is touching."

"Seriously. Say you're right about this cult, whatever..."

"*Say* I'm right. You still don't see it?"

"I see someone tried to take you out. We don't know who, or why."

"I know."

"Okay. It plays, I grant you that. More reason why you ought to have some cover, just in case these flakes decide a payback is in order."

"I don't need a watchdog. Thanks, but no thanks."

"Yeah, I figured that's the way you'd see it." Fishing in a pocket of his coat, Grant found the snubby .38 and placed it on the stand beside Carr's bed.

"What's that?"

"You have to ask, with all the practice you've been getting lately?"

"No, I mean—"

"We're holding yours until the inquest, right? Okay. There's nothing in the rule book that says I can't provide a loaner when a citizen's life is in danger."

"I hope it won't be necessary."

"Yeah, me too. The piece is registered to me. I'll want it back before you fold your tent and ride off into the sunset."

"Sun*rise*," Carr corrected. "I'm an Eastern boy, remember?"

"Right."

"You getting everything you need?"

"I think I'm covered. Rubber chicken from the microwave, reruns of *Gilligan's Island*, a bed pan. What more could I ask for?"

"Beats me." Grant felt awkward in asking the question that came to his mind, but he got it out anyway. "Listen, does this kind of thing happen often?"

"What's that? Getting shot in the ass?"

"An attempt on your life."

"Not so much. It's a risk, but with most of the threats you can tell they're not serious."

"This time they were."

"Yeah, I'd say."

"You believe all this stuff, about cults linking up coast-to-coast? You're convinced?"

"Bet your ass. If I wasn't convinced I'd be sitting at home with a brew and the ball game, collecting my pension in peace."

"It's a hard thing to grasp."

"That's their strength. Who believes in the bogeyman these days?"

"I wonder sometimes."

"It's a start."

"You're sure about that guard?"

"I'm sure." Carr took the .38 and broke its cylinder, examining the load before he slipped the weapon underneath his blankets. "Thanks. I'm covered."

"Fair enough. You've got a nurse right down the hall, but if you feel like anybody's giving you the bad eye, drop a dime, you hear me?"

"Right."

"I'll see you."

"Sure."

Outside, the evening's visitors were starting to collect around the nurse's station, bearing flowers, candy, fruit in baskets wrapped with brightly colored tissue paper. Grant scanned faces—young, old and in-between—in search of anyone who might be stalking Amos Carr. He couldn't shake his feeling that the wounded man was still in danger, but Grant's own troops were spread out thin enough already, with the recent spate of homicides. He was in no position to insist that Carr accept a bodyguard.

The goddamned guy was on his own. Grant wished him luck. He had a feeling Carr would need it.

DENVER HAD BEGUN to wear on Lucian Slate. Before they came to Colorado everything about the Slaughter Tour had been running as smooth as glass. The money had been rolling in, his hunters had performed their tasks efficiently and Braithwaite's strident sermons had been worth a fortune in publicity.

In Denver things had changed dramatically and for the worse. His confrontation with the pastor was a minor thing, a simple test of wills that Slate was bound to win, but he had other problems now. The death of Arthur Trent had homicide detectives sniffing all around Braithwaite's crusade, and there was always the unnerving possibility that one of them might stumble on a vital piece of evidence. Worse yet, the bungled hit on Amos Carr had left two hunters dead and their backgrounds subject to examination by authorities.

The dark man felt uneasy, realizing circumstances had begun to slip beyond his grasp, escaping his control. York's brash experiment with multiple abductions was a case in point; the man had started thinking for himself again, and that was always dangerous. If he couldn't eliminate a sitting duck like Amos Carr, could he be trusted with the care of living hostages?

There had been so much death already, in addition to the sacrifices. Trent, the hunters, an employee from a cemetery. And the woman. Had he learned her name? If so, Slate's memory was failing him. A Wiccan snooper, she deserved to die, but it was simply one more problem at the moment, one more opportunity for fatal error.

Death, per se, had never troubled Lucian Slate. Whenever possible he left the execution of the deed to others, knowing there were always willing hands available. But death was necessary for the Master's pleasure and the satisfaction of his followers. There could be no eventual success without the blood.

So thinking, Slate removed the thermos bottle from the small refrigerator in his room. The boys would be waiting for him down in Clay's suite. It was feeding time.

The rapping at his door was soft, insistent. Frowning, Slate replaced the thermos. He hadn't ordered anything; the beds were made. Who could it be?

A tall man in expensive clothes stood in the threshold, studying Slate's face with eyes that held no spark of warmth.

"What is it?"

"Lucian Slate?"

"That's right."

"We need to talk."

"I'm rather busy at the moment. If it's not extremely urgent—"

"You could say it's life-and-death."

"Oh, really? Whose?"

The pistol seemed to come from nowhere, fastening its muzzle to his forehead like a limpet.

"Yours."

INSIDE SLATE'S ROOM, the door locked tight behind him, Bolan made a rapid scan for weapons, saw none and propelled his captive toward the bed.

"What is this?" Slate demanded.

"First rule," the Executioner declared. "I ask the questions, you supply the answers. Any deviation from established rules of play could seriously jeopardize your health."

"You can't be serious."

A backhand drew blood and laid Slate out on the king-size bed. The dark man shook his head as if to clear it, tried to wipe the blood away, but only smeared it on his face.

"This is outrageous."

Bolan held the Beretta steady. "So is human sacrifice. But I respect your civil liberties. In fact, you have the right to remain silent forever."

"Wait!" Slate saw his death in Bolan's eyes and raised a bloody hand as if to shield himself. "Just tell me what you want to know. I'll answer anything."

"Your hit team," Bolan said. "They've taken prisoners. I need an address."

Slate gave a number and a street in Englewood. "An old two-story job," he told the Executioner. "Big basement. It could use a coat of whitewash."

"So could you. My second question. Why?"

Slate didn't seem at all confused. "Why not?" he countered. "Power, wealth, the pleasures of the flesh. We don't believe in all that crap about how suffering on earth will guarantee eternal satisfaction in the afterlife. Far better for the sheep to suffer, while the Master and his chosen people relish every moment of the here and now."

"Including human sacrifice?"

"The ritual release of energy at death invokes the spirits who would do our bidding. Blood is in the nature of an offering, a bonding ceremony."

"Bonding?"

"Flesh and spirit. Man and Lucifer. It's not unlike the Roman Catholic communion ceremony."

"And the band?"

Slate sneered. "Spoiled children. Oh, they have their uses, but they're soft." The dark man chuckled to himself. "They still believe we're drinking calf's blood in our celebrations.''

"What they don't know, mmm?"

"Precisely."

Slate was smiling, warming to his topic, confident that nothing he might say under the gun could be used against him later. Bolan took advantage of the new, expansive mood and played a hunch.

"Why Braithwaite?"

"Once again, why not? The man's a pompous ass, but he has followers. Enough, perhaps, to put him in the White House—or at least a senate seat. With adequate promotion and support, the reverend has possibilities."

"Did he approach you first?"

Slate shrugged. "I've never been precisely clear on all the details. Overtures were made, by one side or the other. Cash changed hands. A schedule was arranged. We've kept our bargain with Braithwaite."

"And the murders?"

"He requested incidents to dramatize his sermons. We complied." A new idea occurred to Slate. "Is that what this is all about? Did Braithwaite send you here?"

"Not even close."

"You aren't with the police." It didn't come out sounding like a question.

"No."

"Well, who then?"

"Let's just say I represent the sheep."

"An altruist?"

"Not quite."

A sudden flash of understanding sparked behind the furtive eyes. "You won't gain anything by killing me."

"You never know."

Slate struggled to his feet. "I'll give you names."

"I have enough already. I'll be calling on them soon."

"For God's sake, don't!"

"For my sake."

The impact of a point-blank parabellum round between the eyes picked Lucian Slate completely off his feet and drove him back against the dresser. Dead before he slithered to the floor, the dark man's eyes were open, staring back at Bolan from across the void. If hell was waiting for him, as reward or punishment, he gave no sign.

The Executioner removed a small recorder from his pocket, let the tape rewind halfway and played a portion of it back to double-check the quality. It wouldn't pass for anything recorded in a studio, but Bolan thought it should serve his purpose well enough.

The battle wasn't finished yet by any means.

In fact, the worst of it had only just begun.

York could have flipped a coin to choose the evening's sacrifice, but he decided on the Wiccan bitch because he hated meddlers. It didn't pay to tamper with the Master's business.

"Felix, you'll be staying here to watch the sheep."

"I hate to miss the party."

"There'll be other parties," York assured him. "Lots of party times in Vegas."

"Sure, Scratch. Anything you say."

"My man." He smiled. "Let's fetch the guest of honor, shall we?"

Thorn was standing watch, a chore they took in shifts whenever they were on the road and hunting. York didn't believe the local cops would ever crack his cover, but while any slight chance remained, security precautions would be recognized. If Manson's tribe had posted sentries in the desert, Charlie might be on the street today, instead of vegetating in San Quentin.

Snake and Felix trailed him through the kitchen, waited while he found his key, unlocked the cellar door. The single light downstairs had been left on around-the-clock since they acquired their captives, and a glance informed him that the prisoners were still in place. The redhead sat against one wall, with her companions lying close beside her, back-to-back. York's choice for the festivities was huddled by herself, approximately where she had been placed upon arrival, though he noted that she faced the staircase now.

So much the better. She would see Death coming for her, and the sight would chill her meddling soul.

"It's party time," he announced, sauntering across the concrete floor as if he hadn't already chosen one of them. Let the bitches sweat a little. Fear increased the ultimate release of energy in sacrificial ceremonies, and tonight York thought they might proceed without the normal tranquilizer. Just for fun.

"I need a volunteer from the studio audience," he said, grinning at their discomfort. "Who shall it be?"

York passed the catatonic specimen and nudged her prostrate girlfriend with his boot. "You up for fun and games tonight, my darling?"

"Why don't you go fuck yourself?"

The redhead, Alix, glared at York with unadulterated malice in her eyes. He liked that in a victim and would certainly have chosen her to grace the altar if his mind hadn't been made up in advance.

"I don't believe that's possible, is it?" he asked Alix, smiling. "Maybe we should all fuck you instead."

"Sounds fair," Snake offered, moving closer.

"I'm for that," Felix agreed.

The young woman sneered. "I doubt you three could get one up between you."

"Ooh, I love a challenge." Stepping closer and leaning forward, York stroked her cheek, his fingers slipping lower, searching for her breast.

She stabbed him then, the movement absolutely unexpected, and he saw the gout of blood before he felt the pain. A chisel, streaked with crimson after slicing through his arm, was aimed at the hunter's face.

He blocked the move in reflex action, swinging up his wounded arm and belting her across the face with everything he had.

"Watch out!"

A shout from Snake, and then a blur of movement in the corner of his eye brought York around. The witch was on her feet, a hammer clutched in both hands, poised to strike. Snake dropped her with a snap-kick to the ribs as Felix was disarming Sarah, holding up a screwdriver the girl had hidden behind her back.

York pulled his sleeve up to the elbow, found his wound was superficial. Some adhesive from the first-aid kit upstairs would put things right. He wouldn't need stitches.

"Next time try the eyes," he said to Alix.

Spitting blood, she told him, "I'll be happy to."

"The problem is, there won't be any next time. I was looking for a volunteer, and now I've decided on an even pair."

"A doubleheader," Felix sniggered.

"Right as rain." He tossed the chisel toward the far end of the basement, heard the other weapons follow it. "A little something extra for our final night in Denver. Two for one."

"That's tasty." Snake was grinning like a junkie in a drugstore.

"Finest kind." York savored the adrenaline rush, looking forward to the greater pleasures he knew were coming. From his belt he drew an automatic pistol, covering the captives while his soldiers went about the chore of binding hands and feet.

"Make everybody nice and cozy," he instructed. "I don't want our guests of honor missing out on all the fun."

21

"There's still no answer, dammit!"

Slamming down the telephone, Clay Deatheridge retreated to a mirror and began to brush his hair with angry strokes. It wasn't like their mentor to be tardy. Slate was punctual above all else, and running twenty minutes late without a check-in call was simply not his style. His room was on the floor above—perhaps a minute's elevator time away—and still they waited while his goddamned phone rang off the hook with no response.

"He's really late, man." Johnny Beamish looked confused, but that was fairly normal.

"Hey, no shit. Where've you been?"

"Take it easy, Clay." Sweet reason came from the lips of Tommy Piersall. Clay couldn't decide if Tommy was relaxed or simply wasted.

"Take it easy? We're on stage in what, three hours? We've got things to do, and I don't mean hanging out here, watching Freddy pick his zits!"

"You're getting hyper, man. He's late, okay? It's not a tragedy. Why don't we zip upstairs and see what's happening?"

"That's not a bad idea."

He dropped the brush and hit the corridor with Tommy close behind him; Beamish, Sykes and O'Neal emerged from the suite as Clay was waiting for the elevator. Crowding into the car, they pushed a button and in a moment were standing in the corridor outside Slate's room.

"Go on and knock, for Christ's sake," Tommy prodded. "What's the problem?"

Clay couldn't have put his feeling into words. Since Slate had joined the band and turned their lives around, he'd been nagged by fear that someday—someday soon—their mentor would leave in search of other fields to conquer, other bands to resurrect. It would, perhaps, be too much to suggest that Deatheridge was hooked on Lucian Slate, and yet....

He knocked, and took a quick step backward as the door responded to his touch. It only moved an inch or so, but that was plenty. All the hotel doors were set to lock themselves the moment they were closed; you needed keys to get inside...unless the door was left ajar.

"That's weird."

"So check it out."

"Go on, man."

Clay stepped forward, hesitant, and pushed the door a little farther open with his fingertips. "Hey, Lucian, man...you in there?"

Nothing.

Clay pushed harder, eased his way inside, the others crowding at his back. There was a little entry hall before you saw the room proper, and Slate was waiting for them as they came around the corner. He was sitting on the carpet, with his back against a dresser, leaking blood and brains from one hell of a head wound.

"Holy shit!"

"He's dead, man."

Clay shrugged off the hands that settled on his arms and shoulders. "Tell me something new," he growled.

"We ought to call the cops," Johnny Beamish offered.

"No! Forget the cops." Clay didn't know why Slate had been killed, but he could read the signs of murder from across the room. There might be something left behind that would incriminate their mentor, lead to trouble for the band.

"We've got to get him out of here," he said at last. "Clean up the place and check around for anything that might cause trouble."

"What do you call this?" Freddy whined. "I'd call *this* trouble."

"Stuff it, man. We'll need to wrap him up in something, take him down the service stairs and put him in the car."

"Sometimes they stick an extra blanket in the closet," Tommy offered.

"Check it out."

In fact there were two blankets folded neatly on a shelf. Clay supervised as they were spread out on the floor, Slate's body lifted into something like a makeshift sling and wrapped securely. When they'd finished, with the corners all tucked in, Slate looked as if he was ready for a burial at sea.

They wiped the dresser down and tried to sponge the crimson carpet clean. It was the best they could do, and gory towels were stuffed inside the body-bundle for disposal. If the maids set up a clamor, they would pay for any missing towels and leave the house dicks to try to figure out where Slate had gone. Police could analyze the carpet stains until they knew the fibers inside out, and it wouldn't prove murder.

"Wipe the place for fingerprints before we go," he ordered, startled by the calm that had descended on his brain. The shock and loss would follow in their own good time; just now, they had a body to dispose of and a gig to play.

"I'll take his feet. Mike, get his shoulders, will you? Someone catch the door."

"Oh, shit."

The tone of Tommy Piersall's voice caught Clay's attention. On the threshold, watching them with interest, stood two men in suits and ties. The taller of them flipped his wallet open to reveal a badge.

"You need a hand with that?" he asked. And smiled.

IT HAD BEEN SIMPLE, as predicted, to obtain the number of his target's room. No fuss, no muss—a phone call to confirm delivery of flowers and a get-well card for patient Amos Carr. The operator shuffled through her files, came up with information that his friend was stable and receiving visitors.

Room 314.

En route, Hacker hedged his bets by stopping off to buy a small bouquet. The flowers might turn out to be superfluous, but he would rather cover all his bets than have another fuckup on his hands. Scratch might not be forgiving next time, and he frankly didn't need the kind of grief that came with exile from the brotherhood.

That kind of grief was permanent, and he'd seen enough of Scratch's work to know that it was more blessed to give than to receive.

He found a parking space reserved for visitors and killed the Chevy's engine. Fishing in the glove compartment, Hacker found the .22 automatic, equipped with a silencer, and tucked it inside his belt. Two extra magazines went in the pocket of his sport coat, just in case. With any luck at all he wouldn't need them, but the afternoon had taught him all he had to know about preparing in advance for the "easy" jobs.

This time there would be no mistake, nothing taken for granted.

Leaving the car, he checked the pocket of his jeans and felt the switchblade's reassuring weight. If possible he would prefer to use the knife and keep the pistol in reserve. The personal approach provided so much more in terms of satisfaction.

Carrying his flowers, Hacker made it through the lobby, past the information desk without a second glance from the operator working the evening shift. He moved directly to the elevators, waiting with a pair of blue-haired matrons, punching the button for number three.

Visiting hours were in progress, with businessmen, housewives and shit kickers all rubbing shoulders, intent on delivering candy and bogus best wishes to Grandma or poor Uncle Harry. The nurses on duty were answering questions and giving directions, their smiles plastered firmly in place as they tried to get on with the jobs they were paid for. He slid past their station, examining numbers, and paused outside a door restricted to Employees Only.

Glancing back along the hallway, making sure the nurses were distracted, Hacker tried the knob and found it open. Once inside he hit the light switch, scanned the shelves of linen, plain white robes and bedpans. Nothing that could be of use.

He was about to leave, had one hand on the doorknob, when he found the lab coat hanging on a hook behind the door. It didn't fit him very well but it was close enough. He ditched the flowers and the sport coat—no ID or labels that would help the pigs to trace him—and became an instant intern by the simple act of slipping on a garment.

He stepped into the hallway and closed the door behind him, striking off toward 314. There was no guard posted, which had been Hacker's greatest fear. Apparently the asshole didn't rate police protection.

Twenty yards later he was at the door, looking in each direction, making certain he was unobserved by anyone who might think twice about his visit to a private room. As usual with hospital rooms, the door had no conventional knob or latch; the nurses needed access to their charges at a moment's notice, any time of day or night, and they couldn't afford the headaches of some basket case deciding that he needed privacy.

Before the door swung shut behind him, Hacker had the silenced .22 in hand. No point in taking chances that his mark might raise an outcry and alert the staff. His finger tightened on the trigger as he stood his ground, a looming shadow in the darkened room.

If Carr was conscious of his uninvited visitor, he gave no sign. So much the better. Tucking the pistol back in his waistband, Hacker pulled the switchblade, snapped it open, moving swiftly toward the bed.

"Sweet dreams," he whispered as he struck.

JORDAN BRAITHWAITE PACED his dressing room with restless strides, head lowered, staring at the faint impression of his footsteps on the carpet. They would call for him in moments—he could hear the music building to its climax even now—and for the first time in his life the pastor wondered if he would have anything to say.

The sheer mechanics of the message were no problem; he could do it in his sleep. The missing element was *feeling*, the desire to move an audience and hold it in his hands, possess the mass emotion of its members for an hour, ultimately send them on their way as messengers of God—and Jordan Braithwaite.

He was losing it, the fire that lifted ordinary sermons from the snoozer category, lending them the strength to seize men's souls. The last two days had left him drained, and Braithwaite knew that he was simply going through the motions, marking time.

With any luck his audience would never recognize that truth.

He stopped his pacing, squared his shoulders and turned toward the door. The notes were in his pocket if he needed them, but Braithwaite knew they wouldn't be necessary. One more night in Denver, after this, and he would have a break before the game began all over in Las Vegas.

Two young women—girls, in fact—were waiting on the threshold, startled as he opened the door. Both of them were blond and might have passed for pretty, in a pinch.

"Excuse us, Pastor," said the taller of the two.

"What is it, girls?"

The shorter, rounder specimen looked nervous as she cleared her throat. "There's something you should know," she said, her voice a whisper.

"Yes?"

"Well...please forgive me, Pastor. I was listening to rock and roll just now, and—"

"Child, it isn't *my* forgiveness you require. Your business is with God, while mine is with a waiting audience. If you'll excuse me..."

"No! I mean...please, wait. I thought you ought to hear the news."

"What news is that?"

"Just now, while I was listening, they broke in on a song with the announcement that there wouldn't be a concert at the stadium tonight."

"No concert?" Braithwaite felt his hackles rising. "Did they offer an explanation?"

"Yes, sir. It sounds crazy, but the members of Apocalypse are all in jail for murdering their manager. According to the radio, policemen caught them carrying his body out of a hotel room."

"Manager?" His heart was leaping, threatening to crack his rib cage.

"Lucian Slate," the taller girl reminded him, as if he didn't have the name emblazoned on his brain.

"Of course."

"We thought, with everything that's happened, you might have to make some changes in your message."

"Thank you. You've been very thoughtful." Braithwaite could have kissed them both, but how would *that* have sounded on the news?

"Oh, Pastor?"

"Yes?" He could afford the smile.

"About the music . . ."

"I forgive you, child. I'm sure that Christ will, too."

His sermon would require some changes, but it didn't matter; he could make amendments as he want along. The pastor felt as if a crushing weight had just been lifted from his shoulders. He was grinning like a schoolboy by the time he reached the stage.

IN TWENTY-SOME YEARS of carrying a badge Norm Grant had learned to trust his instincts, listen to his hunches. You would never find it in the manual, and if you publicly admitted it, your cases would be booted out of court before a liberal judge could reach his gavel, but the plain fact was that cops *knew* things, sometimes in ways civilians couldn't fathom.

Soldiers, he suspected, picked up something of the same sixth sense in combat, making life-and-death decisions on a daily basis, knowing one mistake could get somebody killed. Grant never laughed at tales of female intuition, ESP or anything along those lines. There were a lot of fakes and hustlers on the street, without a doubt, but the lieutenant also knew the human mind was capable of picking up on messages, vibrations, that the eye and ear could never grasp.

Right now the vibes were bad and getting worse. Grant's instinct told him Amos Carr was still in danger. Never mind the guy's pretense that everything was fine and dandy. If the former cop's suspicions of a homicidal cult were accurate—and Grant was now ready to accept the substance of them—then he was looking at a heavy payback situation. Carr had iced not one, but two John Does with likely cult connections, both of whom were definitely hitters. At least one had managed to escape, and there was every reason to believe that he would be communicating with superiors, requesting new instructions, drawing orders for a second try.

Disgustedly Grant dropped his greasy burger in its plastic basket, scrubbing off his hands with paper napkins. No matter how he tried he couldn't find a way around the problem. He would have to have another talk with Carr and make the guy accept protection.

Leaving money on the counter, Grant made his way toward a pay phone near the door. On second thought, he pocketed the quarter, stepped outside and headed for his car.

No point in waking Carr if he was sleeping. On the other hand, it wouldn't hurt to check in on him, have a quiet word or two if he was still awake. Or Grant could take a look around the place, discuss security with the nurses on duty, perhaps order up a uniform from patrol, just in case. Carr wasn't going out this evening anyway; he didn't have to know that he was being watched, unless somebody spilled the beans.

Grant turned the volume on the squawk box and put his car in motion, rolling through the night.

THE HOUSE IN ENGLEWOOD identified by Lucian Slate was big and old, its weathered face the dominating feature of a narrow residential street near Progress Park. Mack Bolan noted the pale light in a solitary downstairs window, one car sitting in the driveway outside a locked garage.

He drove around the block and found himself an alley, cut between the rows of older houses to permit a weekly garbage pickup in the rear. Proceeding with his headlights out, Bolan counted rooftops, had no trouble picking out his target as he coasted two doors past and killed the rental's engine.

He was dressed in blacksuit for the probe, his face and hands blacked with camouflage cosmetics. The Beretta 93-R hung in shoulder rigging, while the mighty Desert Eagle

.44 rode Bolan's hip on military webbing. Canvas pouches at his waist held extra magazines for both weapons, a bandolier across his chest providing ready access to the backup ammunition for the Uzi submachine gun he carried on a shoulder sling. A Ka-bar fighting knife and several stun grenades completed the ensemble, clipped to Bolan's harness where his hands could find them instantly.

The hour was growing late, and Bolan knew the odds were long against discovering his targets—or their captives—all at home. If they were operating on their normal schedule, there would be another sacrifice that night, and some of them might be en route to its location at this moment.

A light inside the ancient rambling house told Bolan there was still a chance, however slim, of finding someone home. The Executioner would take whatever he could get at this point, and be thankful if the mission didn't blow up in his face.

He'd selected stun grenades, instead of fragmentation or incendiaries, with the prisoners in mind. If they were still alive, he didn't plan on jeopardizing their survival for the sake of bringing down the house.

A covert entry was the key, and Bolan trusted that the hit team hadn't wasted any time on installing alarms. He scaled the wooden fence and hit a combat crouch on touchdown in the yard. He spent a moment checking out the house, alert to any sign that he'd been observed. Then Bolan closed the distance in a rush, flattening himself against the rough wooden siding.

The back door opened onto a spacious kitchen. It was locked, but age and rust collaborated with his pick as Bolan worked the tumblers. The hinges gave a tiny squeal as Bolan entered, and he held the Uzi ready to respond if he was challenged from the shadows.

Nothing.

Bolan moved through darkened rooms, along a musty hallway, homing on the only source of light. A lamp was burning in the parlor, but the room was empty. The warrior cast a glance in the direction of the stairs, prepared to try the second story next, but he was diverted by a sound emanating from the rear.

Retracing his steps toward the kitchen, Bolan veered hard left, into a pantry, and found another staircase that led to the basement. With its door closed, the stairwell would pass for a closet, but the door was standing partly open now, faint light spilling through the aperture. He could make out muffled voices from below.

Correction: one voice, male, its tone reflecting something like amusement.

He held his breath and eased the door back, slipping through to stand at the top of the stairs. He had a clear view of the basement, two girls bound and huddled on the floor, a young man kneeling in front of one and fumbling with her clothes.

"No reason we can't have a little party of our own," the guy was saying, chuckling to himself.

Bolan let the Uzi dangle on its sling and unsheathed the Beretta as he started his descent. Surprisingly the risers made no sound. He hesitated halfway down the stairs.

Downrange his target had the girl's blouse open and was working on her bra. "Come on, babe. Party time."

"The party's cancelled," Bolan told him.

He expected a reaction, but the guy surprised him, swiveling and springing backward, digging for a weapon underneath his jacket as his mouth dropped open, scared eyes going wide.

An automatic filled the guy's hand when Bolan fired, the Beretta whispering its single word. A parabellum crusher closed the gap between them, drilling through the target's shoulder, spinning him around and spraying blood in all directions. Bolan heard his side arm clatter on the concrete as the guy fell facedown.

He gave the girls a glance in passing, found one watching him with nervous eyes; the other seemed to be catatonic. Neither looked to be in any danger at the moment, and he moved on to his adversary, stretching out on foot to flip the young man over on his back.

The cultist's face showed all the elements of early shock, but he was conscious and he tried to rise before he focused on the pistol, realizing it was hopeless.

"Man, I need a doctor."

"So I see."

"You gotta help me."

"Wrong. The only thing I have to do is watch you bleed, unless you tell me what I need to know."

"So ask."

"There were two more prisoners."

"Too late, man. Gone."

"Gone where?"

"You missed 'em. They've been chosen for the ritual."

"How long?"

"You missed 'em," he repeated, drifting, losing focus.

Bolan helped him back to reality by stepping on his shoulder. Pain worked wonders when it came to clearing out a mental fog. The cultist gave a shriek and squirmed away from Bolan's touch.

"How long?"

"I didn't time them, dammit. Ten or fifteen minutes, I don't know."

"Where were they going?"

"That's the beauty of it, man. The cops'll never scope it out."

"Why's that?"

"They never count on lightning striking twice, you know? They won't have any piggies staking out Mount Olivet."

"How many in the party?"

"Scratch, Snake and Thorn. Two sheep. They got a double-header, man."

The soldier straightened, spending several precious moments in consideration of the news.

"I need a doctor. " He was fading in the stretch.

"I called one," Bolan told him.

"Yeah? Thanks. What did he say?"

"You didn't make it."

"Hey—"

He put another round between the glassy eyes and backtracked to the prisoners. The first one flinched as Bolan drew his knife, slicing through her ropes, but there was no response from number two. He didn't have the time to spend on therapy.

"There's a telephone in the kitchen," he told the girl who had her act together. "Call the operator and ask for the police. You understand?"

"I hear you."

"Do it now."

He left her kneeling on the floor and put the place behind him. Every heartbeat counted now, and he was running well behind the pack. Ten minutes was a lifetime in the hellgrounds, and he couldn't count on fate to intervene.

22

Amos Carr had never learned the trick of using bedpans. They were cold, uncomfortable and threw his body so off balance that he was inclined to soil himself, his bedding and the floor instead of letting the device fulfill its function. Maybe, he had thought from time to time, if they designed the beds with little cut-out holes, like toilets, where the bed pans could be nestled flush—so to speak—with the mattress...

As it was, when Mother Nature came to call that night, the former captain of police knew he'd never have a prayer if he relied on the bedpan that a "thoughtful" nurse had planted on his nightstand after dinner. He'd have to reach the bathroom on his own, in spite of any pain that might result from his nocturnal prowl.

For starters Amos used the bed controls to help himself sit up, then lowered it again when he was in position, pale legs dangling toward the floor. It was a bitch to scoot across the mattress, feeling for the icy vinyl flooring with his naked toes, but Carr was able to negotiate the move by slow degrees.

My first time shot, he thought, and it *would* have to be my ass.

He made it to his feet and teetered for a moment, waiting for his balance to return. Carr hadn't walked a step since he'd been extracted from his car by paramedics, and he felt a little like a child, compelled to learn the art anew.

He took a pair of shuffling steps, returned and fetched the little .38 from underneath his pillow. It was silly, packing heat to use the head, but Grant had gotten to him, just a little, with his obvious concern about another attempt on his life.

If anything Carr's brush with death was overdue. In more than twenty years behind a badge he'd escaped from several rugged situations with no more than minor cuts and bruises. On the two occasions he'd used his weapon, prior to this afternoon, his adversaries hadn't fired a shot in Carr's direction. Since "retirement," working with the cults and crazies, he'd listened to a nonstop flow of threats from heavy-breathers, superpatriots and lunatics who honestly believed they were in touch with God, or His equivalent. Carr had been alternately damned by televangelists and Satanists, assorted Aryans and Hare Krishna freaks who carried automatic weapons underneath their saffron robes. And through it all, he had emerged unscathed.

Until today.

The toilet seat was cold and hard, but Amos clenched his teeth and did his duty. Finished, he was reaching for the stainless-steel lever when a scuffling sound beyond the door caught his attention.

He rose, the linen johnny gaping open at his back, and pressed one eye against the narrow opening where he'd left the door ajar. The hairs on his nape rose as he watched a tall young man in doctor's white attack his bedding, stabbing at the rumpled blankets with a long, thin knife.

It took perhaps a heartbeat for the would-be killer to discover his mistake. He cursed and glanced around the room, his eyes immediately settling on the bathroom door.

By that time, Amos was emerging in his knee-length flapper, bringing up the .38 in two big hands. "Hold it right there," he growled.

The young man dropped his knife and slipped a hand inside his lab coat, digging for another weapon.

"Don't."

Carr fired on instinct, twice, before the other man's pistol cleared his belt. The impact rocked his target, speckled crimson on the snowy jacket, spinning him around. Incredibly he didn't fall, but rather made it to the door, used spastic hands to yank it open, disappeared outside.

Carr hobbled after him, a wounded bear, prepared to finish what he started.

GRANT HAD TROUBLE with a parking space and finally nosed his cruiser in against a stretch of bright red curb, tossing a cardboard Police sign onto the dashboard as he exited and locked the driver's door behind him. He would only be a moment, and emergencies were routed to another entrance far removed. Besides, he told himself, rank had its privileges.

He waited for an elevator to disgorge its human cargo, found a corner for himself adjacent to the door as late arrivals tumbled in behind him, anxious for a flying glimpse of incapacitated friends or relatives. Inside the rising box, it smelled like hairspray, perspiration and Vitalis.

Grateful for the opportunity to disembark on three, Grant watched the doors slide shut upon the sweaty load and made a sour face. The public. In his oath of office Grant had vowed to serve them, with his life if necessary, but he often wondered who the hell "they" really were. The public he encountered on a daily basis was a ragtag mob of me-first assholes, shoving one another—often killing one another—as they grappled for a place in line, a bigger slice of pie. It seemed preposterous that Grant should owe them anything, much less his blood and last dying breath.

He moved along the corridor, avoiding contact with the drifting individuals who blocked his path. He recognized the nurse on duty—an attractive blonde—and smiled at her in sympathy as she directed a quartet of heavyweights to their appointed destination. If she saw the smile, she gave no sign.

Carr's room was less than forty feet away when muffled gunshots echoed in the corridor. He drew his .38, was closing, when a scarecrow in a bloody lab coat staggered through the door, an automatic pistol in his hand.

"That's far enough!" Grant warned him, aiming his revolver from a combat stance.

The young man fired at Grant, missing by a yard, and Grant responded, squeezing off a round that struck his target just above the belt line.

Reeling, clutching at himself, the shooter went down on his knees, still firing, sprinkling the floor with empty cartridges. Death whispered past the homicide detective, left and right, before he emptied his revolver at the dying gunman. The impact twisted Grant's assailant, blew a ragged mouse hole in his shoulder. But the guy refused to fall.

A figure with pale, knobby knees staggered into the corridor behind Grant's assailant, squeezing off two rounds in rapid-fire, dropping the gunner in a heap. By the time Grant moved forward to scoop up the guy's .22, Carr was clutching the back of his robe, going red in the face from exertion or plain old embarrassment. The detective couldn't tell.

"You were right," Amos said. "They came back."

JINX HAVERSHAM had once suggested that he ought to pack a firearm on the night shift, and his supervisors at the cemetery had been scandalized. What sort of trouble could he have with corpses?

It took a human sacrifice and reams of bad publicity to change their minds, but Jinx was armed this night, despite the fact that homicide detectives airily dismissed the possibility of any further incidents. The killers didn't work that way; they never hit the same spot twice.

Okay.

Suppose the dicks were right. So what? It made Jinx feel a whole lot better, strapping on the heavy Smith & Wesson Magnum that he hadn't fired in years. The weapon and its Sam Browne rig were legacies of other times, when he had played night watchman at a warehouse in Chicago. It had been a cushy job, until the night he got a bit too comfortable, dozing at his post, and let a pair of thieves waltz off with several thousand dollars worth of merchandise.

Tonight Jinx Haversham was wide awake.

Each time he closed his eyes the image of a naked, mangled body popped up in his mind and banished sleep. The bastards who could violate a teenage girl that way were capable of anything, and Jinx knew all about the watchman who was missing from Arvada Cemetery. There was speculation in the papers that he might have killed the girl discovered there the previous night, but Jinx wasn't persuaded.

He was betting that the watchman had been killed, as well, his body carried off to camouflage the crime.

So much for the eternal-rest routine.

Death came on soon enough without an invitation, and for all his run of sorry luck Jinx Haversham wasn't about to cut his own time short through negligence. It bothered him that someone had invaded his domain, and he was sick about the girl, but he wasn't prepared to join her yet. The gun was basically for his protection, and he wouldn't hesitate to use it if the need arose.

With any luck, Jinx thought, he'd be worrying for nothing. If the cops were right the killers might be miles away by now, already looking for another town to terrorize.

But if the cops were wrong...

He paused beside the lighted mausoleum to check his weapon, swinging out the cylinder to verify its load. That done, he revved the golf cart's small electric engine and continued through the darkness on patrol.

THE GAG PREVENTED Cass from speaking, but her captors hadn't bothered with a blindfold this time. Obviously they didn't intend to leave a witness to their crimes.

Her back was turned to Alix, but she felt the girl nearby, her slender body trembling with fear. Her tough facade had broken down as they were loaded in the van, and Cass could hear her weeping softly, whimpers stifled by the gag that cut into her cheeks.

She closed her eyes and concentrated on their three abductors, trying desperately to read their auras, find a weak point she could take advantage of. The driver, Felix, had been one of those who snatched her from the shop, and he'd been excited then, keyed up. Tonight he seemed relaxed, almost sedated, and Cass wondered if the cultists had been taking drugs. She mentally prepared herself to take advantage of impaired reaction time.

The watcher, known as Snake, seemed perfectly alert, a little agitated—hungry. He was anxious for the ceremony to begin, aroused by thoughts of blood and violent sex. He wouldn't make it easy for his captives, but in ardor there was room for error.

Cass was most concerned about the leader, formally addressed as Scratch by his companions. It wasn't his name, but she immediately recognized the label's dark significance. The Devil. This one was devoted to his mission at a deeper level than the others. He was sane, albeit twisted, capable of channeling his rage, inflicting death and suffering with surgical precision.

He was evil, and his aura reeked of carrion.

Escape wouldn't be easy—and in fact might prove impossible—but Cass was bound to try. She wouldn't let herself be meekly led to slaughter. Working on her bonds, she prayed that Alix would have nerve and strength enough to help her when the time was right.

At some point, she supposed, their captors must untie them for convenience in the preparation of their sacrifice. Outnumbered as they were, there would be little chance of breaking free—no chance, perhaps, of actually outrunning their abductors, but if Cass could reach a weapon, like the pistol she knew Scratch carried in his belt...

Her last attempt at self-defense had been a pitiful performance, and her ribs still ached from where the one called Snake had kicked her. Sluggish off the mark, she had allowed her fear to overcome the anger she felt inside, and she hadn't been quick enough to make the kill.

A gun would turn the tables, though, reducing the advantages of strength and numbers. Any child could pull a trigger, and at point-blank range she wouldn't have to worry about her accuracy, either. If she registered determination, let them know she was prepared to shoot, there was a chance she might not have to kill.

A fantasy, Cass realized. Her enemies were guilty of at least two Colorado murders, with their "special circumstances" making Scratch and company eligible for the gas chamber. An arrest would mean the end of freedom; life inside a cage would be the very best they could expect.

And they would fight. She knew that. If Cass succeeded in disarming Scratch, she'd be forced to use the gun, kill all of them.

So be it.

When they freed her hands, however briefly, she would make her move, and they would have to kill her this time to regain control. If nothing else she would deprive them of their sacrifice and spoil their ritual.

When they released her hands.

Cass closed her eyes and waited for the moment to arrive.

YORK HALF EXPECTED guards outside Mount Olivet, and he was grateful for the open gates. He remained alert as Felix piloted the van through darkness, switching off the headlights, navigating by the moon and the light that managed to escape the mausoleum behind them. There was still a chance that cops might have the place staked out, so York kept one hand tucked inside his jacket, inches from the pistol, as they made their rounds.

"This is good."

As Felix parked the van, York flexed his arm, refusing to acknowledge pain from where the little bitch had cut him. She was quick, but careless; with a little forethought, better aim, she could have blinded him or sliced his jugular. Impulsive action was the hallmark of a child, and she would never have a second chance to learn from her mistake.

The Wiccan was another story. Fear had slowed her hand, and Snake had intervened before she found the will to strike with purpose. Given time she might become a formidable adversary, but he had no time to spare. The contest would be ending here tonight, and she would serve the Master as a graphic lesson to her spineless friends, a warning for the meddlers of the world.

"Let's get set up." ·

The family crypt was small but it was adequate. York snapped the padlock with a crowbar, spent a moment on the latch and then he was inside. His flashlight beam illuminated dusty caskets, stacked on shelves to either side like bunk beds where the campers never answered reveille.

He stood aside as Felix started hauling in the gear, arranging candles. He shook a spray can and handed it to York. As leader it was his task to inscribe the circle, and he set to work immediately, long experience permitting him to do it freehand, coming close to geometrical perfection. Stepping clear, he spent another moment on the pentagram and its attendant symbols, standing back to let the whole thing dry before they proceeded.

"We need an altar," he announced. "These ought to do."

The newest-looking caskets were extracted from their shelves, laid side by side within the magic circle. One for each of their reluctant sheep.

He slipped on his robe, waited for a moment while his two attendants made themselves presentable. It was the smallest group of celebrants that York had ever seen, but it would have to serve, considering the circumstances.

"Bring them in."

York stood by and watched as Snake and Felix fetched the prisoners, a sharp knife severing their ankle ropes, but leaving wrists securely tied, their gags in place. It would be easier to drug them, but he liked the thought of seeing terror in their eyes. For safety's sake their wrists and ankles could be tethered to the coffin handles, leaving them immobilized while he got on with the ceremony.

It was perfect.

He could feel the old, familiar racing of his pulse, the tingling in his fingertips. A few more moments now. Not long at all.

THE HEADLIGHTS HAD ALERTED Jinx at once. The intruders would have to use the pavement, thereby giving Haversham an edge. His golf cart was designed to travel over grass, and he could take a shortcut, gaining time if he was careful to avoid the headstones.

Steering in between the markers, racing through the open spaces, Jinx ran down the possibilities. A mourner calling late, for instance, visiting the gravesite of a loved one…but would any mourner try to navigate without his lights? It made no sense at all, and Haversham was certain that the van meant trouble. Maybe not the killers—other ghouls might be attracted by the bad publicity, as well—but Jinx was spoiling for a fight.

The thing to do, he realized, was double back and telephone for the police. It was the reasonable, safe alternative, but he couldn't forget his first sight of a young girl's mutilated body sprawled among the headstones. If her killers *had* returned, it meant another lamb for slaughter, and a lot could happen in the time it took to call police, sit back and wait for their arrival.

People could get killed, for instance.

Sure, like me, Jinx thought, but anger and determination conquered any fear he might have felt. He had a job to do, and he wasn't about to delegate the task to anybody else.

The van had stopped, its outline a smudge against the lighter foliage, half-concealed within the shadow of a family crypt. Jinx slowed his golf cart, finally parked it, fearing they might hear him coming and make a break before he had an opportunity to bring them under fire.

He circled through the darkness on foot, closing from a hundred yards. He kept the van in sight as much as possible, detecting movement there, a flash of dome light revealing human silhouettes. He didn't have a chance to count his enemies, but numbers had no meaning for him now. Jinx owed the bastards something, and he meant to pay his debt.

At fifty yards he caught the sound of muffled voices, but the words were unintelligible. Frightened, determined not to let the fear take over, Jinx drew his revolver from its holster, moving forward in a crouch that made his legs complain.

You're out of shape, he told himself, and wasn't that a news flash? Pushing sixty, and he still expected all his joints and muscles to perform like he was twenty-one. Some joke.

Tonight, however, Jinx expected all the old reserves to function on command. He might not have another chance to prove himself, make good on his responsibilities, and he was damned if he would blow the chance.

The shoe was on the other foot, and anyone who tried to make him play the fool would have a few surprises waiting. Painful ones at that.

Before they made a fool of Jinx again, the little shits would have to kill him first.

And that, they would discover, was easier said than done.

23

There seemed to be no easy way around Mount Olivet. The cemetery was a large one—second largest in the Denver area—and Bolan had no hope of pinning down his enemies by cruising the perimeter. In any case, two-thirds of the perimeter was inaccessible by car, and he wasn't about to sacrifice mobility by running laps around the place on foot.

That narrowed his options drastically, and Bolan kept his eyes peeled as he drove through wrought-iron gates, extinguishing his lights as a concession to security. He cranked the windows down in hopes of hearing something, anything, above the grumble of the rental's engine. To his right the track wound off through darkness, and he followed it, aware that he could never tour the grounds in time to pick the hunters out by serendipity alone.

The gunshot sounded from somewhere on his left. He guessed it was a Magnum. A lighter semiautomatic fired seconds later in response.

He stood on the accelerator, tossing caution out the window. Someone had engaged the enemy ahead of Bolan, and he didn't mean to miss the party. Following the asphalt, scanning ranks of monuments and markers for any sign of action, Bolan's night eyes picked out the van at a hundred yards.

He tapped the brakes, then killed the engine, coasting to a stop. No point in advertising his arrival if the troops were otherwise engaged. A second Magnum round went off as Bolan left the car, and this time he could see the muzzle-flash downrange.

Someone was crouched beside the van and firing in the general direction of a smallish crypt, with those inside the house of death returning fire. It looked to be a standoff for the moment, but the Executioner couldn't afford to let it ride. Police might be en route already, and he knew the consequences of giving up his prey to the authorities.

The case would be a show trial, like the Manson circus in Los Angeles, and the eventual results would be the same. A few specific agents of the cult would be imprisoned for a while, and on the street their brethren would continue with business as usual.

It wasn't good enough, by half.

The Executioner heard doomsday numbers falling as he went to even up the score.

JINX HAVERSHAM HAD WORKED his way around the crypt to reach the van, his progress unobserved by those inside. The door was standing open, giving him a view of men in flowing robes, and a pair of females who were obviously not too thrilled about their role in the proceedings. Having seen the end result firsthand, Jinx didn't blame the girls a bit.

His hands were trembling as he aimed his Smith & Wesson. Three men, at least, and there might still be others he hadn't seen. Jinx didn't like the odds, but he had come in search of trouble, dammit, and he'd found what he was looking for.

Two options, then. He could retreat and call the cops, after all, with no attempt to help the prisoners, or he could get up off his ass and *move*, do something right for once and make it count.

The choice was easy, since he really had no choice at all.

He rose on creaking knees, was ready to advance when something—some*one*—blocked the candlelight, emerging from the crypt. A tall man, blond hair hanging to his shoulders, straightened his robe and moved toward the van. Jinx saw his margin of surprise go up in smoke.

"Don't move!" he barked, emerging from the cover of the van, his Magnum gripped in trembling hands.

The blonde reacted like a pro, immediately feinting left, then right, retreating as he dragged a pistol out from underneath his robe. Jinx fired—too late—the combination of his weapon's recoil and a moving target throwing off his aim. He heard his bullet ricochet off marble, whining into space, and then his target was returning fire, a near-miss driving Jinx back under cover.

He could hear them babbling excitedly inside the crypt, although he couldn't make out the words. An angry voice was rasping orders, trying to regain control, while Haversham's assailant popped another round in the direction of the van. This time the slug exploded window glass.

Jinx risked a glance around the fender, saw his target framed in silhouette and fired a shot one-handed, smiling as the head ducked out of sight. Another miss, but ricochets inside the crypt would at least keep the bastards hopping.

Four rounds left in his gun, and twelve more in the ammunition pouches on his belt. Jinx hadn't come prepared to lay a siege, but he would do his best and hang on while he waited for—

For what?

Mount Olivet wasn't exactly downtown Denver. There were residential streets adjoining Eldridge, on the west, but that was close to half a mile away. The Magnum should be audible, assuming anyone was outside listening, without a television, stereo, or screaming kids for background noise. Assuming, right, that anyone who heard the shots cared half enough to call police and send them... where?

Jinx knew how a noise could sneak around and fool you in the dark, confusing distance and direction, making it impossible to trace the source. From half a mile or more, the sound of shots would be a phantom, echoing from everywhere and nowhere.

Which left him on his own, to see it through.

Jinx caught a slight movement on his flank and prepared to turn. When the muzzle of a weapon pressed against his cheek, images of a wasted life began to pass before his eyes.

"Relax," a strong voice told him, "I'm a friend."

As if to prove it, unseen hands withdrew the weapon, granting him the liberty to turn.

The new arrival was a big man, dressed in black, with guns and knives all over him. His face was smeared with war paint, like a jungle fighter.

"I'd say we've got a situation here," Bolan said, shifting so that he could watch the crypt.

"I'd say."

"All right, here's what we do..."

THE FIRST SHOT startled Alix, images of freedom flashing through her mind with scenes of grim disaster following in hot pursuit. Her guard, the one called Felix, had untied her hands a moment earlier, propelling her in the direction of the caskets, when his sidekick, Snake, had cursed and muttered something underneath his breath.

"What's wrong?"

"The chalice, man. I'll be right back."

No sooner was he out the door than a new voice barked, "Don't move!" A heartbeat later thunder echoed in the crypt, and Snake was dodging backward through the open doorway, holding a pistol and popping off three rounds in rapid-fire.

For several seconds Alix was forgotten by her captors, both of them retreating toward the door, where Snake was crouching, squeezing off another shot into the darkness. A bullet struck the marble wall ten feet in front of Alix, whining off in ricochet and battering around the walls like something from a bad cartoon.

She hit the deck and scrabbled toward the corner where Cass lay, still bound and waiting for the knife. Forgotten prayers were surfacing about the time the bullet spent its force and clattered to the floor beside her face.

A strong hand caught Alix by the collar, hauling her to her feet. A knife was pressed against her cheek.

"Come on, bitch," Felix grated. "You're my ticket out of here."

She twisted in his grasp, kicked backward, found his shin. The knife bit through her earlobe, drawing blood, but he released Alix long enough for her to reverse her stance and aim a solid kick at her assailant's groin.

She caught his thigh instead, and Felix staggered back against the shelves where the coffins had been lifted out, a kerosene lamp planted in their place to supplement faint candlelight. His thrashing elbow caught the lamp and knocked it to the floor, where it shattered, liquid fire expanding in a pool around his feet.

His robe went up in flames, the knife forgotten as he tried to shed the burning garment, beating at the fire with blistered palms. A shriek of panic tore his comrades from the entryway as Felix made his break, a human comet streaking through the door.

YORK LEAPED BACK as Felix staggered past him, trailing sparks and screams. A flash of heat against York's face, and he was gone, his footsteps smoking in the grass outside.

The burst of automatic fire was short, precise. It brought the human fireball down, and simultaneously ushered in a whole new ball game.

York wasn't about to stick his head around the corner to chance a look. He would be a sitting duck if he peered into darkness from a lighted room. In fact, the lights were problem number one, and he immediately moved to snuff the ring of candles, trampling them underfoot. When he was finished, only traces of the spattered kerosene still burned, providing dim illumination in the crypt.

He shoved the little redhead toward the corner where his other captive lay, then slugged her with his pistol, putting her away. It hadn't felt like lethal contact, but he wasn't worried, either way. It really didn't matter who survived the night, as long as York was one of those who walked away.

Escape was paramount. If he was taken into custody, the network would be forced to disavow him, turn their backs and let him take the fall alone. It was established policy—York had no quarrel with that—but he didn't intend to be treated like another head case, sitting in the dock while shrinks and lawyers made their reputations trading on his name.

He reached the older captive, Cass, and dragged her to her feet. She tried to pull away from him, but it was hopeless. Tangling his fingers in her hair, York pulled her head back, brought his lips close against her ear.

"We're walking out of here together," he informed her. "You're my ticket. Any tricks, you're canceled, understand?"

She nodded—tried to nod—and finally muttered, "Yes."

"That's fine. You do your part, you might survive. A bonus, mmm?" He turned to Snake and said, "We're leaving, man."

Snake grinned and fed his piece another magazine. "I'm ready."

"Great. You first."

Snake held his gaze for several seconds, nodded, moving toward the redhead. He tried to lift her, then shook her like a dusty throw rug, getting no response.

"Goddammit!"

"What the hell, she's finished. Do it."

"Yeah."

The tall blonde braced himself beside the open doorway, took a few deep breaths to stoke himself for action. When he smiled at York, there seemed to be no animosity at all.

"I'll see you, man."

"I'm coming."

"For the Master."

"For the Master."

JINX HAD SHIFTED toward the rear end of the van, and he was crouching in its shadow when the burning erupted from the crypt, flapping arms like wings of fire, as if he thought it possible to fly. The jungle fighter dropped him with a well-aimed burst before Jinx had a chance to aim, and that was just as well. His hands were *really* shaking now, and Haversham wasn't convinced that he could hit the broad side of a barn if he was given half an hour to aim.

Inside, someone was busy putting out the lights, a few stray flames imparting eerie shadows to the crypt's interior. Jinx caught a hint of movement near the door and wrote it off as his imagination. More than ever, with that heap of laundry burning up on the grass, he wished that he had telephoned the police.

Too late. His ass was on the firing line, and it was *way* too late for bugging out.

Whatever else he might have been, Jinx Haversham wasn't a quitter.

Shadows in the doorway blotted out the fitful firelight as another figure broke from cover. In his mind, Jinx thought he recognized the blonde from moments earlier, but there was no way to confirm ID before the running figure started blasting with an automatic pistol.

He was firing toward the front end, pinning down the jungle fighter, never giving Jinx a second thought, when Haversham reared up and squeezed off two quick rounds, the recoil thrumming in his wrists and rattling his dentures. Number two was wasted, but the first round clipped his target on the run, a shoulder wound that knocked the guy off stride.

Incredibly the runner didn't fall. He turned on Jinx, his pistol wavering, then found his target, squeezing off so rapidly that three shots came out sounding like a single blast.

Jinx took one round above his belt line, left of center, and he heard the others pass him by like hornets. Startled by the lack of pain, he emptied out the Magnum, scoring one more hit before his rubber legs betrayed him and he sat down, hard.

The leading blonde was lining up a kill shot, breathing through his mouth and through a chest wound, when the jungle fighter dropped him in his tracks. Jinx felt the Smith & Wesson slipping from his fingers, grimaced as it clattered to the pavement. You could spoil a weapon's finish, tossing it around like that. He hoped the pistol wasn't scratched.

A snatch of childhood prayer came back from nowhere.

"Now I lay me down to sleep..."

So MUCH FOR SNAKE.

York gave the witch's hair a painful twist. "We're on."

She struggled briefly as he pushed her toward the open doorway, got the message when he jammed the muzzle of his automatic in her ear.

"Hair trigger, bitch," he growled. "If you wiggle too much, you could be a topless dancer."

Edging through the door, he caught a glimpse of Felix, smoldering, a mess the dead man's mother wouldn't recognize. Snake's broken body lay between York and the van, leaking blood onto the grass. Behind the van a guy in a khaki uniform was stretched out on the pavement, dead or wounded.

Shifting his position, York released the witch's hair and looped an arm around her body. He clutched her tight against him, ducked his head to compensate for differences in height and maximize her value as a human shield.

There had to be another gunner somewhere.

A tall man dressed in black stepped out from behind the van. He held an automatic pistol in his fist.

York stopped, secured behind his prisoner.

"What's shaking, man?"

"Show's over," Bolan said, angling for a clear shot with his .44.

"I think you've got it backward. I'm the one who says it's finished."

"Look around. You're running short on troops."

"Who needs them? I've got life insurance."

Bolan saw the autoloader prodding Cass's cheek. A shot from his position would be sure to take her down before it nailed his target.

"Let her go. We'll play this one-on-one."

"Can't say I like the odds."

"They're all you've got."

"Don't push me, man. I'll waste this bitch."

"Your funeral."

"Don't push it, man. I haven't got a lot to lose."

"Fact is, I know of several agencies that wouldn't mind a deal. Your testimony in return for limited immunity."

"No thanks. I'll play the cards I've got."

"You're looking at a dead man's hand."

The shooter's laughter sent a chill down Bolan's spine.

Cass knew that she was dead if she got in the van. She didn't think Blanski was prepared to shoot her, but she knew her captor wouldn't hesitate to silence one more witness once they made their getaway. And she was running out of time.

Gambling, York pushed her forward, taking two steps toward the van.

"Don't try it," Bolan cautioned.

"Lighten up, man. You're not going to shoot this bitch."

Another step, and Cass contrived to stumble, one leg slipping out in front of her, the other folding back. Behind her, tethered hands were splayed against the denim fabric of her captor's jeans.

"Get up, goddammit!"

As he hauled her up the pistol wavered, and she found his crotch with fingers flexing into talons, digging deep. He gasped, and his weapon cracked across her skull, propelling her through the darkness streaked with fire.

The woman's move had taken Bolan by surprise, but he recovered in a heartbeat, squeezing off a round at thirty feet. The impact punched his target through a full three-sixty, shattering his shoulder joint and nearly ripping off his gun arm.

Cass was out of it but breathing. Bolan found her pulse, and it was strong. A recon of the crypt revealed another prisoner in much the same condition, stunned but stable, and he placed her gently on the grass beside Cass.

Bolan moved to stand above his fallen adversary, leveling his .44 at a fact that showed the symptoms of advancing shock.

"You think it's finished?" Delving into hidden reservoirs of strength, the wounded man put on a fair approximation of a smile. "You haven't even scratched the surface."

"It's a start."

"Too late. You're all too late."

"We'll see."

The earth was soaking up York's blood, and he was rambling. "Second coming, man. Forget it. New world taking over."

"It's a pity you won't be around to see it."

Sudden anger cut through the haze, and crystal clarity reclaimed the eyes. "It isn't finished. Nothing's finished, man."

"You are," the Executioner reminded him.

"The Master's waiting."

"Bon voyage."

The Desert Eagle's thunder echoed back and forth among the headstones, almost loud enough to wake the dead.

EPILOGUE

The audience was on its feet when Jordan Braithwaite came onstage. He waited for the sound of voices to subside, the thousands to be seated. Leaning toward the microphone, he tried to moderate his voice and keep it gentle, reverent.

"I'm sure that most of you have heard about last night's events," he said. "It isn't in the Christian way to say 'I told you so,' but there are times when truth cries out for recognition. Times when God's omnipotent design must be revealed."

He felt them hanging on his every word, prepared to buy what he was selling. For the first time in a year the minister experienced a sense of absolute control.

"Last night—"

The microphone went dead. He registered the difference with his ears and saw the faces of his flock, impatient for the message that had been delayed. He turned to scan the wings, eyes searching for his new technician, hired that afternoon. It seemed a relatively simple thing to keep the PA system functioning, and yet . . .

"Your hit team," a voice he didn't recognize said, amplified a thousand times. "They've taken prisoners. I need an address."

The audience began to stir, and Braithwaite tapped his fingertips against the microphone without result.

He recognized the voice of Lucian Slate, reciting an address in Englewood. "An old two-story job," the dark man answered from beyond the grave. "Big basement. It could use a coat of whitewash."

"So could you. My second question. Why?"

"Why not?" Slate countered, disembodied tones as strong as ever. "Power, wealth, the pleasures of the flesh. We don't believe in all that crap about how suffering on earth will guarantee eternal satisfaction in the afterlife. Far better for the sheep to suffer, while the Master and his chosen people relish every moment of the here and now."

"Including human sacrifice?"

Braithwaite felt beads of sweat collecting on his forehead, underneath his arms. The audience was stirring now, a number of people rising from their seats. He shouted to be heard, but Slate's voice drowned him out.

"The ritual release of energy at death invokes the spirits who would do our bidding. Blood is in the nature of an offering, a bonding ceremony."

"Bonding?"

"Flesh and spirit. Man and Lucifer. It's not unlike the Roman Catholic communion ceremony."

"And the band?"

This can't be happening, Braithwaite thought, but he found no comfort in the thought that he was going mad.

"Spoiled children," Slate was saying. "Oh, they have their uses, but they're soft. They still believe we're drinking calf's blood in our celebrations."

"What they don't know, mmm?"

"Precisely."

Braithwaite had a stranglehold around the microphone, to no avail. The booming voices overwhelmed his efforts to be heard.

"Why Braithwaite?"

"Once again, why not? The man's a pompous ass, but he has followers. Enough, perhaps, to put him in the White House—or at least a senate seat. With adequate promotion and support, the reverend has possibilities."

Members of the audience were weeping now, some shouting, others staring at the podium with eyes reflecting stark betrayal.

"Did he approach you first?"

In vain, the pastor shouted, "It's a vicious lie, I swear."

"I've never been precisely clear on all the details," Slate responded. "Overtures were made, by one side or the other.

Cash changed hands. A schedule was arranged. We've kept our bargain with Braithwaite.''

"And the murders?''

Wailing from the crowd. An usher tried to keep a burly man from moving toward the stage, and he was flattened for his trouble.

"He requested incidents to dramatize his sermons. We complied. Is that what this all about? Did Braithwaite send you here?''

The pastor fled, before his flock could rouse itself and reach him. Brushing past the hangers-on who gaped at him in horror, he was halfway to his dressing room when the detectives—Grant and Miller, he recalled—moved in to block his path.

"I have a warrant here for your arrest,'' Lieutenant Grant informed him.

"This is nonsense.''

"You have the right to remain silent,'' Miller recited. "Anything you say can and will be used against you in a court of law. You have the right to an attorney. If you can't afford one—that's a laugh—the court will choose a lawyer for you prior to any questioning.''

"That won't be necessary,'' Braithwaite told them, trying to preserve some vestige of his dignity. "I'm not afraid to speak. I *will* be heard.''

"That's fine,'' Grant said, producing handcuffs from a pocket of his coat. "They tell me confession's good for the soul.''

Nile Barrabas's most daring mission is about to begin . . .

THE BARRABAS BLITZ

JACK HILD

An explosive situation is turned over to a crack commando squad led by Nile Barrabas when a fanatical organization jeopardizes the NATO alliance by fueling public unrest and implicating the United States and Russia in a series of chemical spills.

Phoenix Force—bonded in secrecy to avenge the acts of terrorists everywhere.

Super Phoenix Force #2

American "killer" mercenaries are involved in a KGB plot to overthrow the government of a South Pacific island. The American President, anxious to preserve his country's image and not disturb the precarious position of the island nation's government, sends in the experts—Phoenix Force—to prevent a coup.
